all the
missing
girls

all the missing girls

LINDA HURTADO BOND

Preview of *The Phantom Pirate of Gasparilla* copyright © 2024 by Linda Bond.

Entangled Publishing, LLC
644 Shrewsbury Commons Ave
STE 181
Shrewsbury, PA 17361
rights@entangledpublishing.com

Amara is an imprint of Entangled Publishing, LLC.

Edited by Robin Haseltine
Cover design by LJ Anderson, Mayhem Cover Creations
Cover photography by Nikada/GettyImages
Interior design by Britt Marczak

Manufactured in the United States of America

First Edition August 2024

All the Missing Girls is a fast-paced, serial killer thriller set in Cuba. There are some elements of horror and non-sexual intergenerational abuse. Readers who may be sensitive to these elements, please take note.

This book is dedicated to my husband, Jorge Figueredo. Not only did he introduce me to the beauty of the Cuban culture and the importance of family bonds, but he stepped up and did the tedious work so I could write this book. I love and appreciate you.

"Those who love you will never leave you behind. Even if there are one hundred reasons to give up, they will find one reason to hold on." Mari Alvarez

Chapter One

The midnight sky, collaborating with the inky Caribbean Sea, acts like a blindfold. I squint to make out land, my skin moist as I grip the dock line. Water batters the boat's sides, until the captain shifts the motors into neutral. The boat idles in like a whisper, barely displacing the water.

Four wooden walkways protrude from the shadowed shoreline. My heart flutters, much like the waves lapping at the hull.

"Mari, now."

The captain's whispered order fuels my fingers. I toss the line toward a dark but moving figure on the closest dock, so I'm pretty sure it's not a piling.

I'm praying it's Tony's cousin, Enrique, with a vehicle waiting.

The figure jumps and catches the line.

I exhale, wiping sweat off my forehead.

Under the cloak of this rare, Black Moon, we enter Communist Cuba illegally, my TV news photographer Orlando Jones and Tampa homicide detective Tony Garcia with me. We're on an unregistered boat, docking at this private, barely lit marina, in search of elusive information— the address of the man who kidnapped my sister Izzy and killed my mamá.

"Secure the boat." The captain's voice is as tight as the line pulling us toward our destination.

I'm here, Izzy. I'm coming to find you.

My younger sister disappeared from Tampa, Florida approximately two weeks ago. After the cigar factory burned down. After Raúl's involvement in our mamá's murder came to light. After I learned Izzy knew about Raúl's guilt and remained silent.

I think Raúl, her ex-boyfriend, forced her to come with him to Cuba either to protect her from the law or from my shock and initial anger. Or maybe Izzy came willingly, to reconcile their romantic relationship.

At that thought, my stomach churns in hurricane waves.

Although I've come to find and hopefully bring my sister home, Detective Garcia wants to haul Raúl back to Florida to face charges in Mamá's murder. Orlando plans to secretly videotape our mission for a documentary.

I have no idea if we'll achieve our goals. Undercover, we have little power here.

"Mari! Grab your bag."

I flinch at Orlando's command.

"Get off!"

My photographer, and best friend, is yell-whispering from the dock. Snapping at me, more like it. But the clock is ticking. I've been so inside my head, I missed O exiting the boat. I grab my backpack and duffel and fling both toward the dock.

They land with a thud.

I still, realizing my mistake. *Make as little noise as possible.* That had been the detective's directive as we approached land. *No one must know we are here.*

Detective Garcia, Tony to me, extends his palm.

I place my trembling hand in his steady one.

On the dock, I situate my backpack, eyes still on Tony, who remains on board. My breath catches. It's not too late — I can jump back on board. We can still go back to Florida.

As if Tony senses my anxiety, his lips move. "I'm coming." The wind carries his whispered words in an eerie delay.

"Forty-eight hours." The captain grabs Tony's arm before he can disembark. "That's it. Any longer, the government will be on to you. You're on your own then. I won't risk my family. Text only in emergency. Meet back here in forty-eight."

Forty-eight hours! My heart smacks my ribs, rattling me even more. *Will that be enough time?*

To find Izzy, we need to find Raúl. We don't even have an address for that gangster. Just a town where he's been spotted by a credible source.

Orlando, lengthy backpack strapped across his six-two frame, holds a GoPro up. It's obvious he's recording "Hey, you can see—"

"Sshh!" The man who tied up the boat holds a finger to his lips. I'm assuming this is Tony's cousin, because the detective doesn't react.

Tony's cousin gestures for us to follow him.

A creak stops us as Tony, heavy gear on his back, lands on the rickety dock.

Enrique turns back. I can't make out his features but can feel the heat of his irritation.

"Sorry, cuz," Tony whispers.

Enrique is risking his family, too. To help us.

I take a few deep breaths, glance around.

Wind whips through the palm trees, fronds dancing in tune with the bursts of breeze, making the shoreline move in hypnotic waves. Water laps the dock, as if Mother Nature is licking the wood, and insects buzz, sounding much like cicadas back home in Tampa.

The island's welcome.

My reporter's intuition senses someone watching us other than the cicadas.

I scan the shoreline and blink a couple of times, my eyes adjusting more. I don't see anyone lurking in the shadows.

Ay Dios mio, what are we doing?

I'm a TV crime reporter sneaking into a communist country with a news photographer and a cop who has no jurisdiction here.

I'm circus performer Nik Wallenda, on a high wire with no net.

Beep. Beep.

A door slides open. Enrique is at the end of the dock with a…looks like a van. My heart does a momentary tap dance. Tony's cousin came through for us.

The detective's hand on my back makes me jump. "Let's go."

I suck in air. Humidity warms my lungs. But the rest of my body catches a chill as the boat motors away.

No turning back now.

Chapter Two

Day One
ONE A.M.
FORTY-SEVEN HOURS LEFT

TONY'S FAMILY FARM

We tiptoe through a dimly lit garage. Enrique goes first, Orlando second, his GoPro out and recording. I'm holding on to Orlando's shirt. Tony walks behind me. We lug our gear with us, so moving isn't easy.

As we enter the house through the kitchen, I take note of one single light bulb hanging without a cover from the ceiling. It sways as we pass, casting light in waves across the bare cement walls.

Towels cover the windows, even though it's still dark outside.

Enrique pulls back a sheet hanging over an open archway, and as soon as we walk through, nervous energy embraces me. Candles burn in place of lamps, and the glow illuminates eager faces. Almost a dozen of them.

"Americano!" A one-armed man, in a faded Nike T-shirt and ripped jeans, pulls Tony in with his stump and slaps him on the back with his good hand. "Americano!"

Tony gives a few pats but pulls away.

The *Americano* seems uncomfortable with raw emotion.

Similar greetings swirl around us, like an emotional tornado wanting to suck Tony up.

They must all be relatives of his, crammed into this living room, moving around so quickly, I can't tell if the floor is shifting or it's me. The heat and humidity add to the feeling the room sways, like I'm riding waves.

Most of those gathered are older men, but there are two women, a couple of teens, and one three-legged dog, an ugly, multicolored mutt with sad blue eyes.

One of the women draws me into her arms, hugging me; Spanish endearments roll into my ear. My heart swells in reaction to the smell of lavender on the woman's skin. The scent reminds me of my Abuela Bonita's Violeta perfume. I squeeze my eyes shut. *I will not cry.*

My clothes, moist from the five-hour boat ride from America, must be dampening her dry clothes. I'm starting to tremble, so I don't want to be held tightly. I really need to pee, but I'm ashamed to ask, because Tony is busy being washed around in this tsunami of a family reunion. Orlando is busy recording. All of that is more important than my needs.

Tony hasn't seen these family members since he left Cuba as a baby. Twenty-eight years ago. It hits me—he, too, has lost family, if not to murder or kidnapping, to separation by both water and politics.

The first time his mother invited me to dinner at her house in Tampa a month ago, Tony didn't eat, because he was too busy caring for his ninety-year-old grandfather. Watching him feed the older man, stroking his hair, helping him to bed, stirred something in me.

His grandfather must have meant a lot to the owners of this house, too, because a painting of a younger version of him hangs on the living room wall. He'd been a dissident, and because of a few rallies against Fidel Castro, he'd been arrested and imprisoned. When he finally made it to America, his physical and mental state had been damaged beyond repair. Tony became his caretaker, a constant reminder, he told me, of Cuban suppression, imprisonment, and torture.

Tony's temporal artery pulses. He didn't come to Cuba only to help me; he came for the revenge against those who wronged his family. And to save those he could.

We stare at each other, no words needed.

His conflicted emotions weigh heavy in my chest. My heart aches. It literally *hurts*. For him. For me. For us.

"This is my Uncle Maximo. Enrique's father." Tony breaks our silence and introduces the man who called him the Americano. "He and his sister Esme own the farm."

"Mucho gusto." I didn't realize we were on a farm. I hold out my hand to shake his but—Maximo pulls me in.

"You have brought my Antonio back to me. God bless you!" His chest heaves with deep breaths. I cannot help but hug him back, his joy infectious. Even at one a.m.

"Thank you for letting us stay here." *I know the danger.*

Orlando's GoPro moves into my peripheral vision, then into my face. I want to push it away. I'm feeling way too raw for this to be documented, but I understand the drill. "I'm so thankful for your help—"

Maximo squeezes me harder.

A short woman, gray hair pulled back into a severe bun, housedress looking freshly pressed, breaks through the group, and throws her arms around Tony.

"Esme." Tony wraps his arms around the frail woman's waist. "I'm so happy to see you." His head lands on top of her head. "Mother wants to see you in person. She sends her love."

When Esme pulls back, tears glisten in her red-rimmed eyes. Tony wants his mom's sister to come back to America with him. He's been working with both governments to secure visas for her and her family.

A high-pitched whine, followed by an uneven sound, pulls me out of the moment. That scruffy three-legged mutt hops toward me.

"Hey, boy." One of the kids, in too tight shorts and socks with a hole at the big toe, slides onto his knees and grabs the dog, keeping him from jumping on me.

"Come on, boy. Settle down."

Not sure the dog could hurt me on three legs, but I appreciate the gesture.

The skinny teen, probably about thirteen, folds his arms around the animal. "This is Freedom."

"Freedom?" Who names a dog Freedom? "What happened to him?"

The teen rubs the dog's head. "Don't know." He plants a kiss on its fur. "Found him on the street." The kid speaks English almost perfectly. "I'm bringing him with me when I go to America with Tio Tony."

"You're not going to America," Enrique interrupts. He's powered back into the room from wherever he'd disappeared to after we came into the house. "Esme can't handle the farm without you."

The teen turns away from Enrique and me and throws his arms around the dog. "I'm not going to pick corn all my life."

"Domingo! Stop." Enrique holds up a hand, leaving no question as to what could happen if the kid, Domingo, continues to press the issue. "I'm back at five a.m.," Enrique says to Tony. "We sneak you all out the way we snuck in. In the dark, in the van. Can't risk you being seen."

Tony had explained to me about the neighborhood watchdogs before we left. He called them members of The Committee for the Defense of the Revolution. Basically, government spies.

"Got an address for Raúl?" Tony asks.

"Someone will make contact with you in Playa Hermosa."

"How will we know who *someone* is?" I ask Enrique.

He doesn't bother to turn and face me. "I'll be with you."

Well, honestly, that does make me feel better, even if Enrique's tone and behavior are a bit off-putting to me. He knows the town and the people.

"I'll walk you out." Tony's arm falls over his older cousin's shoulder. "I have a few questions." They walk through the back door, and the family members buzz around, going back to the business of the night. Whatever that might be for each of them.

I'm not sure what to do next.

"Domingo," Esme says, "can you show our guest to your room."

Heat hits my cheeks when I realize the kid may be giving up his bed for me tonight. "Oh no, I can't."

He shrugs. "This yours?" Domingo grabs my bigger duffel bag.

Once in his room, I place my backpack gently on the floor. I have precious cargo inside. The mutt, who finally makes it to the bedroom, starts sniffing it. "Hey, stop!"

Domingo reacts by pulling the dog away, pushing him out the door and closing it. "You got something in there that's illegal?"

Does the kid think I'm going to smoke pot with him? "My abuela's ashes."

"Oh." He blanches, steps back, his gaze secured on the black backpack. "Oh."

I don't elaborate. I'm too tired and really want to use the bathroom we passed in the hallway. "Thank you for your help." My fingers find my black azabache charm dangling off the bracelet Tony gave me. I twist the charm three times to the right, three times to the left. Muscle memory. "Maybe we can talk more after the festival."

I don't know where I'll be after we head into Playa Hermosa. I don't know who or what we'll find. I don't know where we might need to go next on our quest.

"Be careful tomorrow." Domingo stares at me, his features thin lines above furrowed brows.

Is he trying to make me nervous? It's working. "Why? It's a big celebration, right? Dancing, singing, food?" A chance to enter town hiding in plain sight, like tourists.

He points to the charm I'm still rolling between my fingers. "Keep that on. It will protect you from the evil eye."

The tiny hairs on the back of my neck rise. I nod as he backs out of the room and closes the door.

Alone, I glance over at my backpack, in which I've carried my Abuela Bonita's ashes with me since leaving America. My other goal while I'm here.

As if she listens to my thoughts from heaven, my abuela's voice forms in my head. *"I will be there, too, mi amor, but do what the boy says. Wear the charm. It will protect you from the malicious intentions of those who wish you harm."*

Chapter Three

PLAYA HERMOSA

Turbulent clouds tumble upward, the morning humidity suffocating before the afternoon thunderstorms build and break. Mother Nature's way of releasing its energy.

I wish I had a better way of releasing mine.

As we enter the main street of Playa Hermosa, Orlando, Tony, and I begin our search and rescue mission. Enrique had dropped us off and told us he'd park nearby and wait for our call should we need him. He didn't want to be seen with us. While many of the people attending would be visitors, enough locals would be around, and if any recognized him, they'd ask questions about us. Makes sense. We're trying to fly under the radar. Blend in as tourists.

Dishes clang as we pass an outdoor cafeteria called Casa

Del Chocolate. A vintage Harley backfires, causing a hitch in my step.

Spanish escalates as more people fill the main street, merging from side streets. A few bump me as they pass, rushing with clear intention toward the center of this beach town.

I twist the black gemstone hanging off the azabache bracelet. I wish I could quit this nervous habit. I catch a chill as I remember Domingo and Abuela's forewarning. *Not taking it off today.*

"Don't worry, Mari," Tony leans in and whispers to me. "We'll find Izzy."

"And Raúl, too." I whisper back. "I'm going to make him pay."

"Alvarez, take a breath." After years of working as a team, Orlando knows when I'm apprehensive.

"I'm cool." *I'm so, not...* My clothes stick to me already, and my white, flat, walking shoes collect more brownish-orange dirt with each step down the main road.

Classic cars, in bright shades of baby blue, cherry red, and even magenta, fill the side streets. No one is driving down the main stretch—too many people form a human road jam.

I scan the crowd. Would I recognize Raúl if I saw him after ten years? Maybe not. But I will recognize Izzy.

Many of the people crowding into the town's center are dancing, driving their limbs outward and around, a flurry of colors moving against the heat—yellow, white, some in red. But the mounting droning of drums fails to lull me into a hypnotic state. I certainly don't feel like dancing.

"What in the voodoo is going on?" Orlando asks. He favors humor under pressure.

"On September eighth Cubans celebrate the Virgen de la Caridad del Cobre," I explain. O knew only that we'd be attending a festival while searching for Izzy and Raúl. "She's the saint of the island of Cuba."

Tony, always the detective, had decided the Celebration of the Virgen would be a great day to move around without drawing attention to ourselves. Enrique had agreed.

Gotta say they were right. No one is even giving us a second look. "They also celebrate Oshun, the goddess of fertility and love." *The goddess of love.* Ironic, since both love *and hate* brought me here.

Despite my efforts to look like a festival goer, happy and carefree, my heart keeps jabbing at my ribs like an angry boxer's fist.

I scan the crowd, searching for Izzy's trademark hairstyle, the throwback Farrah Fawcett flip many girls in their early twenties are favoring today. So many brunettes are here, many who look to be Izzy's age. Hard to focus with all the moving parts. In fact, the middle of this rural town is otherworldly to me, having its own rhythm, beating fast like my heart, music pumping dancers in and out of the center square.

Drummers line the right wall, men dressed in white cotton Guayabera shirts, with red scarves tied around their necks. They bang on various percussion pieces—a bongo, two congas. One plays the shekere, a dried gourd with beads and cowries woven into a net covering, the sand swishing inside it, between the rhythmic pounding of drums.

A dark-skinned man, weathered and so skinny he looks anorexic, sings lyrics about devotion, hitting high notes unusually smoothly, while a chorus of middle-aged women chant. A few laugh as they dance.

I grab Tony to steady myself and squeeze his arm. He's my human stress ball.

He side-eyes me but says nothing, and the drums make speaking nearly impossible.

Orlando walks two steps ahead of us. This morning, he'd hidden cameras in both his baseball hat and the T-shirt with a smiling face on the front. The camera peeks out of one of the eyes but you'd never see it if you weren't looking for it.

I walk up behind him. "You recording?" He nods but keeps looking ahead, not acknowledging me.

I pick up the smell of bubbling oil mixed with garlic and onions. Sofrito, for sure. And cinnamon? Yep, definitely cinnamon. Also, food frying, probably in oil hotter than the air. The aromas of this festival remind me of the state fairgrounds in Tampa, Florida, during the annual state fair. My heart stretches with painful yearning, remembering how Izzy loved to eat all the food on the midway and then challenge me to ride the roller coaster without throwing up. We were not even teenagers then. The memory makes me chuckle.

The drums start up again, a faster, darker beat.

A woman bumps me.

I twirl away.

But as I check her out, her white teeth in her beautiful, relaxed, bronzed face releases the energy balled up deep in my center. I roll my lips inward, embarrassed at my, I don't know, my edginess. I've got to relax, pretend that I'm *excited* to be here. I wipe sweat off before it drops into my eyes. Sweat. Sometimes a sign of stress, but in Cuba, everyone is sweating. Even in the morning.

The woman reaches into her basket and hands me a flower. One perfectly formed, yellow and brown sunflower. I don't take it. *"No tengo dinero."*

She tilts her head and pushes the flower into my hands. "I don't want money," she says in accented English.

Ay Dios mío. Heat hits my cheeks, and I'm sure they look sunburned. Only in America does everything have a price.

"Estas orando por amor o barriga?" she asks. *Do I pray for love or fertility?*

I glance at Tony. He knows Spanish. His eyes find mine,

and my breath catches. "I…I pray…" I take the flower, placing it to my nose like the woman would expect me to. I smell earth, dirt—nothing pretty or floral. "I pray for peace."

I pray for retribution. No, I pray for revenge.

The woman's eyes widen.

I didn't say that out loud, did I?

"She prays for peace, as we continue to pray for her fertility." Tony grabs my hand, entwining his fingers in mine. "Our fertility," he says in Spanish.

His skin is warm. My heart skips beats, and my breath flutters.

"I…I… He's right." Tony and I agreed we would *pretend* to be a romantic couple coming to the festival to honor Oshun.

The woman bows to both of us and leans in, whispering to me in Spanish, "May the Goddess Oshun bless you both with children."

Tony's fingers twitch in mine like he heard her. Instinctively, I clutch his hand, afraid to let go of our charade. More afraid to let go of him.

"May Oshun bless your family." The woman spins around, dancing back toward the center stage, the *swish, swish, swish* of the shekere weaving in between the lyrical voice of a woman wailing with want.

The drums chime back in with a warm, sensual beat; seductive, like Oshun herself.

I glance down a side road and spot something close to where the lane meets the main street. I stumble.

A group of men, deep in conversation, almost run into me.

Tony pulls me aside, so I'm not hit by the surging crowd. *"Qué pasa?"*

I point to what caught my attention. A good-sized poster is stuck to a stone indention built into the wall. A corner flutters, as if tape came off one area. The paper is posted lower to the ground, in what appears to be an altar.

My pulse picks up, pounding at my temples. Then the sound of drums fades in my head and a ringing takes over. But oddly, I can still hear the sexy, singing voices of the Oshun worshippers and the intermittent rolling of thunder.

Tony's fingers freeze over mine.

He must see it, too.

The poster contains a picture of a girl. From this distance, she could be my missing sister, Izzy.

Chapter Four

The girl in the picture has a wrinkle-free face with no smile, a serious girl with long brown hair feathered away from her youthful, round face. Could be Izzy, but I can't be sure from here. Still, my heart races at NASCAR pace.

"What's with the coconut heads?" Orlando asks as he joins us on the side street.

*Coconut head*s?

On the ground, as part of a man-made altar, I count eight dried coconut shells. They've been cut in half, placed topside up, in wooden bowls. Each of the brownish shells have two eyes and a mouth made of cowrie shells. A variety of black feathers stick out of the top of each coconut face like a headdress. Four more coconuts sit on a raised stand, an animal's head—*severed*—in the middle. I step back. Tiny hairs lift all over my arms. "Think that head is real?"

"Don't go closer." Tony grips my hand again.

Icicle-like chills run through me. "But that may be a picture of Izzy." I point. "And there's more posters."

"*That* is nothing you need to toy with."

"How do you know what *that* is?"

O lets out a low whistle. "Picture looks like Izzy to me, too, bro."

Tony doesn't respond. He walks back to the main road and glances around the corner. Festival goers move past him.

What's he looking for? Probably anyone who looks suspicious. Must be muscle memory for a cop.

I turn my attention back to the altar. The wind flogs the flyer, and the fluttering makes a whipping noise, kind of like my pulse. Both beat in time with the bongos.

I grab the flyer.

"Marisol!"

Tony, back by my side, uses my full name. The last time he called me Marisol was when we were cop-reporter adversaries, not friends. These days, it's usually Mari. But he's never used that sharp tone with me. Maybe I'm possessed by what I recognize instinctively to be an altar to the dark side of the Cuban religion Santeria: Brujería.

*Witchcraf*t.

I know better than to touch anything else in this altar—Abuela Bonita taught me that. But this is for Izzy. I stretch out the paper.

"It's a missing person's flyer." My fingers are trembling. "Not Izzy." My heart takes a giant leap. *Thank God.* "Some girl named Teddy Meyers." My pulse stops accelerating, and the world is no longer wiggling under my feet, because it's not Izzy's face above a dead goat's head, with flies buzzing around empty, partially eaten eyes.

"You don't think *that* belongs to Teddy Meyers, do you?" O's eyes are wide in a way I rarely see.

Is he talking about the goat's head? I follow his gaze. Air stalls in my lungs, and I can barely get out, "Is that a...looks like a...that's a...can't be a *human* heart? Can it?" And why does the drumbeat now morph into the sound of a human heart in distress? *Boom-boom. Boom-boom. Boom-boom.*

O's got a hand on his stomach, but he's aiming his hat down.

"Are you recording that?" Tony asks, glancing around as he says it.

"Hell, yes. If you were that girl Teddy's mother—"

"I would *not* want to see it." I can't believe O is—

"It's plastic." Tony says.

"You sure?" The organ wasn't bloody, or smelly, or—

"Could be plastic, I guess."

"Maybe this is an altar to love?" O asks. "Like part of that Oshun-Santeria thing?"

"For missing girls?" My stomach turns over. "That would be sick." I rip another flyer off the wall, realizing the whole altar may be about missing girls. "This is a different girl. A blonde. Looks like a college girl, too." As I read out the name Arianna, I'm distracted by what's behind the flyer.

"Now *that* looks bloody real." Orlando's dark complexion pales.

Blood drips down the wall, sprayed against the concrete, like someone had been shot. The fresh blood trickles down the stone, landing behind the bowl holding the heart.

My own blood rushes through my ears. "Could be goat's blood. Santeria incorporates animal sacrifice."

Tony's silence speaks to me.

"Buscas a alguien?"

I jump. "Sorry?" I flip around, startled by a new voice behind me. "Am I looking for someone?"

The stranger, who has walked up behind us so quietly none of us heard him, is wearing a typical white, wrinkled guayabera shirt, but his khaki pants are perfectly pressed, and his tennis shoes are white. And new. Odd, since the street is made of red clay.

The older gentleman points to the flyers I hold in my

hands. "Looking for a friend?"

He looks Cuban but speaks English. Perfectly.

"No." Tony puts out his arm, like he's protecting me from a car accident. "No, we are on our way to the festival," Tony speaks in Spanish. "We couldn't help but look at—"

"You don't live here." Not a question from the stranger. "If you find yourself in need of information—" The man hands me, not Tony, a business card, which is weird for Cuba, because who has personal business cards? And why hand it to me?

Our hands touch, and his flesh is heated like his skin is on fire.

I jerk away.

His eyes burn with urgent intent, large, dark ovals lacking empathy.

I look down at the card he handed me. I gag. Can't help my reaction. On the front side of the card is an evil eye with a tongue sticking out of the bottom half of the eye; a knife pierces through the tongue. There's no name, only a telephone number with nothing on the back. I clench my stomach muscles. Is this a threat?

"Marisol!"

My full name again? Who but Tony's family would know me here? I spin around, looking for someone I may have met before in Tampa. There aren't many people who travel to Cuba to see relatives these days.

"There you are."

A dark skinned, heavy-set woman makes eye contact with me as she walks my way, her arms wide open as if she were my Abuela Bonita coming to comfort me. I'm sure I do *not* know her. I freeze, not sure how to react. Then, I remember what Enrique said. *Someone will contact you.* I sure hope it's this lady and not Mr. White Shoes we'll be working with. The woman could be my grandmother, but her face lacks wrinkles. Her eyes sparkle, her hair, hidden under a white wrap, has a red rose attached. She is a Santera, a female practitioner of Santeria, the Cuban mix of an African religion and Catholicism. The good side my Abuela raised me to believe in. This I *do* know. My shoulders drop, and I relax a bit. Santeria itself is used for good.

I walk toward her awaiting hug, hoping she's indeed trying to protect me from the stranger with the scariest business card I've ever seen. Probably the government watchdog I've been warned about.

As she reaches out to pull me into her arms, I breathe in a sofrito-tobacco mix. It's comforting because it reminds me of the Babalawo who'd visited our West Tampa neighborhood. He always had a real Cuban cigar in his hands.

The man in perfectly pressed pants steps between the Santera and me, pushing us apart, without touching either of us. "Josefina, you know these three?"

Her name is Josefina.

"Of course I do. This is my niece—come to visit. She and her husband"—Josefina gestures toward Tony— "are trying to have a child."

O's eyebrows shoot up, and I hide my ringless hand. We all say nothing.

The man nods but points to the altar and says in Spanish, "They are praying to the wrong saint. Perhaps you should *warn* them."

My heart lurches.

The Santera clicks her tongue.

It's the same sound Abuela Bonita used with me when she thought I was saying something silly. The noise triggers longing in my soul. My chest literally aches with how much I miss her.

The Santera waves the man off. "Mind your own business for once, Alfonso."

Alfonso. I make a mental note.

She gestures for us to head back to the main road, and we blindly do as she says, following her, not looking back to see if Alfonso, with his pressed pants and perfect English, is following us.

As we turn the corner onto the main street, the hairs on the back of my neck alert me to his approaching energy.

We've arrived in Cuba, and already I feel like dueling forces are after me. Good versus evil. Each pulling a different way. Right now, I'm hightailing it after the good. Still holding the missing person poster, I fold and pocket it. Orlando is walking beside me. "You get all that weird stuff on video?"

"That Stephen King, pet cemetery stuff? Sure did." Orlando jerks the business card out of my hand. He looks it over as we walk. "What the freaky-fuck?"

I roll my lips in and shrug.

O passes the card to Tony. "Is this like a Cuban mafia way of saying they'll cut off our tongues if we talk?"

"Talk about what?" My stomach is somersaulting. "We don't even know anything yet."

Tony pockets the card. "He's the neighborhood snitch."

The Santera nods but says nothing. She still hasn't formally introduced herself.

Someone bumps into me, and I wonder if I'm being pickpocketed. *Ay Dios mío.* It's Alfonso. He passes us, and I'm freaking out, thinking maybe he heard us talking about him and the CDR.

But he doesn't look back. Once he makes it to the main road, he plants himself in a doorway across the street. Perfect place to watch us and see where we go next.

I don't even know where we're going next. We still have no idea where Raúl lives, and now we probably can't ask around without this watchdog guy catching on as to why we're here.

"Well, shit." Orlando moves his body, so his camera faces

where the government snitch is standing watch. "What now? I don't feel like getting my tongue cut off."

"Follow me," the Santera says, leading us to a general store on the main road, the opposite way from the festival. There are no Targets or Publix grocery stores in small-town Cuba. Instead, this store looks like a third world CVS, a pharmacy that also sells fresh fruits and vegetables, clothes, Cuban sodas, and snacks. Just about anything you might need. As soon as we enter, it hits me—I'm starving, and so thirsty I could stick my face under a faucet in the bathroom and drink for a day. But I'd rather have a Fresca, Izzy's and my favorite drink. I'd challenged her to taste Fresca in front of her girlfriends as we watched Netflix one night more than a decade ago. Izzy never could resist a dare or a challenge. It became our go-to drink together. Don't see any. I do see TuKola, the Cuban Coca-Cola alternative. I grab one, even though it's not my favorite. "May I?"

Josefina waves off my offer of payment. "This, I've prepared for you." She puts two plain paper bags on the counter.

They are both full of... "What's this?"

"They are things you will need when—"

A bell rings, and a female customer walks in with a toddler dragging a stuffed purple Barney dinosaur behind him.

Josefina doesn't finish her sentence, leaving me wondering what the heck are in those brown bags in front of me. I feel her energy shift, and she drops her eyes, pushing one of the bags across the counter toward me.

Should I grab it? I mean—I'm at a loss as to what I'm supposed to do.

"When you're ready to pray for the love from Oshun," Josefina raises her voice, "these ingredients will help you conceive." Raises it like she *wants* the lady who entered to hear her. "I've included instructions."

Ah, we're acting. "Gracias." *Another government watchdog?* "I will follow the instructions."

The customer is wandering the store, holding the hand of her son, but not putting anything into her shopping bag. Orlando is following her, maybe to get her on video? Tony stands watch at the door. Probably keeping an eye on the neighborhood snitch, who's down the street surveilling us.

It all feels very James-Bond-like.

"Don't open the envelope until you are home."

I nod.

Josefina glances at my wrist. She reaches for the black gemstone dangling off the chain. "You have an azabache charm."

"A gift, yes." *From Tony.*

"Bueno." She lets the charm fall and leans forward to whisper, "When you find what you are looking for, you will need the azabache's power."

I swallow and step back. Second time I've heard that, and I've been in Cuba less than twenty-four hours. I twist the black charm three times to the right and three times to the left. "I always wear it. Always." *Hear that abuela? Are you here with me? Can you send me a sign?*

"Time to go." Tony grabs one of the bags the Santera prepared for me.

I jump at his abruptness but grab the other.

Leaving, I almost trip over something. The Barney. The boy dropped his stuffed dino. I spin around.

Tearful, the toddler is clinging to his mother's leg. She's ignoring him, still asking O questions. *Where he's staying. Who he is visiting.* What the—?

I need to stop the interrogation, so I walk over and hand the little boy his lost toy.

He stops sniffling. The mom eyes me. In silence.

As soon as we've cleared the store, and I make sure neither the customer from the store or the government watchdog are following us, I put my bag down on a closed trash can and go through it.

"Don't do that here," Tony says.

But I can't wait. I must know what the Santera wanted us to have. I pull out yellow paper, a graphite pencil, a small pumpkin, some brown and white sugar, a container of honey, a cinnamon stick, and some yellow powder.

Orlando takes off his hat, obviously videotaping the items.

"There's also red ribbon and two yellow, heart-shaped candles." I look to Tony for an explanation. "I don't know what all these ingredients are for."

"Didn't she say it was for fertility?"

"Right, but you don't really believe that, do you?"

"There's also an envelope," Tony says, while keeping his eyes on the area where the snitch had been standing. "He's disappeared."

"Good." I grab the envelope out of the bag and open it. "There's an address." But I freeze before I speak the next two words written on the paper.

The Santera knows exactly why we're here. Not only that, but it's also apparent she *is* the person sent to help us.

Next to the street address, a printed name: Raúl Martinez. "I've figured out our next move."

Butterflies dance across my heart. Black butterflies with razor wings that whip wildly in anticipation.

Chapter Five

Day One
10:00 A.M.
THIRTY-EIGHT HOURS LEFT

RAÚL'S HOUSE

We've located the address the Santera Josefina gave us. We think the house must be at the end of this dirt road, about five minutes away from the center of Playa Hermosa.

No other homes are in sight.

The perfect place to hold my beautiful sister Izzy hostage. Or, the perfect place for my stubborn sister to hide from her own shit.

As we walk down the driveway, my thoughts drift to the text I got from her a couple of weeks ago. When she first disappeared, I thought she'd run away with Raúl, because she feared getting arrested after the truth about Mamá's murder came out. Raúl may have pulled the trigger, but Izzy kept the secret from the police and me, making her an accomplice.

Part of me was okay with Izzy vanishing—even making a new life with Raúl in Cuba—if it meant she'd stay out of trouble and jail back in Tampa. Despite our differences after Mamá died, I love her fiercely. But then I got a text message from an unknown number:

Don't come looking for me. I'm safe in a place. Don't come looking for me. Izzy.

I'm sure it was Izzy, because she used our secret sister code—say something twice, and it means the opposite.

I smile, remembering how she made up the secret code in high school so my crush, who was always trying to grab my smartphone, wouldn't really know how much I liked him. I chuckle. Silly, but it stuck, and as we aged, we used that system to alert each other in more serious situations. We used it when we didn't want others around us to know what we really meant.

This text led me to wonder if Raúl forced Izzy to come to Cuba and was now holding her against her will. Maybe shame made her flee. I simply don't know, but I must find out. I'm her big sister. And her only family left.

And, there was Abuela's last request: "Promise me you'll stay in touch with Izzy. Forgiveness heals."

My heart squeezes.

I'm here looking for you, Izzy. Where are you? Where is this safe place? Or did you mean the opposite? Are you somewhere NOT safe?

The faint sound of conga drums can still be heard, as the festival lasts until sundown. The storm clouds continue to build. Humidity clings to my skin like a leech.

An engine revs nearby, followed by clanging. I glance toward the car sounds, but a tree line blocks what's next door. Someone's working on a vehicle, maybe a motorcycle? That wouldn't be unusual. Most Cubans fix everything in their own driveways. The question is can *they* hear *us*?

I shudder, nerve-induced sweat shimmying down my back.

I inspect the surrounding woods but see nothing unusual, other than the brush and palms swaying in the pre-storm rush of wind.

"What if we're trespassing?" Orlando's words are barely audible.

"I don't see any property lines out here." I hate the way my voice snaps, even in its lowest volume, because it stings O's pride. We've become like brother and sister; we've been working together so long. And right now, I'm so anxious, it's making my stomach sick.

Thunder rolls overhead, moving past like a sound wave.

I glance up at the darkening sky, bumpy with simmering clouds about to boil over. Maybe the electricity making my hair stand is coming from those climbing cumulonimbus rainclouds. Or maybe it's my reporter's intuition kicking in.

Something doesn't feel right.

People disappear in this country.

I twist my azabache charm three times to the left, three times to the right.

Tony, walking to my left, side-eyes me. His gaze drops to my wrist and the black gemstone dangling from my gold bracelet. My by-the-books homicide detective doesn't believe the azabache charm protects you from evil. But he knows I believe it, and that's probably why he gave it to me. I resist the urge to keep twisting my anxiety away while he's watching. It's important to me that he thinks I'm up for this mission.

I glance down at the gun holstered on his belt. Once we left town and the busy festival, he uncovered it, and his hand grips the butt now. He doesn't intend to use his weapon unless necessary. Tony's intentions are pure, like he is. He wants to convince Raúl to do the right thing and come back willingly to face murder charges in the U.S. I don't think we're going to get that miracle. But if we find Izzy, and we get her back without any problems, that would be enough. For me, at least.

Are my intentions as pure? That question has been

driving around my head, like a wound-up race car, ever since Izzy disappeared from Ybor City. My raw desire for revenge against Raúl, especially if he forced her here, terrifies me. I hide it like a well-guarded secret.

At the end of the driveway, the three of us stop in front of a neglected, wood-framed farmhouse. A tin roof covers the faded wood, once painted white with bright pink trim, I think. Flecks of the pink color stick to the wood. Shutters hang off the front windows, slapping the side of the home in the same rhythm as the pre-storm gusts. One might think it abandoned except for the pair of jeans and a still-stained, white work shirt hanging by clips on a single laundry line, drying in the whistling wind.

I steal a look at Orlando. But his wide eyes miss my gaze, instead darting side to side, scanning the wooded area to the right and left of the farmhouse. One of his hands clutches a small, hand-held TV camera he'd added to his undercover arsenal of cameras hidden in his hat and shirt.

"We need permission to go inside?" O asks.

Tony looks back and shakes his head.

I step in front of Tony and gently pull on the doorhandle. "We're not trespassing. Not until we're told to leave, anyway." The door doesn't budge, even as I jerk on it. "Locked."

"Of course," Tony mumbles. "I'm heading out back."

"Coming with." As much as I trust O, I feel safer with the man who has a gun.

Tony's hand flicks open the snap on his gun belt. As he walks around the house, his eyes never leave it. He's watching the windows. A side door. He eyes every entrance.

A flash of light in the distance and a deep roll of thunder blocks out the sound of festival drums temporarily. I look at the sky.

"Check this out," Tony says as I round the house into the backyard. He's squatting next to what looks like a burn pit.

"What's in it?" I ask, coming up behind him.

"Someone recently burned stuff." Tony picks up a stick and pokes at the ashes, still smoldering. "That"—Tony points—"looks like a cell phone."

My heart compresses. Could be Izzy's. "Only one reason to burn an expensive cell phone, especially when they're harder to get here. Someone wanted to destroy what's on it."

Tony squats down and uses a portion of his shirt to pick up the find. "Let's see if they left the SIM card. You got something I can use to pop it open?"

I hand him a bobby pin I have in my hair.

He uses it to pop out the tray that holds the SIM card. His shoulders drop. "Someone ejected the card."

Disappointed, I exhale. "So there's no way to prove if it's Izzy's?"

Tony doesn't answer.

I realize what's grabbed his attention—he's holding a bottle of bleach not burned in the fire pit.

"Empty?"

He nods.

"Looks like someone burned up some flooring, too." O is videotaping.

Tony uses the stick to pick up a half-burned T-shirt. "UGA."

"University of Georgia? We've got to get in that house." Acid burns the back of my throat, and if I'd eaten anything lately, I'd be throwing up. "Now."

I take off for the back door. I'll kick it in if I have to. If this home belongs to Raúl, it's the most likely place I'll find my sister. And all these clues we've found in the backyard lead me to believe someone tried to cover up something.

Bleach.

Burned cell phone.

Half-burned T-shirt.

Ripped up flooring.

Someone could be trying to cover up a murder.

Chapter Six

I use the full force of my fear and anger to push my foot against the back door. Not needed. The door, apparently made of thin wood, isn't locked. It flies open under the pressure of my kick, leaving me off-balance. I fall forward and grab the doorframe in a desperate attempt to stop from face-planting. My foot, airborne, finds the floor, and I steady myself.

"You okay?" O asks, his voice full of what sounds like both awe and concern.

I *am* acting a bit out of character. Never kicked down a door before. "Fine. I'm fine." Not really. Just pulled a back muscle. And made a shit-ton of noise. *Not good.*

The kicked-in door leads to a sitting room next to a tiny, rundown kitchen. Despite Tony's effort to pull me out of the house, I'm already inside.

And I'm staying.

Tony steps in front of me, placing a finger over his lips.

I get it. Be quiet. Although I've busted open a door, so I'm pretty sure I've alerted anyone who's here that they have company.

Maybe that's why Tony draws his weapon and points it in front of him.

We all freeze, waiting to hear a mad scramble of footsteps, an eruption of cursing, or the calculated cocking of a gun being loaded.

A snap of angry thunder rattles the windows. The dull lull of drums drones on.

Nothing else.

Well, my heart. My heart thumps madly.

The inside of the farmhouse is simple—wood floors, bare walls, except for a few paintings. There are two rocking chairs and a basic coffee table. A fan and a 1980's tube TV on crates, instead of a stand.

Tony motions for us to stay in the kitchen, probably to clear the house with his gun drawn. We wait in silence, but I don't take my eye off the door Tony walked through.

O watches the back door we busted.

Seems like forever for Tony to return.

I mouth the words, "Any sign of Raúl or Izzy?"

He shakes his head, holsters his gun, and picks up a cigar in an ashtray on a table, lifting it to his nose.

Looks to me like a Cohiba. Half smoked. I lift my eyebrows.

"It's cold."

My shoulders relax. Then I notice it—a can of Fresca sitting on the coffee table. My hope rises. Izzy loves Fresca. *She's here!* I point to the can, and Orlando nods. He knows Izzy well enough to know she drinks Fresca like I do.

"Izzy!" I yell. No movement. No sound.

My hope falls like a boulder.

Tony clears his throat.

I look up and catch his disapproving stare.

I know. I know. I need to be quiet. "She's been here," I whisper, knowing a Fresca can may be a stretch, but my reporter's intuition tells me I'm right.

He nods and puts a finger to his lips.

How can I be silent when my baby sister may have been here or is still here? Freaking out won't help. I intentionally focus on other potential clues.

The Fresca can sits on a brochure. *Oshunvilla*. On the cover: *A Cuban artist reclaims his impoverished neighborhood by creating a folk-art kingdom where dreams come true*. I've heard of this place. A Cuban Disneyland made of ceramic and tiled art, minus the rides. Below that quote, a timetable for state-run buses leaving from Havana's airport to Oshunvilla. I have no idea why Izzy, if she lives here, would have this. She hates art. Maybe it's Raúl's? When I knew him, he was into crime, not art.

Fire fills my center. I *need* to know more about what's going on here.

Also on the table—a missing persons flyer. My breath catches, and the room sways. *Arianna Johnston*. The blonde from the flyer at the goat altar. Why would *that* be here? Could the cell phone out back belong to this Arianna? Not Izzy? I exhale in relief, but instantly feel guilty. Arianna Johnston may be someone else's sister.

Tony walks over and acknowledges the poster but picks up the brochure.

"Might be a clue that my sister, the one I'm trying to rescue from an abusive situation, is here of her own free will, coming and going, drinking Fresca and visiting tourist attractions like she's on vacation." *Carajo*. Heat runs up the back of my neck.

"That would be better than her being dead," Tony says. "Or even missing."

I glance at the flyer. *He's right*. I exhale my frustration.

Orlando holds up a slip of paper.

I grab it. "Looks like Izzy's handwriting."

O nods.

"Hostel Paraiso, along with a phone number." Maybe she was trying to get away? "I'll call the number."

O taps my shoulder again, this time pointing.

I follow his finger. My breath catches, and my knees go slack. In the far corner of the family room, an altar is built into the wall. The first image I recognize is a statue of Saint Peter, the Catholic saint credited for creating the Catholic church. But the statue is probably a front for the real religion the person who lives here practices: Santeria. My abuela told me most Cuban American families have altars to Santeria saints. I remember Raúl's mom had one in her living room, much like this one.

Next to the statue of the saint is a bowl the size of a cereal bowl. Inside, a collection of iron tools. A sharp knife, larger than one you'd keep in your pocket. Three cast iron nails, longer than the ones you'd use for home repair. Thicker, too. Like ones you might use for torture. There's also a sword, about the size a large toy soldier might carry.

Thanks to all the lessons on the saints from my Abuela Bonita, I grasp that this is an altar to Ogun—a fierce Santeria saint who lives in the woods. He's considered by the Cubans and Africans who worship him to be a skilled surgeon who cuts cancer out of bodies. Others see him as a bloodthirsty warrior who swings machetes and decapitates his enemies. I squeeze my eyes shut, remembering the severed goat head, and force the rising acid down my throat.

When I open them, Orlando is shooting video, like a TV news photographer should be doing. He didn't see my reaction. I'm glad O doesn't know what we might be walking into. Or what Izzy might have gotten herself tangled up in. Santeria or Brujeria? This altar makes me think it could be both, the latter being dangerous, potentially deadly.

"Doesn't look like Izzy is here against her will," Tony

mouths the words.

Even though I'd already come to that conclusion, I bark-whisper back, "What does that mean?" My chest hurts. *Take a breath*. These are your friends. They care about Izzy, too.

Tony gestures for Orlando to come closer. He whispers, "It means we may have to force Izzy to come home with us." He is holding a framed picture in his hands. It's of a man who looks like the older version of the Raúl I knew in our old neighborhood, still tall, lanky, with new facial hair, but a familiar sleeve of multicolored tattoos. "This Raúl?" Tony asks.

My shoulders fall. "It could be." Tony checked Raúl's background record, his file, etc., after Izzy confessed Raúl killed my mother a decade ago. "What do *you* think?" He'd vanished from Tampa right after my mamá's murder. But I'm beginning to think Izzy and Raúl kept in touch during his decade here in Cuba.

"It looks like him. Sleeve of tattoos looks similar to what's in his file. But he could have—"

"Gotten more here," I finish for him. "What do we do now?"

Orlando places a hand on my shoulder. "We'll wait here until she comes back."

"Or we check if she's in there." Tony is no longer mouthing words or whispering. He's pointing to a door at the right side of the room, past the kitchen. It takes me a moment to realize why he wants to check that room when he's already walked around the house. This room has a thick board across it. It looks like the board is screwed into the wall. From the outside. Like someone inside was or *is* being held hostage.

Chapter Seven

Tony found a knife in the kitchen and uses it like a screwdriver to twist at the screws embedded in the thick piece of wood across the outside of the door. He's grunting, and a sweat stain is spreading across his back.

Orlando is videotaping, but he keeps glancing at the front door, like he's worried Raúl may return.

I hope the bastard does come back. I can't wait to look him in the eyes and tell him I know he killed my mother. And the police back in Tampa know it now, too.

I finger the pendant of Saint Barbara hanging around my neck, another gift my Abuela Bonita handed down to me while she was still alive. To protect me. I pray if we find Izzy behind that bolted door, she's still alive.

I close my eyes and think back to the time Abuela Bonita explained to both Izzy and me why she wore the pendant of Saint Barbara. She told us how slaves, brought over from Africa, wanted to practice their African religion, but many Cubans forced Catholic beliefs on them. So they developed a way to please their owners and still stay true to themselves.

They gave their orishas, or divine spirits, the faces of Catholic Saints. Saint Barbara is Changó, my orisha, Abuela told me. Her favorite, too. Which Izzy knew. But instead of being jealous of my connection to Abuela, Izzy studied the saints and their counterparts in Santeria. One afternoon she told me, "Changó teaches us that there is still a chance to change and redeem oneself after a lifetime of mistakes. That is so you, Mari. Always trying to seek justice for others. Always seeing the potential in others. I'm proud of you."

My eyes water at the memory. That, of course, happened before her boyfriend killed our mother and Izzy covered for him. I hope my sister wants more for her life than to hide out here. She'd told me, "I hope I can see the good in people one day, just like you do. Maybe eventually I'll have something worthy to offer. Some skill or life experience. A purpose, you know."

It's still not too late for her. I just need to find her.

A clap of thunder vibrates through me. I didn't even see the lightning preceding it.

"Got it!" Tony stands up and shows me another screw is out. "One more."

I nod, my throat too parched to speak. Nervous, needing something to do as we wait, I reach into my backpack and finger a small box with its precious cargo. If we find Izzy in that room, healthy enough to leave with us, I can accomplish one last thing for our abuela. She'd left her last wish in a letter I opened after her passing. She wanted her ashes spread over the garden she tended as a child behind her farm home on the outskirts of Havana. I have the address. I carry her ashes with me in a heart-shaped metal container. I'm literally carrying around what's left of the most important person in my life, other than Izzy. My heart stretches, yearning to make a connection like the one I shared with my abuela. At times, I still smell the lavender Violeta she pressed onto her skin after showering, even though it was meant for babies, the same scent one of Tony's relatives wore last night. In times of stress, I feel Abuela's bony, cold fingers embrace my cheeks, all her love and concern apparent in her warm eyes. I exhale slowly, hoping to let go of a little more of my ever-present grief and anger when we find Izzy. Abuela Bonita would have wanted that, too. She wanted us to lean on each other.

"Done!"

The wooden board falls to the ground at Tony's feet.

"Open it." I zip my backpack. My mouth remains dry as dust. "O, I'm not sure I want you to video this."

"Sorry, Mari."

He won't meet my eyes. We'd agreed ahead of time he would record everything he could. We'd decide later what to air. But now that we might see my sister hurt, held captive, maybe even dead, I can't stomach the thought of that living on in video.

The door creaks open.

Gun drawn, Tony enters like the homicide detective he is. He takes two steps in.

I can no longer see him. Should I go in, too?

"Clear."

"Izzy?"

"Not here," Tony says.

My whole body relaxes. It takes me less than three steps to join him in the center of the room. "What is—"

"Probably a storage room."

Coño. My shoulders, heavy, drop. The room is full of stacked furniture, none of it matching. And boxes, lots of them, mostly labeled from a produce farm, but obviously not filled with fresh fruit. "Great. A dead end."

"Maybe not," Tony says. "Orlando, come videotape all of this. Just in case."

O is already in the doorway, doing that.

"What do you see?" Tony asks.

Tony and I learned to work together as a team during the weeks we followed clues left by a serial killer in Tampa. I slowly spin in a circle. "A bunk bed. Weird, if Raúl really lives here. Unless he has kids. He'd be in his late twenties now."

"Or maybe female captives," O says.

I shiver at the thought. "What else?" I exhale, because what's obvious to me is, "A shit ton of stuff we don't have time to go through."

"We're looking for Izzy." Tony's voice is calm. Almost too quiet. "What in this room relates to your sister living here or being held captive here?"

Another boom makes me jump. My foot lands on something, and my ankle twists. I drop my gaze to the floor, trying to figure out what the hell I stepped on. *Ay Dios mio.* A knot forms in my throat. *Izzy.* I use my shoe to push a box aside. Then another.

"The flooring is ripped out." All the boxes covering the floor hid it but I say, "Someone ripped up whatever flooring used to be here. So, probably the stuff burned out back?"

Tony nods.

If I were Izzy, and I was trapped in a room with a piece of wood screwed in across the door, how else would I escape? The window? The window. *The window.* "The window has a board covering it. But I'd bet it's also bolted from the outside. Like the door."

"You make a great detective." For the first time all day, Tony smiles at me.

That makes my heart sing, but also hurt. These clues are not good for Izzy. Or that other missing girl. These clues lead me to believe someone had been held here against their will.

"Ay Dios mio."

That gets my attention because Orlando is using my catch phrase—in Spanish—which he rarely speaks. He points to the window.

I cringe. Underneath the windowsill, I find something that roils my stomach. I pull it off the wall.

"A fake nail." Long, white tip—pink and whites they call them. "Probably broken when some…someone…some girl—" I need to catch my breath. "Probably some girl who tried to pull at the plywood on the window. *Ay Dios mio* is right."

"Izzy didn't have fake nails."

O's right. "Oh my God, it wasn't Izzy stuck in here."

"We don't know that yet," Tony says. "Bunk beds." He points to them. "He could have held more than one girl."

The thought makes me gag. Raúl was a gangbanger, into drugs and pretty girls, but I never thought he'd kidnap them. But he killed my mother so she couldn't keep him and Izzy apart. Raúl could be capable of anything.

Orlando, across the room, moves a desk away from the wall. "Looks like someone scratched letters into the wall. That's how a fake nail fell off, maybe? T. E."

"Teddy?" The first girl in the poster above the goat's head.

"Shit if I know. Looks like someone punched a hole in the wall where the rest of the name probably was."

That twists my gut. "Well, like you said, probably wasn't Izzy."

"What do we do now?" Orlando asks.

Tony walks around the room, stopping to move a box and push a piece of furniture to the side. "We wait."

"In here?" I ask because the raindrops ping like bullets ricocheting against the tin roof.

"Not a bad idea." Tony continues his search of the room, opening a big box next to the door. "We can start going through stuff in here. Trying to prove Raúl lives here."

"Well, that was him in that picture you showed me. I'm pretty sure." Another boom. "Wait!" This time the boom sounded more like a door slamming. "That wasn't thunder."

"No," Tony heads for the door.

I run after him. He's already out the front door.

A man is hauling ass away from the house. He's lanky and lean, dressed in jeans and no shirt.

"Can't tell if it's Raúl," Tony says.

"It's him." He has a sleeve of colorful tattoos. Like in the picture.

Tony has his hand on his gun but stalls on the front porch, maybe contemplating whether it's worth going after someone he can't identify?

I run up behind Tony. "It's him." And I've waited too long to see him get what he gave. "It's him." He killed my mother and kidnapped my sister. Or killed her, too. My abuela died because she buried the secret of Izzy's complicity in her soul. I am left. I am the one who must right this wrong.

Tony takes his hand off the butt of his gun.

I have the cojones to do it. I do. I do. I do. Those words beat into me like the dull lull of Oshun's drummers.

I grab the gun out of Tony's holster and aim at the coward. My reporter's intuition is telling me Raúl is running because he knows I'm here and knows I'm *not* afraid to even the score.

I'm not letting him get away again.

My finger finds the trigger.

Chapter Eight

"Marisol, what the—"

Tony covers my hands with his. His palms are damp.

My hands are shaking.

His body presses up against mine, his breath hot on my neck. "What the hell are you doing?" he whispers.

He never whispers.

"I'm going to kill him." *Am I?* I blink a drop of sweat away.

His grip tightens on mine. "We don't know that's Raúl."

"He's getting away." My voice cracks.

"Breathe, Marisol."

"He won't come back."

Tony's body stiffens. "Take your finger off the trigger."

"This is my only chance." Now *I'm* whispering.

The tension in his grip tightens. "We didn't come here to kill anyone."

You didn't. "Maybe I—" I can't even say it. My lungs lock up. My finger, on the trigger, twitches. "He's going into the barn."

"Take your finger off, Marisol."

"What if he's going to get a gun?"

"I'm serious."

So am I. "Can't see him anymore."

"Jesus, Mari what the freaking-fuck are you doing?"

Orlando. He's taping me?

"You lost your mind?"

"Stop, O, I—" *Maybe I have.*

Tony's breath is in my ear. "Before you embark on a journey of revenge, dig *two* graves."

The hair on the back of my neck rises.

"Pulling the trigger won't bring back what you've lost," Tony says.

Hot tears burn my eyes. "What I've lost." *A mother. A father. My abuela. Maybe my sister, too.*

"And it won't help us find Izzy."

"You wanna get us all thrown in a Cuban prison?" Orlando's voice escalates. "You kill that piece of shit—you fuck up your life. And ours, too."

O is right. What would I do if I lost Orlando, my work sidekick for five years. Maybe my best friend? And Tony. I don't even know what he is to me, except I can't fathom doing this without him.

My hands still shake. My throat is chalky. *If I shoot Raúl, I'm no better than he is. I become a murderer, too.*

This is what I've become? An angry woman, willing to shoot a man. Hoping I'll get away with it, because no one knows I'm here, and the Cuban government isn't going to cause a problem with the U.S. government over, as Orlando put it, "a piece of shit"?

"You need to forgive Raúl." Tony's voice is steady.

"Yo perdonar a Raúl?" I swallow and look at Orlando. He *is* videotaping me. "I'll never forgive Raúl." I look right into the camera.

"Forget him, then." I catch the plea in Tony's tone. "Let's

go find your sister," he says, "spread your grandmother's ashes—"

"Get the hell out of this place," O jumps in. "We're putting our lives in more danger every hour we're still here."

Light flashes, followed by the instant clap of thunder.

The house shakes.

That message from Mother Nature rattles me back to reason. *I am not a murderer.* Killing Raúl would make me as evil. One person's justice becomes another family's trauma.

When does the violent cycle end? Isn't that what I learned from the serial killer I fingered, who disappeared that night the cigar factory burned down in Ybor City? Here I am acting like that killer. I can't believe rage brought me to this brink. I take my finger off the trigger.

A car engine revs. The barn door opens, and out comes a car from the fifties. A quick maneuver and the driver takes off down the driveway, kicking up dust and dirt. Raúl's getting away.

"I'm not ready to forgive you." I flick on the safety. "But I don't want to kill you either." Relief unweights my shoulders. "I just want my sister."

Tony takes the gun out of my trembling hands. I let him, even though there's a small part of me that still wants to use it. That little devil in my ear whispers, "Raúl will never pay the price for his murderous actions. You've spent years dreaming of revenge. But you let him drive away."

Tony holsters the weapon he taught me how to use before we came here. Does he regret that now?

We stand in silence.

Until thunder rocks the windows again.

"Maybe we should go," Orlando says. "We can check the rest of the house, but I don't think Izzy is here."

"Alive, you mean." All three words crack.

Tony takes my hand and squeezes. "I've got a plan."

Chapter Nine

Day One
Noon
Thirty-six hours left

TONY'S FAMILY'S FARM

Tony's plan: head back to his cousin's farm, about thirty minutes away, to regroup.

He wants another shot at convincing Esme and Maximo to come with him to America, or at least let Domingo leave with him. I catch snippets of conversation, so loud the words walk down the hall as if they have legs.

Orlando and I are hunkered down in the back room of Esme's house, which is barely more than a closet. One bed, a sheet with permanent stains, and one flat excuse for a pillow. No shades for the window. A beat-up desk, with a wobbly leg that creaks when you move past it, and one chair, the back broken.

Domingo's room. Where I'll be sleeping for only one

more night, hopefully.

The house steams with moisture. My clothes are damp, and I'd give anything for a cool shower and a hot meal.

Anything.

I sigh and plop down on the bed. The box springs seem to reach up and pinch me in the butt. "Ouch!"

O's already lying down next to me, one arm thrown across his face, equipment on the floor, shoes safely off the bed.

I chuckle, because the bed isn't long enough for his whole body. His feet hang off the edge. Imagine if he had to sleep like that.

Tony's voice, coming from the kitchen, escalates. I want to smooth over the situation, but the swooshing in my gut tells me Tony wouldn't appreciate any interference.

"This may be your last chance!" His voice crescendos, the tone of his words razor-sharp.

I stand. Ready to intervene.

"I cannot leave the farm." That is Maximo. Old and without an arm, but still running the farm.

"The government runs your farm," Tony says, "and takes half of what you grow here."

Probably more. I've never heard Tony this angry.

"Let's stop eavesdropping." I jostle Orlando, feeling a bit voyeuristic listening to Tony's argument with his resisting family and knowing how upsetting this is to him. I feel a sudden urge to get on with things and get out of this country. It's bringing out a side of Tony I'm not sure I like. It's brought out a side of me I don't like—I've never pointed a loaded gun at anyone before.

"What do you have in mind?" Orlando asks.

"When I couldn't figure out who was killing people in Tampa, I took the clues and put them up on the wall, you know, like they do on *Law & Order.*"

That brings a long exhale out of Orlando. "I saw your

morbid murder wall. This is different. No one has been murdered."

"That we know of." At least Orlando is now sitting up in bed. I visualize the empty bottle of bleach, the burned vinyl flooring, the boarded-up room, Raúl fleeing the house, and I shudder. "Let's start with what we found at Raúl's. Let's build a wall of clues and at least make some suppositions about what they could mean. Maybe it will help figure out where Izzy might be." I pull the picture of Arianna from my backpack and put it up on the bare wall with duct tape, the only thing I could find in the house. I use my teeth to tear it. Couldn't find scissors. "Arianna Johnston. Her missing person flyer found at both the altar in Playa Hermosa and at Raúl's house."

"We *think* it's Raúl's house." Orlando is up now, organizing his gear. But he's moving as if in slow motion.

"It *is* Raúl's house. We saw him there." I stare at the pretty, college-aged blonde in the flyer. "Who is Arianna Johnston? Why was her missing person's flyer up over an altar to Brujeria? Why was her flyer also at Raúl's? We can assume Arianna either knew Raúl or Izzy."

"Or both." Orlando chimes in. "Where is Arianna now?" He's got his GoPro camera out and is recording me for his documentary.

"We can assume Arianna is missing."

O circles around me. "Clue Two?"

"That brochure for Oshunvilla." I pull out the booklet and flip through it. "A tourist place Izzy may have visited. It's a famous artist's house." I've looked over the brochure a couple of times already. Nothing really stands out, in terms of Izzy. "Mosaic tiles, statues of people, mostly women, archways all covered in bright colored tiles." I tape the advertisement up next to the missing person flyer. "Reminds me a little of the artist Dali. Ever been to the museum in St. Pete?"

"Not my jam," O says.

"Not Izzy's *jam*, either. So, why would she go there?"

"Who says she did? But another good question. Clue Three?"

"Clues Three and Four, I'd say, would be the picture of Raúl and the Fresca." The last word gets stuck in my throat. "Who drinks Fresca in Cuba? *Izzy*. I introduced her to it."

"Maybe that's a clue Izzy was with Raúl at some point. Not that she's living there now or—"

"Spare me, Orlando." I'm too tired to put up with him trying to manage my fear or hurt. "Izzy could have been the victim locked in Raúl's room."

Orlando exhales. "Arianna could have been, too." Then he says, "Next clue?"

"Clue Five: the collection of potential murder cover-up clues we found out by the fire pit?"

O purses his lips, nods but says nothing.

"I have pictures of each item. Once we find a printer—"

"Won't forget those images." He points to his temple. "Got 'em right here."

My shoulders hike up as electricity shimmies down my spine. That visceral reaction always happens when I'm on to something. "I won't either." I shake my head to clear the images. "Moving on. Clue Six: the name and address of a hostel in Havana: Hostel Paraiso." I pull out that piece of paper, ripped from my backpack, but still enough intact to add to the wall. "Could Izzy be staying there? Was Arianna staying there? Should be easy enough to find that out. What's the connection? And who is Teddy Meyer? Remember, the first missing girl on the poster at that creepy altar?"

O doesn't answer. I put up Teddy's missing person flyer and walk in a slow circle, thinking, fully aware Orlando is recording me, and this could end up on Netflix, which is kinda sick if you think about it, but it is what it is. *This* is what we, as reporters, do. "Why did Izzy write the name and address down? Was she trying to escape and wanted to stay at the hotel? Was she trying to help one of these girls escape?" I stop moving and look directly at Orlando's GoPro. "Let's assume the missing girls were staying at that hostel in Havana. Let's start there."

A door slams shut.

I jump.

I no longer hear Tony, only a soup of distressed Spanish from various family members, probably still in the kitchen.

Orlando puts the GoPro away. "Do we wait for him to cool off?"

"No." I'm already grabbing my backpack. "We grab Enrique and the car, and we head to the hostel. We can't waste any more time. We grab Tony. It will distract him. In a good way."

Orlando is making sure his gear is gathered and his personal backpack, as well. "I don't think we should leave anything behind." He nods toward my missing girl wall. "I keep thinking about that guy who showed up at the altar. Watching us. How did he know who we were?" O shrugs. "We don't want to get Tony's family in trouble."

I just put the clues up, but I get what he's saying. We discussed this before we entered Cuba. Leave nothing behind. No pictures. No proof. We need to be invisible. I stare at the clues. Take a picture with my smartphone.

I gently, but quickly, take down what I put up. Fold the flyers and arrange them in a side pocket of my backpack.

Truth is, it's better I take all of this with me. I don't know where we'll be tomorrow.

I only know where we'll be in an hour. A youth hostel in Havana called Hostel Paraiso.

Chapter Ten

Day One
ONE P.M.
THIRTY-FIVE HOURS LEFT

HOSTEL PARAISO, HAVANA

The three of us sit in the lobby of the Hostel Paraiso located in the center of Havana. The outside of the hostel would scare any American traveler with its chipped paint, downed electrical lines that could be live, and broken windows, probably an indication there's no air-conditioning.

Inside the lobby, the young people buzzing around don't seem to mind the heat and humidity. The rain has stopped. The sun shines angry and hot. Accordingly, the hostel clients wear shorts, tank tops, and flipflops, and carry on with excited, on-vacation enthusiasm.

Sky-blue painted walls welcome us. A map of Cuba covers a divider in the main lobby, destinations dotted in red marker. A few tourist brochures paper shelves.

Tony, Orlando, and I observe from a simple metal table with four un-cushioned chairs, sipping piping hot Cuban espresso in mini ceramic coffee cups. Tony's and mine are whipped with sugar. Just the boost I need, despite the heat of the drink matching the heat outside. I'm also feasting on cheap Cuban bread and butter. My mouth literally waters as the coffee meets the bread in my mouth.

Tony remains moody and silent. He may still be dwelling on his fight with Maximo and Esme, but, always the cop, his gaze darts from the door to the stairs and back to the street outside the window where we sit.

Orlando films what's going on around us. I can tell by the way he keeps adjusting his Tampa Bay Rays baseball cap.

I'm asking the young people who enter and leave if they've seen Arianna or Teddy, because that may open a door to finding Izzy. I hold both flyers up as new travelers pass by. Some stop and ask questions, but most barely pay me any attention. Young people are so consumed with their own adventures and immortality. Aren't they concerned that this, too, may be them one day?

Missing.

Forgotten.

Ignored.

So far, the young woman working the front desk hasn't interfered. Hair pulled back in a tight bun, lips in a thin line, she seems curious but calm. My reporter's instinct tells me her cool demeanor means she's already told someone we're here. Maybe she told her parents. Maybe she told the manager of the hostel. Maybe she told the neighborhood watchdog. But she's told someone. Her duty has been done. She's too relaxed. Too quiet watching us ask questions of people staying where she works. She's probably biding time till someone gets here to shoo us away. Or worse. Arrest us. We aren't doing anything illegal. But that may not matter in this communist country.

"You're asking about Teddy."

My back straightens, and I turn toward the voice behind me. "Excuse me?"

Two travelers, who look like stereotypical college sorority girls, stand behind me. My shoulders relax. Not the police armed with questions.

One of the girls is flashing a matching missing person's flyer. My breath catches. It's Teddy Meyers. If not for my ribcage, my heart would have leaped out of my chest. I point to Teddy's picture. "Is she a friend of yours?"

"Met her here a couple of weeks ago when she arrived at the hostel," the girl holding the flyer answers.

I call her a girl, because she's about five foot four, skinny like a teenager, with no make-up on, which makes her look younger, and she's pulled her hair up into one of those *I don't care* buns a lot of college kids wear these days.

"I'm Olivia." The young woman points to the other pretty blonde standing next to her. "This is Samantha." Samantha looks as skinny and as ready to go seek adventure in a foreign country on Daddy's money.

"We've been rooming with Teddy and Mandy for about two weeks," Samantha says, twirling a piece of her blond hair as she talks. "You know Teddy?"

I whip out my cell phone and show Olivia a picture of the altar, with the goat's severed head and flies eating out the eyes. Teddy's pic is hanging right above it.

Olivia's eyes bulge. "What is that?" She steps back.

Orlando has slowly, silently, lifted his GoPro and is now actively recording Olivia's surprise.

"It's an altar."

Tony sips on his espresso, but his eyes are focused on both girls. He's observing their reactions as well.

I've learned his silence doesn't mean he's not lasering in

on the task at hand. He's attacking our goal from a different direction. "Probably Brujeria," I add.

I get no raised eyebrows. No thinning lips. No gasps.

So I follow up with, "Witchcraft."

Samantha exhales, and the color drains from her face at the same pace as her exiting breath. She places one hand over her heart, and I can hear the words she isn't saying, "Holy shit? Witchcraft?"

"Was Teddy involved in anything," I ask, "odd or questionable?"

"Well, she doesn't have a goat's head or blood in our hostel room." Olivia's voice rises as she answers. "If that's what you're asking."

I'm reaching, "Nothing that set off any alarms?"

Samantha shakes her head. "No, she's a kid from Orlando, Florida who grew up near Disney and water parks and stuff like that. I don't know, I guess she said she didn't have a Disney princess upbringing. Parents divorced. Financial problems. That's why she's staying here. She had a few issues, but I've never heard her say anything about brew— whatever you called it."

I'm heading down the wrong path. I shift focus. "Did she take her stuff when she left the final time?"

"Only her phone," Olivia says. When I stay silent, she adds, "She had plans to meet a guy."

"So her stuff is still here?" I'd like to go through it, but it may be too soon to ask.

"Teddy's backpack is still here," Olivia says. "Clothes still in it. Her journal—"

"Have you read it?"

Silence.

I raise both hands in surrender. "No judgment here. Just looking for any information that might help find her."

"Guilty," Samantha says. "I read it when Teddy didn't

come back that night. I looked for clues."

"Like I said, no judgment."

"The police have it now," Olivia adds.

"The police?"

"The front desk called them when we reported Teddy missing."

So, the Cuban police know. Interesting. "Do you remember what was in it?" I inhale, hoping pretty Samantha has a brain and a memory.

"Mostly stuff about her asshole boyfriend who broke up with her right after they graduated."

"And a new guy she met here," Olivia added.

"You have Teddy's cell phone number?" Tony jumps in, sitting forward in his chair, espresso finished, cup resting on the saucer.

Olivia nods.

Tony hands her his cell. "Type it in for me."

She does. I'm kinda surprised, but Tony has that *trust me* kind of face.

He calls the number, but it goes straight to voicemail. "I'll get someone to see if they can find where it last pinged."

I notice he didn't use cop language and say, "my source." The man is smart.

"Maybe her location services are still on?" Orlando says while circling us.

"We can check geolocate, her Gmail if she has an account, and iCloud," Tony adds. "Check her credit card history, if she left a card in her stuff."

Now he sounds a little like a cop. "I wonder if she had Find My iPhone on? That would be the simplest and quickest way to track her," I say.

"She turned it off," Olivia says. "We checked when she didn't come back that night."

"Why would she turn it off?"

"Maybe *she* didn't turn it off." Olivia purses her lips.

"What do you mean?" I lean in.

"Teddy left to go see this guy she'd met here." Olivia looks at Samantha. "Raúlito, right? That's what she called him."

The air literally stops in my lungs.

"Yep," Samantha nods. "Maybe he turned it off, because he didn't want her to be tracked."

I'm on the edge of my chair, my heart zigzagging. I pull out my cell and scroll to photos. I call up the picture of Raúl and Izzy from ten years ago. I should have taken a snapshot of the pic Tony found at the house. Of the man with a sleeve of tattoos. "Is this Raúlito?"

Both girls look at it. "Not sure," Olivia says.

Samantha shrugs and goes back to her phone.

"I never saw him," Olivia continues. "Teddy never introduced us. She'd always meet him places. She'd take, like, an Uber, you know, a drive service."

"That's odd, don't you think?" *I do.* "Where did Teddy go the day she disappeared?"

"Oshunvilla," Samantha and Olivia say at the same time.

The brochure I found at Raúl's house. I'm up on my feet. So is Tony.

Another connection.

"You okay?" Samantha asks.

I nod and wave for Olivia to continue.

"The place is famous, you know." Olivia points to the rack of tourist info. "Got brochures on it over there. They have this wishing well—"

"Wall," I correct.

"Where you're supposed to be able to go and leave a wish. They say after a week, when the messages come down and are burned, your wish is supposed to come true." Her eyes light up like she's entranced by the thought of having one's wishes come true so easily.

"What did Teddy wish for?" Not even sure if it would matter. "Do you know?"

Olivia's eyes are glassy. "What do most girls wish for? We wish for love."

Tony's body stiffens.

Orlando, to his credit, is like a fly on the wall, silent, stealthy, capturing everything.

"Her college boyfriend broke up with her right after they graduated," Olivia says.

"I already told them that." Samantha is growing weary of this. I can tell by the way she's scrolling on her phone. Probably Instagram.

I need to speed this up.

"They were supposed to come here together," Samantha continues. "But he dumped her."

Olivia jumps in, "Teddy's been depressed, been looking for a new high, maybe a hook-up, you know?" Olivia seems to really have liked Teddy and cares about where she is. "Teddy said she likes hot Cuban boys, because they're supposed to be good lovers." She raises her shoulders, but a smile lights her face. "Like I'd know? But she met this guy Raúlito and, you know, Teddy wanted love, like you read about in romance novels."

Tony exhales, and I stifle a smile. "So Teddy went to this wishing wall so she could—"

"Can I see that picture again?" Olivia asks.

"Can we go, already?" Samantha sighs.

"Sure." I hand Olivia the flyer of Teddy.

"No," she says. "I mean the picture on your phone."

"Sorry." I put down the flyer, pull up my phone, and swipe to the picture of Raúl and Izzy.

"I don't recognize the guy," Olivia says and points. "But I have seen her before. Saw her here the other day."

Olivia is pointing at my sister, Izzy.

Chapter Eleven

I point to Izzy's face on the screen on my smartphone. "This girl. You've seen her? You're sure? It's an old picture." My increasing heart rate brings sweat to my already heated skin. "When?"

"She was here, I don't know, Samantha, how many days ago?"

Samantha sighs loudly and starts picking at her cuticle. "She came here a couple days after Teddy left for Oshunvilla, but she was looking for another girl. Hmm, I think her name was…" Samantha exaggerates a shrug. "I don't know. Annie. Amy. Started with an A."

"Arianna?" My breath hitches, and my voice cracks in the middle of Arianna's name. I put down my phone and pick up the second flyer I'd been showing around.

"Yes, yes. Arianna sounds, right." Samantha makes eye contact, finally. "She stayed here, too, in a different room. I did see her around."

"This girl?" I hold up the flyer. "You saw this girl, here?"
Both nod.

I glance at Tony. He's taking notes on a small notepad he always carries with him. Our personalities are so different. My body reacts with a cortisol dump in times of excitement or stress. Tony grows quiet, reins in emotion, and commands control.

"That girl is missing, too?" Fear taints Olivia's voice.

"Yes."

Samantha's eyes pop wide.

They get it, now. College girls are disappearing. They know two of them. I reach for the rest of my espresso and throw it back. It's cold, and even the sugar doesn't make it go down easier. I call up the picture of Raúl and Izzy again. I gotta make sure. "You are sure *this* girl"—I point to Izzy—"came looking for this girl?" I point to Arianna's flyer.

"Yes," Olivia confirms for me. "That girl wanted to make sure this girl was okay."

"Did she say why she felt worried?" I envision a broken fingernail and torn-up flooring.

"No. But that's when we told this girl"—Samantha points again to Izzy—"our friend Teddy also left and hadn't come back." Samantha is reengaged. "We showed her the flyer Teddy's mom made."

"Teddy's mom is here?" I ask.

"Well, not at this hostel," Samantha says. "I think she's staying downtown."

"When we told that girl on your phone—"

"Izzy," I choke on her name. "My, my sister."

"Your sister?" Both girls say in unison.

I nod, because the knot of emotion lodged in my throat since they recognized Izzy chokes off my words.

"When we told Izzy, your sister," Olivia corrects herself, "that Teddy left to meet a guy named Raúlito, your sister seemed to get nervous."

What is the chance Izzy's Raúl is also Teddy's Raúlito? If

you factor in ripped up flooring, bleach, and a fingernail near a boarded-up window, the chances are good, even though Raúl is a common name here. I'm going to throw this out there. "My sister Izzy may have been kidnapped by a guy name Raúl. He may have brought her here to Cuba against her will. I have evidence now that she's here. You saw her. I'm trying to find her. Your friends aren't the only missing girls."

The group falls silent, both young girls staring at me.

I'm fully aware of their silence, encased in a bubble of otherworldly noises, like doors slamming, conversations flowing, a horn honking right outside.

Orlando continues to move around as he records.

I sit down, a little dizzy.

Olivia places her warm hand on my bare shoulder. "I'm sorry."

I look up at her and nod.

"The tie between Izzy and the girls, and Raúl, if it's him, is interesting," Tony says. "But what I don't understand is if Izzy came to Cuba with Raúl willingly, why would she bother with these girls she barely knows? Wouldn't she and Raúl still be in the honeymoon stage, reuniting after a decade? Having fun? Going to places like Oshunvilla? Like tourists?"

"Good point," Orlando chimes in.

"Maybe she didn't come to Cuba willingly, and she learned of a connection between Raúl and these girls and tried to warn them or something. Izzy and I haven't been on the best of terms lately, but she's always had a big heart, especially for troubled girls." Izzy and Abuela Bonita would often cook for some of the West Tampa neighborhood girls who'd fallen into toxic relationships or were victims of abuse by their parents. Izzy had practically adopted a foster girl living across the street. She'd loved the role of guardian angel to struggling girls. She'd taken on that role after Mamá died and Raúl fled to Cuba. Maybe her helping others reflected what she'd wished she'd had before her gangster boyfriend murdered our mother—someone to look up to and help guide her out of a bad situation without parental threats. "At one point Izzy was a broken girl, and maybe she trauma bonded with these other girls, due to similar problems."

"Teddy seemed a little messed up after getting dumped. That's for sure. Your sister asked where Teddy last met Raúlito. I remember that. I told her she used a driver to go meet him at Oshunvilla."

"A driver?" *Oshunvilla again.* "Like an Uber?"

"They call it Bajanda, here," Samantha adds. "But I don't think that's what she used."

Her voice softens and compassion shines through her eyes now.

Olivia walks up to a corkboard next to the map of Cuba. She unpins a business card. "She took this independent driver. He charges less than Bajanda. And the front desk always recommends him." She hands the card to me. "Maybe he gives the hostel a cut?"

Before I grab it, I take a picture of the front. "What did Izzy do next?"

"She called the driver and told me she wanted to go to Oshunvilla. I'm pretty sure she wanted to make sure someone knew where she'd be."

"In case she didn't come back," I say to myself.

"We need to ask for surveillance camera footage." Tony is pointing to a camera above the entrance to the door leading into the hostel. "Bet there are cameras outside as well." He waves Orlando over. "Make sure we get all the places cameras are." He turns toward Olivia. "How many days ago did you see Izzy here?"

"Maybe a week ago?" Olivia says.

"Something more specific would help." Tony's voice remains even, not pushing.

"Teddy disappeared a week ago," Samantha answers. "Your sister showed up a couple of days after. I'd say five days ago, give or take a day."

I glance at the girl working the front desk. She won't be of any help. I'm sure of that. "We've got to talk to the manager here. Ask about surveillance video. We can see who Izzy left with." My pulse pounds at the possibilities of what else surveillance video might show us.

"We might get a license plate from that camera." Tony is pointing to one outside the window.

"We already asked for the video. We gave it a couple of days, thinking she might be shacking up with the Raúlito guy. Here's the prob."

My shoulders drop, waiting.

"Footage is overridden every forty-eight hours."

I can't breathe. "Let's ask the manager, anyway." We are so close to seeing if Izzy left with the same person Teddy did. So close to knowing who that person is. So close to maybe finding them. *So close.* "What the hell do we do now?" I'm thinking out loud. "While we wait to check with the manager, we call the number for this independent driver." I answer my own question.

I glance at Tony. He's nodding.

My heart swells. I'm so thankful he's here with me. Watching out for me. Helping me find Izzy. I honestly don't know what I'd do without him—his calm balances out my anxiety. "And tell the driver what? That we want to question him?"

Tony shrugs. "Tell him the truth. We want to go to Oshunvilla."

"Like Izzy did." I put my hand over my heart. *Follow the clues.* "Maybe it isn't Raúl we need to find and follow. Maybe it's the unknown driver."

"We follow in the footsteps of both Teddy and Izzy—"

Tony takes the card and uses his cell to dial.

"And maybe Arianna, too." I often finish Tony's sentences. At times, *we're like one mind.* My pulse picks up as he orders the car, because maybe we haven't reached a dead end. Maybe this is a new start in a different direction.

After hanging up, Tony turns to Olivia and Samantha. "Ladies, can you hook us up with an extra bottle of water and maybe some candy—some kind of food?"

I stop and stare. "You're hungry?" We devoured coffee and thick slices of Cuban bread with real butter not too long ago. My stomach is, gratefully, full.

"No," Tony says. "Trust me."

If you only knew how much I trust you. I glance over at him, trying to keep my heart out of my eyes. He's no longer looking at me, but I catch something else that triggers my heart in a much different way.

A man standing in a doorway across the street has a hat low over his forehead so you can't see his face, but I recognize the body language and those unusual clean white tennis shoes. Palpitations rock my ribs. The neighborhood watchdog is out of his neighborhood, away from the Brujeria altar and the Oshun festival. "He's *here.*" Why?

Tony turns to see what I'm talking about.

Orlando gets in position to record him. As soon as the GoPro goes up, the watchdog pushes away from the door and power walks away.

"Is he following us?" I ask out loud. "Or is he also looking for Teddy, Arianna, or Izzy?"

Or is he, too, a suspect, making sure we don't find and rescue all the missing girls?

Chapter Twelve

My first instinct is to do what any good reporter does. In this case, that means haul my *colito pequeña* across the street, catch the government watchdog before he disappears again, and ask him, "Why are you following me?" Josefina called Mr. White Shoes, Alonzo, no, Alfonso, that's it. I want to run and catch Mr. Alfonso and start firing off questions like: "How are you following me? Who told you to follow me? What will it take to get you to stop following me?"

But Tony, who must be able to read my mind and also feel the fire in my belly, takes my wrist and pulls me back.

I squint, sending him a narrowed eye look that says, "Don't try to stop me."

But he simply shakes his head. "Driver is here. Focus on the plan. Trust me. We'll figure out that guy's deal later."

A cherry red vintage car, with Chevrolet on the front, pulls up.

"Wow. Fast service."

"Probably lives nearby." Tony hops in the front passenger seat.

Because I trust him, and his cop's intuition, I jump in the back.

Tony turns to the driver. "What is your name?"

Ay Dios mio. My detective is jumping right into tough cop mode. I'm ready to counter with my good cop persona like he taught me before we left America.

"Angel Sanchez," the driver answers Tony, but doesn't look at him.

Angel? You gotta be kidding me. This driver doesn't look like an angel. First, he's thick like a body builder, with grayish-black tattoos all over the back of his neck. Looks like faces of Santeria saints, not angels, covering his skin. Probably all over his body, but I can't see more from where I'm sitting. He's got a bald head and a skull earring dangling from his left ear. At least it looks like a skull. Can't be sure. I only know the energy this man is releasing is not holy, or even kind. His lips, which are visible in the rearview mirror, look thin and wrinkled, like those disgusting earthworms on the driveway after a good rain. His jaw is clenched, and I bet he's grinding his teeth as we speak.

Orlando plops down next to me in the back seat, nods at the driver, and adjusts his hat, which, I'm sure, means the hidden camera is on and recording.

I wish I had Tony's calm energy or Orlando's chill vibe. I'm a coiled snake, untrusting, ready to strike to survive.

"Hi, Angel," I say in my best, fake singsong voice. I give him what I hope looks like a carefree wave. I'm twenty-eight years old, but I need to pull off a young American-on-vacation-with-my-two-friends look. Hopefully, Angel focuses on the fact we probably have mucho dinero to spend.

"Thought you said one girl?" he says in Spanish.

Tony must have called and told him it would be just me. To fit with the driver's pattern. *Smart.*

"Well," I keep up the cheery, high-pitched voice, "I am

a girl." I answer in Spanish, but decide to switch to English, to see if Angel can speak it, but also so Orlando's future documentary viewers can understand it. "I had my—" *What do I call Tony?* We're deep undercover here. "I asked my boyfriend to call you." I stick my arm over the front seat, as if to shake hands. "I'm Mary." *Not Mari.* And not sorry for giving you a fake name.

Angel glares at me through his rearview mirror. He doesn't smile, nor does he shake my hand.

Still, I hold up my flirty grin and hold out my tired hand and try like hell to make my face look like an innocent tourist's should.

"You going to Oshunvilla?" the driver asks me. So, he does speak English. And it's pretty good, despite the thick accent.

"Oh, yes. I've heard so much about it."

The driver takes off with a jolt.

I lurch backward and jerk my hand over the front seat, bracing myself with it instead. Angel isn't going to be won over with my good looks or American charm. I'm a failure so far at "good cop" and "cheerful American tourist." I'll switch up my strategy. "What's it like?" I lean my chin on the red and white seat as if we're old friends. "I mean, it will be my first time at Oshunvilla." I blink a few times and widen my eyes. "I heard it's such a cool place." I really have no idea. I pull out the brochure and thrust it at him. "You need the address?"

The man shakes his head.

I put the brochure away.

The silence settling over the car creeps me out. Like we're being driven into a horror movie. So, I keep talking. "It's like this artist's home, right?" *Remember what Tony said. Keep the conversation going. Make it light, nonthreatening. Win him over. Make him trust you.* "I understand it's open for tours, and you can buy artwork, and they have a wishing wall." I laugh. It sounds fake to my ears. "I've got wishes. Plenty of them."

The driver mumbles.

I can't make out his words.

"I know nothing about the place," Angel says, this time louder. "I, I take people there." The driver's voice remains flat, emotionless. And he looks everywhere but at Tony, as if he senses the threat sitting next to him.

Tony always carries a gun. Either his work-issued or, in this case, his personal weapon. But you'll never see it. Unless you force him to use it. And you won't see it coming.

Tony goes quiet before the chaos.

He's gone quiet.

"How far is it?" I make myself bounce up and down in my seat. "I can't wait. I want to see it all before it closes."

"Oshunvilla never sleeps."

That answer makes me sit back and sit still. "What does that mean? Oshunvilla never sleeps? Thought it closes at sundown?"

The driver grunts but doesn't answer my question. Instead, he says, "I charge more for extra people."

"Okay." I shrug. "That's cool. We've got cash." Keepin' it light, here.

"Do you remember picking up this girl and taking her to Oshunvilla?" Tony comes out of his silence with unexpected aggression, shoving his phone in Angel's face at a stop sign. "About a week ago?" He's pulled up a picture of Izzy.

Angel guns the car, never looking at Tony's phone. The vehicle sprints, surprising for what may be a '57 Chevy.

We barely miss another vintage car turning in front of us.

I grip the back of the seat in front of me and bite the inside of my mouth to keep from making a sissy sound. My stomach swooshes from both the car's motion and my nerves.

"At least look at the picture, man."

"Don't know her."

"You didn't even look."

Angel's gaze darts to Tony's phone. "I don't remember."

"Because you were tired, stoned? On medication?" Tony asks. "'Cause it would be hard to forget this beautiful girl."

I cringe at the way Tony is talking about my sister, but I get it. *Bad cop.*

"This girl called you, and you came to pick her up at the hostel."

Angel remains silent.

Tony continues, "We have surveillance video to prove it."

Angel would have no way of knowing whether Tony's telling the truth. His grip on the steering wheel tightens. "You a cop?" The car speeds up. His knuckles go pale, on their way to white.

I hold my breath.

Visible beads of sweat have formed on Angel's forehead. "You ain't no Cuban cop."

An idea sneaks into my head. "Would you like a water?" I pull out the water bottle Tony requested at the hostel, totally getting it now. A way to change the subject and the energy. My way to win the driver over to my side. This is what it means to be the good cop. "I have an extra." I shove it at him, over the seat.

To my surprise, the driver takes it.

I smile. Tony and I are a good team.

"Hey, listen," I continue, "this girl we're looking for"—I point to Izzy's picture on Tony's phone—"she's more than my friend. She's my sister. If you know something, anything, it's cool to tell us. I won't tell anyone. I don't want to get you in trouble. Maybe you two liked each other." I cringe while I say it. "I want to find my little sister. She's the only—" My voice cracks on the word "only." "She's the only family I have left."

That word catches again. I don't mean to get so emotional, but the words are all garbled in my throat. "Her name is Izzy. Well, Isabella, but she goes by Izzy. She's my sister." I touch her picture on Tony's smartphone. "Izzy." I'm blinking back real tears, pissed at myself for not keeping it together. Who am I kidding? I'd never make a good detective.

Through the rearview mirror, the driver blinks, too. But he won't make eye contact with me.

"Listen, we know you picked Izzy up at the hostel." Tony keeps his voice flat and nonemotional. "We want to know what happened next."

"I don't, I didn't, I—"

Tony pulls his phone away. "She wanted to go to Oshunvilla." He leans in. "Did she ever make it?"

"I did…I don't remember her, man." Angel moves his hand over his scalp as if he had hair to brush back.

"There will be surveillance video of you dropping Izzy off at Oshunvilla." Tony isn't asking a question.

"Never seen her."

A person lies, on average, ten times a day, according to Tony. Probably some FBI statistic. How many lies has Angel told in the last ten minutes?

I say, "My sister was looking for another girl who's gone missing." I pull out the missing person flyer of Arianna, the one we found at Raúl's. "You must remember this girl, right? Blonde. Gorgeous. Unforgettable."

"Never seen her." Angel answers too fast, in my opinion.

"Listen man," Tony's voice hardens. "Help us, or I call the government and tell them you're operating an illegal ride service, and that you're picking up young girls who disappear."

The driver's eyes fire as if a light flicks on inside them. "You tell them that." The corners of his lips lift.

The sly smile is so subtle, it makes my legs move restlessly.

Something is off. I dig my nails into my palm.

"Tell the cops." Angel glares at Tony. "See what *they* do."

Oh, I don't like that answer.

"Who exactly is *they*?" Tony demands, in the intimidating detective voice I remember from our first meeting.

"Hey!" I reach over the front seat and smack Tony on the shoulder. "Stop harassing the guy. I want to find my sister." I hope I didn't take this good cop/bad cop thing too far. I ramble on, softening my voice for Angel. "Why do you take the girls to Oshunvilla? Maybe they disappear there? What happens at that place?"

"It's a tourist trap," the driver snaps back. "I've never been inside."

That I don't believe.

"Come on, man. Help us out," Tony takes the next shot at him. "You want to. It's in your eyes."

I should check the rearview mirror to see what his eyes look like, but I'm distracted by the street we've turned down. A bench at a bus stop is made of painted tiles, like a piece of art you might see in the famous Dali Museum in St. Petersburg, Florida. Yellow tiles create the legs of the bench. White tiles cover the seat. Flower tiles dot the whole bench, making it look almost like it belongs in a garden in Alice's Wonderland.

A wall behind it is painted like a mural, ocean blue. "We must be close to Oshunvilla." A mermaid, made of multicolored tiles, is being chased by some type of fish. While an ornate orange octopus looks on in a bemused fashion. "Is the whole town like this?"

Angel doesn't answer.

We pass a building with a tiled archway that reads MEDICO DE /FAMILIA. "Does the artist ask people first before he makes their storefronts into pieces of his artwork?" The medical clinic is painted forest green, with a big heart made of red tile on the side of the facility. "Does he charge people for these creations?" I look up at the rearview mirror.

Finally, the driver makes eye contact. "You ask so many questions."

I almost say, "I'm a reporter," but I bite back my words. I realize I threw so many questions out at once I gave him no time to respond.

We drive up to an extended mansion spreading over four blocks and up four levels. It's connected by what looks like a maze of rooms, walkways, archways, passages, fountains, pools, and more sculptures of females than I've ever seen. *In. My. Life.* The colorful creations make up a psychedelic playground.

This is the famed Oshunvilla. The artist must have a love for all things Caribbean, because his work is littered with palm trees, ocean themes, chickens, and crocodiles dotting the walls. The female sculptures look to be nods to both the indigenous people who first inhabited this island and the Santeria beliefs that now rule. Cuban flags and political sayings are also splashed throughout the murals, like signatures.

I've never seen any place like it. And I live in Florida, close to Disney World and Busch Gardens.

Angel pulls up to the front gate and slams on the brakes. I brace myself by sinking my fingers in the crevice between car and car cushion, holding on for dear life. My fingers hit something hard. "Ouch!"

"Get out."

"Hey man," Orlando jumps in. "You wanna hang out and give us about twenty minutes or so. You can take us back?"

"Get out," the driver's voice escalates. "Don't call me again."

Orlando opens his door and exits, walking toward the

back of the car.

Tony hands the driver cash.

He rips it from Tony's fingers, leans over, and opens Tony's door. "Get out."

I'm afraid the guy will take off with me alone in the car once Tony is out, so I jerk my door open and pull myself out.

As soon as my feet hit the dirt, the driver takes off, wheels spinning, kicking up dust in my face. I cough and turn. Exhaust fumes whoosh up my nose. Now I'm gagging.

"I got his tag number," Orlando says, nodding his head like a proud papa. "We're gonna find that dude again."

Tony is watching the driver speed away. "I'll have my source here run it. We'll get an address, at least."

"He was lying. The whole time." I'm pissed, because I don't think we learned a thing from him. But I did learn *something* new.

"Of course, he lied about not knowing both girls," Tony says. "We have witnesses who say Izzy and Teddy called him. Those girls at the hostel may be able to identify the driver— not that it's going to help us find Izzy or the other girls. That driver will probably never cooperate. And we still don't know if Arianna had a connection to him."

My pulse picks up. "We can safely assume she did." I hold up a keychain, keys dangling from it.

"University of Georgia?" Tony asks.

I pull out the flyer of Arianna, the photo of her in a UGA sweatshirt. Tony and Orlando's eyes widen. "I found the keychain in the crevice of the back seat. We can now assume Teddy, Izzy, *and* Arianna used the same driver. It's a connection. We have a new suspect. Or at least another suspect."

Tony nods, "Nice, Mari."

My pulse buzzes through me like hungry bees. I care so much about his opinion, it stings sometimes. My cheeks heat, and I turn away.

"What do we do while we wait for your source to run his tag and give us an address?" Orlando is walking in a small semicircle, videotaping with his hidden hat camera.

"We do what we came here for." Tony is also looking around, but probably for surveillance cameras or anyone who may cause us trouble. "We explore Oshunvilla and look for any signs of our missing girls."

Chapter Thirteen

Day One
THREE P.M.
THIRTY-THREE HOURS LEFT

OSHUNVILLA

Walking into Oshunvilla, I feel a bit like Alice in Wonderland. Maybe the artist who created this artistic, architectural fantasyland knew those willing to travel far to get here would come seeking something serious. Maybe salvation? Maybe healing? Maybe love? Maybe family? Maybe, like Alice when she followed the rabbit down the hole, a new identity?

The words painted in bold, red strokes on the archway leading into Oshunvilla hint at what one might find here: LOVE. SUCCESS. PROSPERITY. PREGNANCY.

But it's a white rabbit made of white tile, wearing a waistcoat, and holding a watch, hopping into Oshunvilla, that catches my attention. It's a small creature, compared to the other giant mosaics, but I'd like to think the artist put much thought into this piece of artwork. What was the artist searching for when he created this giant rabbit hole for others to fall into?

That question makes me curious to meet him.

Because I've been drawn here, too.

Why did this place call out to Izzy? Surely, she didn't want to get pregnant. Maybe it's as simple as she wanted to find Arianna. She always loved being someone's savior. Like Raúl's.

Look how that turned out. I shake my head of negative thoughts. Maybe Izzy came here looking for change. Maybe she wanted to find a new identity, like Alice in Wonderland.

And what about me? Who am I, if not the girl searching for Isabella and seeking revenge for the ruination of my family.

Like Alice in Wonderland, I'm Mari in Oshunvilla. *Just as lost.*

Tony's fingers entwine in mine. I'm not sure if he's falling into our "we're a couple trying to get pregnant" alias, or if he's holding my hand because he senses my unease. I fight the urge to squeeze his fingers or run my thumb over his flesh. I love the feel of his skin, rough but not wrinkled yet by life. His touch is firm and reassuring, and when his fingers are wound up with mine, I feel safe. Even entering this unknown, whimsical, and wickedly wild place.

I glance up at Tony and catch him observing me.

He looks away immediately, his cheeks a little flushed.

From heat or embarrassment? Or something more?

Standing inside the archway of Oshunvilla, I can't help but think this feels like Kismet. For some reason we have been led here, Tony and I, together.

My fingers tingle, and I wonder if he can feel the energy.

He lets go of my hand and wipes his palm on his pants.

He doesn't reengage.

My center aches at the loss of our connection. It physically hurts that he can so easily pull away from me, leaving me longing for more.

A flurry of movement hijacks my attention.

A cat shimmies over my toes. Not the Cheshire cat with its stripped fur and mischievous grin. A real, golden cat, meowing and rubbing up against my leg. I am not in a Tim Burton movie. This is real life. And that cat is probably hungry and looking for food from tourists. I lean down and pet its silky fur.

"Where do we start?" Orlando asks me.

"Begin at the beginning," slips out.

Both Orlando and Tony stare at me like I'm losing my mind.

"And go on till you come to the end. Then stop."

Orlando places his hand on my forehead as if I'm ill.

I laugh it off. "It's a quote from *Alice in Wonderland*."

"There you are, Alicia."

Alicia? Tony raises his eyebrows. He understands that's the Spanish way of saying Alice. Now I really do feel like I'm tumbling down the rabbit hole.

"Who are you?" An elderly woman, I'm guessing in her seventies, approaches us, her gait a bit uneven and slow. "That my Alicia finds comfort with you?" The old woman is about my height but slouches in an osteoporosis way, the curve in her back looking almost painful. Her gray hair is held away from her face in two childlike ponytails held with yellow ties gathered on either side of her face. Her bangs are held back by a headband of yellow flowers. Fake, I'm assuming. They look too perfect. She wears round glasses, smudged, maybe from ash, since she's holding a thick cigar between her teeth and talks while smoking it. She's Cuba's version of an aging hippie, and something about the combination of her style and her flamboyance causes me to like her instantly.

"I'm, I'm Mary." Not going to tell her my real name, though.

"I'm Anthony," Tony says. "And this is our friend, Orlando."

O purses his lips, nods at the woman, but says nothing.

"Welcome to Oshunvilla."

I continue my observation while Tony makes small talk.

The old woman has on plastic earrings, also yellow, and a bright colored shirt, yellow and red, with loose fitting blue jeans. The type of stretchy jeans your grandmother might wear. She has an infectious grin, but her teeth are stained by tobacco and she's missing two teeth on the left side of her smile. Still, the woman exudes warmth. And I'm a pretty good judge of character, having to sum up people I'm about to interview all the time. Asking myself, *Will this person embarrass me on live TV? Will they lie and get me in trouble?*

"Your first time?" The old woman is talking to me.

"Yes, yes, it is." I'm curious that this woman knows to speak to us in English. Do we scream American? We've been trying hard to fit in.

"You are looking for the Fertility Fountain." It's not a question.

Tony reaches for my hand again, squeezes it, and smiles down at me. "We are."

My heart flutters, but only because I realize the connection I've been feeling is probably part of our act to him. Nothing more. I want to pull away but don't. I'll suffer through my own physical yearning for Tony, if it helps me find Izzy.

The woman grabs the cigar from between her teeth, blows out smoke, and beams as she nods. "It is as I thought when I saw you two. Holding hands. Sneaking looks at each other. Lovers. But not yet parents."

Tony's fingers flex within mine, and I fight to hold a

straight face. We are not lovers. Guess we're playing the part convincingly.

"And you are…?" Tony asks the woman.

Orlando is close now, adjusting his hat down over his forehead. The woman should have no idea he's recording her.

"Graciela Gonzalez." She puts the cigar back into her mouth with almost a twirl, puffs on it, and says in a cloud of smoke, "But people call me Granny."

The smell of cigar smoke makes me ill. "Granny," I repeat, after catching my breath, thinking it's odd strangers would call her that, but who am I to judge? "Do you work here?"

"Ah, that's a good question, my love." She pats me on the cheek.

I step back at her familiarity.

"The artist doesn't pay me." She throws her head back and laughs, a deep, rich sound with a little crackling that is probably the result of years puffing on tobacco. "I'm the historian, I guess you could say."

The cat, Alicia, is no longer purring or rubbing my leg. She's now swirling around Graciela.

"I love Oshunvilla and all the stories woven into Jimagua's works," the old woman says between puffs.

"He-ma-gwa." *So that's the artist's name.* I let the sound roll over my tongue. "He-ma-gwa." Even his name is like artwork.

"Follow me." Graciela gestures. "I will take you to the Fertility Fountain."

"Let's go." Tony pulls me forward, his other hand finding the curve in my lower back, pushing gently.

As we walk down the mosaic tiled pathways through the art kingdom, we pass a colossal floating eye and many swooping curlicues that climb into the air like the smoke from Graciela's cigar. References to daily life here are abundant.

People playing dominoes, an outdated fan on the floor by their feet. Vintage cars next to the Virgin Mary. A Cuban flag next to the words VIVA CUBA. All made with tiles or clay. I'm silent, because words would distract me from absorbing all the magical details of the artist's genius. He must be mad. Only a mad mind could create such a place.

I glance at Orlando. He's silent, too, turning his head side to side, his chest as well. But he's also pulled out the GoPro. That doesn't scream media, as most tourists have them now.

We stop by an elongated pool with a fountain at one end. The fountain is full of floating sunflowers. On the side nearest to the wall and the tiled statue of a goddess, pumpkins sit in a line, with what looks like honey and some food dishes I don't recognize. They must be offerings to the goddess.

"This is Oshun?" I point to the enormous creation looming over us.

"Oshun, yes," Graciela says. "Oshun is the queen of the waters of the world. She is also the personification of love, wealth, and fertility."

The goddess is adorned with gold jewelry, bracelets and beads, mirrors, and other elaborate decorations. She has a gold crown that looks more like rays of sunshine beaming outward from her head. Under her gold gown, she has the tail of a mermaid—gold, not green or blue. And in her arms, Oshun holds a beautiful, bronzed-skinned baby.

"You pray to Oshun to be blessed with children." Graciela has both of her hands across her own belly, staring reverently at the vision of Oshun.

Next to Oshun, a statue of a tall and powerful woman reaches out across the fountain, reaching out to me it seems. I point to the statue. "Who is this?"

"Ah, this is where my job as historian comes in." Graciela no longer has the cigar. "This is Adora, Jimagua's mother."

I catch the twinkle in Graciela's eyes. "She's, she's—" I

can't ask if the woman is dead. That would be rude, right? So, I cover with, "She's beautiful."

Graciela smiles but says, "She is no longer with us."

I want to say, "What's her story?" Instead, I ask, "What happened?"

"Adora was pregnant with twins. A boy and a girl. She had a condition that is rare called twin-twin syndrome, where in the womb the stronger twin, Jimagua, takes the nutrients of the other twin. The baby girl died in the womb. Born dead."

I shiver. I can't imagine delivering a child that is already dead. I lick my lips, thirsty for more information, dry and full of empathy for this mother who lost her baby before she even had a chance at life. How unfair. Under the statue is a headstone with the name Adora on it. Is that where her ashes are? Or did the mother name the dead baby after herself?

"Adora focused all her attention on Jimagua, treating him like a king, because she couldn't have any more children, after the...after the incident. But Adora still longed for a little girl."

As I look around, I realize most of the statues in the courtyard by the pool and fountain are females. Young females. Some even babies.

"Adora, like many Cubans, practiced Santeria," Graciela continues.

I get the feeling she's more than the historian here. She's a tour guide and has given this talk many times before. To many tourists. Is she expecting money? *Probably.*

I need to get back to searching for Izzy.

"Adora prayed to Oshun every day. Jimagua grew up watching this, and the young boy began creating art to dedicate to Oshun to please his mother, whom he loved with his whole heart. His artwork began to take off, getting noticed all over the world. The Cuban government recognized his talent and began demanding more. Jimagua branched out, making artwork that symbolized the great details of the Cuban lifestyle. From the ocean and sea creatures to—"

"The evil eye," I say, paying attention while also scanning the crowd for anyone who looks like my sister. As I circle around, I catch Orlando shooting me an evil eye of his own.

I ignore it.

"You will see many images dedicated to the practice of Santeria here."

"He's amazing," I gush. "I mean, I can really see why tourists travel from all over the world to see his art." *Kill 'em with kindness.* And it isn't a lie. Maybe she'll help me find Izzy if she likes us.

"Adora decided they would turn not only their home, but their town, into an art wonderland that would draw in tourists from, as you say, all around the world. It worked. The Cuban government changed the name of the town to Oshunvilla, and they now pay Jimagua to keep his home open and keep changing it up with new artwork."

"Jimagua's mother must have been a genius." I stare at the statue of a beautiful, bronze-skinned woman with blonde hair and dark brown loving eyes. "What happened to her?"

"She never got over the death of her daughter and eventually died of a broken heart."

Or maybe a regular ole heart attack. Broken heart is a better story for tourists, though. "Is she buried here?" I point to the headstone that reads Adora.

"Jimagua couldn't bear to let his mother go, so he had her cremated and placed her ashes in the concrete base of this statue. Now, when women come to pray to Oshun, Adora stands watch over them, protecting them, and praying with them that they will get their wish to have a baby."

My heart stretches, thinking of my own mother, gunned down and taken from us so cruelly. I feel a connection with this Jimagua instantly. "I'd like to meet the artist."

"Oh no. He works only at night." Graciela waves her hand, dismissing my request. "All night. And sleeps during the day. He doesn't meet people."

"But you've met him?" I ask.

"What's that?" Orlando asks. "The baby's gravestone?"

I'm a little annoyed at O because he and I used to have a better rhythm. Orlando would never jump in and ask a question when I just asked one and am still waiting for an answer.

"Yes. This is where baby Adora is buried. Two hearts still connected. Never apart."

Electricity shimmies across my skin. Reporter's intuition. *There's more here.*

Next to the headstone is a coconut bowl with two plastic hearts in it. I elbow Tony and try to get his attention without pointing. Two hearts, one baby sized, the other adult sized. *WTH.* I envision the plastic heart we saw earlier at the altar in the town where the festival took place. How many hours ago? Seems like a whole different lifetime ago. I mean, how many fake plastic hearts does one see in a lifetime? I've seen three today. The whole thing gives me the heebie-jeebies.

"How do we go about praying to Oshun?" Tony asks.

Leave it to the detective to stay on track.

Something fires in Graciela's eyes. Not sure what it is. Passion for helping couples conceive?

"Usually one brings an offering," Graciela says.

"A sunflower," I say. I should have kept the one given to me during the festival.

"But it is not necessary, if the intent in your hearts is real."

My breath catches. Can this woman see my feelings for Tony on my face? Or does she read energy? Some people have that gift.

Graciela grins. "Take my hand, young one."

Her skin is rough and weathered, the opposite of Tony's. But I don't fight her. I hold her hand and look right into her eyes.

"I will say the prayer. Later, when you are alone, you finish the ritual."

I remember the bags of ingredients the Santera gave me at her grocery store. Honey, candles, ribbons, a variety of typical Santeria ritual items. Does Graciela know about that? How could she? But everything that has happened so far today seems to be connected and seems to have brought Tony and me here. And that scares the heck out of me. I don't want to get pregnant.

Does this stuff really work? Is Tony wondering that, too?

Doesn't matter. Getting pregnant would require sex. Which we aren't having.

"My goddess, patroness of fresh waters, wife, mother of all your devotees, I turn to you and your abilities, with all the humility and devotion that my being can give. I ask you, Mother, to help this woman become a mother with this man."

It's subtle, but I know Tony so well, that when his muscles tense, I feel it. When his energy shifts, I know. He's as uncomfortable with this as I am. Why? Because this woman, this person we've never met, is hitting on issues we've not had the courage to address.

"I ask that you come closer to this woman, squeeze her belly with love."

Graciela places her other hand on my flat stomach. I flinch. Even though I try to stand perfectly still.

"I want you to turn this into a fertile belly, so that she can carry this man's future child and bring her to Earth."

Her?

"Hear my prayers and guide me along the path of the good mother. Amen."

Something about this spiritual moment calls up the image

of my Abuela Bonita. Her last words to me, "I leave you with one last thought. Broken girls blossom into warriors. Be a warrior, Marisol. Be a warrior."

Why would I think of that right now when a woman is praying for my fertility? Because, if I ever do have a baby girl, that is what I will teach her. To be a warrior. Not a victim.

"Hey, ah, not to intrude on the ceremony and all. I mean it's peachy, but"—Orlando is fidgety— "who is this person?"

O is pointing to another statue on the other side of Oshun. A younger person, brown-skinned, beautiful. Also reaching out, not to us, to Oshun.

Graciela's face darkens.

"I do not know. The artist does not speak of it."

Okay. I'm making note of that.

O certainly does. He's videotaping the statue with his GoPro.

Graciela's smile comes out again. "Even I do not know the history of every single piece of art. Can you imagine if I did?"

The sudden feel of fur on the bare part of my leg makes me jerk. It's so startling, I drop Tony's hand. The cat is back to rubbing on me again, and as I reach down to pet it, the cat takes off, sprinting. It scampers across the courtyard to another woman across the pool from us. The woman has a frantic face, at least that's what it looks like from this distance. She's handing out papers. Maybe *missing person flyers*? Worth checking out. "I'll be right back," I say to whoever is listening.

"Hey, wait—" Tony says, reaching for my hand. Again.

Is he trying to control my actions? Or trying to keep our connection? I step away. Because I don't want him to stop me.

"I'm coming with you," O says.

"Thank you, Graciela. We will—"

The older woman raises her hand. "Don't leave without

visiting the Wishing Wall. Leave your wish for a child. Pin it to the wall. The messages come down tonight. They'll be burned and offered up to Oshun in tribute later this evening. To rise into reality."

"You burn the messages every week?" I ask.

"Yes, or the wall would be overrun with papers. The messages are delivered to the heavens when they turn to ash. Wishes from the fire go from death to life. To rise into reality, a wish must first die."

The woman with the flyers is walking away. I need to see whose face is on those papers. Is it her daughter's? Maybe Teddy's? Maybe Izzy's? Maybe some other missing girl?

"Okay, I'll—"

I turn around and Graciela has disappeared.

Chapter Fourteen

As I approach the woman who appears to be handing out something, her gaze darts side to side until it locks on me. Something must resonate with her because her cheeks, already rosy, appear to darken. Maybe it's the late afternoon steam, post storm. Her mouth drops open and sweat drops from her face onto the flyers she clutches in her hands.

She's white-knuckling them. Her chest rises and falls like she's completed a difficult sprint.

"My name is Mari." I place my hand on her shoulder, trying to ease her tension. "I couldn't help but notice you handing out flyers. May I have one?"

The woman blinks back tears. Her eyes are red as if from nightmares. "I'm Cynthia Meyers." Her wrinkled clothes tell me she's been wearing the same sundress for days. Her feet, in sandals, appear dusty and dirty, and her fingernails have dirt under them. "I'm looking for my daughter, Fredericka."

I tilt my head because that's not a name—

"Her friends call her Teddy."

I exhale. My chest hurts for this woman. I take the flyer

and look at it—it's the same one up on the altar in Playa Hermosa. "How long has Teddy been missing?" I don't tell her I first saw her picture above a severed goat's head with half-eaten eyeballs.

"Two weeks, I think. Mandy called me when my daughter started seeing this local guy."

Raúl. A strike right to my gut. Where the hell did he run to? We must go back to his house and see if he's returned.

"She worried the guy isolated Teddy, keeping her away from the hostel."

Some things never change. Raúl isolated Izzy, too, when they were teens. And probably forced her here to Cuba as an adult.

"Then one day, Teddy didn't return to the hostel, and she hasn't been heard from since."

The pattern is similar. I look away, sick to my stomach. Sick, because I don't know what to do next.

"Who is Mandy?" Tony asks.

"Mandy Preacher. Teddy's best friend. They're traveling together. You know college kids. They want to see the world. Cuba is so exotic. They convinced me they needed to start checking things off their bucket list. Everything is cheap here, which is one of the reasons they came."

Are traveling together. She still has hope. "Where is Mandy?" She may have seen my sister at some point at the hostel. I still have hope, too.

"I spoke with her right before I flew into Havana but, since I arrived, Mandy hasn't answered her phone. She hasn't been seen at the hostel." Ms. Meyers rolls her lips inward, drops her gaze to the flyers she's still gripping. "I don't know. I made up flyers with Mandy's picture, too."

She hands me one.

"Another missing girl," I say mostly to myself, because I can't believe what's happening. This mission should have been so simple. Find Raúl. Find Izzy. Bring her home. Shouldn't take more than forty-eight hours.

Now we've got four missing women to find.

"Holy shitzo." Orlando is using his GoPro to video what Ms. Meyers is saying. He gets it, too.

His documentary is about more than Izzy now.

It's about all the missing girls.

The woman looks so beaten down, so frazzled, she doesn't seem to care that Orlando is recording her.

I check out the second flyer. Mandy is another college-aged girl, with auburn hair and bright blue eyes and freckles. She has an innocent smile, if also world-weary eyes. A purplish hemangioma covers a portion of the right side of her face. That will make her hard to forget, which might help us. My heart squeezes, thinking about what might be happening to these young women, Izzy included.

"This is Orlando Jones and Tony Garcia." I don't fill in details of our professions because right now, we're simply friends on a mission. "We are here looking for my sister, Isabella. She's missing, too." I can't believe I'm saying this, standing in the middle of a mystical mansion with another woman looking for another young girl.

"How long have you been in Cuba looking for her?" Tony asks.

"I've been here for about four days."

"Teddy's dad?" Tony's firing off questions like he's the reporter.

"I'm here alone." Ms. Meyers takes a long, slow deep breath. "Teddy's dad isn't in the picture. Neither is Mandy's. She's a foster child whose been living in the system."

Ms. Meyers doesn't need to say more. Both young women are vulnerable. Easier targets. Like Izzy.

"Teddy met Mandy in high school. They're both free spirits, and not very focused on the big pictures in life."

She shrugs and bites her bottom lip. "They wanted to travel together for a gap year. Live in the moment. Seek adventure and love, you know." She shrugs.

I feel the weight on the woman's shoulders. She can barely move them. "I do know." Izzy is also a romantic. Always believed the best in Raúl. Or at least believed she could change him, show him a better way. "Now we have four missing girls." I leave out *and two possible suspects: Raúl and the driver, Angel.*

"Where else have you looked?" Tony asks.

"The hostel they were staying at. Everyone there has been most helpful. I've gone to the local police. They have my baby's journal. But they aren't being helpful. I've been to a few other tourist attractions where I was told they've visited. I came here again today, because Teddy said she wanted to visit Oshunvilla."

"Did she say why? Like, what she was looking for here?" I spin around, and my foot lands in some uneven part of the ground. I fall backward. I hit something hard behind me, feel it teeter and shatter as it hits the ground. "Ouch! Uh-oh. What did I just—"

"Stop!"

The high-pitched wail freaks me out. I'm spinning around, trying to see what the hell I knocked over. Then trying to see who's screeching at me.

"He will know. He will be angry with me." The man talking is thin, scrawny. His stick arms are covered in a brown monk-like dress over jeans and a long coat. It's like ninety-eight degrees out. His head is covered, and he is wearing sunglasses and a wrap around his lower face and neck. Like a fisherman might wear to protect his neck from the sun.

I can't see his facial features, so I focus on his energy. "I'm, listen, I'm really sorry." *I am.* "I'm sure the artist worked hard on the piece I knocked over. I can pay for it."

"This piece is new." The man falls to his knees. He's going to cut himself on those sharp tile and clay edges. "It's priceless."

Ay Dios mio. Is he setting me up to sue me? "I'm sure they are all special."

"Don't move!"

I freeze and throw my hands up like a guilty suspect in a bank robbery. "I'm sorry." Whatever the art piece used to be, once it hit the ground, it shattered into tile and clay pieces of something totally unrecognizable. "I'm sure it was beautiful." I'm also pretty sure it can't be glued back together.

"Don't step on anything." Still on his knees, he fingers a few of the shattered pieces, staring at them as if precious diamonds. "Stay where you are."

"Can we help?" Tony also has his hands out, empty, in a show of cooperation. My eyes fall on the bulge near his belt, where his weapon is secured. I'm glad it's there. Should we need it. I'm not sure what this man's deal is, but he's obviously upset. Angry, even.

"I will clean it up. I will clean it up. I will clean it up. Or he will punish me."

I recognize this pattern. It's OCD, a need for control. I reach for my azabache charm and twist it three times to the right, three to the left. I don't look at Tony because he won't approve. But I get it. This guy's got anxiety. For whatever reason, it's transferring to me.

"He's going to punish me." It's a whisper now.

"Who is 'he?'" Tony asks but doesn't move.

"The one."

"Jimagua?" It's the artist he is referring to, but I want to make sure.

The man looks up at me, and his eyes clear. It's like he sees me for the first time. "No. Luis." He stops his obsessive collecting of clay pieces, and his gaze holds mine. "It's my job to take care of the art."

He's clutching clay pieces so tightly I'm afraid his palms will start bleeding.

"Protect the art. At all costs." He keeps pawing the pieces in his palms. "No one must break it."

"I... I'm sorry, I... This wasn't *your* fault. I'll take responsibility." What could that mean? *No one must break it.* This is a tourist destination. I'm sure this isn't the first accident here.

"Luis will know." The man stares at me. Then, it's like curtains slide across his windows, and he sees me no more.

"Luis will know what?"

"Excuse me."

Someone is tugging on my shirt. *Ms. Meyers!* I forgot her.

She swallows and fidgets with her flyers. "Can I get your phone number?" She gestures toward the exit. "I need to keep looking for the girls."

She's looking at the strange man on his knees, gathering pieces of shattered art, like maybe he's a little crazy. This must be heightening her anxiety, as well.

"Sure, of course." I take her phone and insert my cell number.

"If you hear anything, find your sister, anything."

I nod. "I'll call you." I want to say more, but my gaze is drawn back to the skinny man with trembling fingers. He's placing jagged remnants of the artwork in a jacket he'd been wearing over that brown gown-like thing, in this god-awful steaminess, and it looks like he intends to carry all the pieces in the jacket to be fixed. His fingers shake.

That's when I notice the tattoos on each finger. Each one has a letter on it. P. E. R.

"What are you doing?" The harsh voice pulls my gaze away from figuring out what the letters spell.

Graciela is back, looking the same, except for the bonfire

blazing in her eyes. That heat isn't directed at me. It's directed at the man on the ground.

"I didn't do it. I didn't." He points at me. "She, she broke it."

Graciela grabs the man by his collar and pulls him to his feet. "You know the rules."

The violence in that one, quick, controlled gesture makes me take a step back.

"What's going on here?" Tony's hand moves naturally to sit closer to his gun holster.

"Don't talk to the tourists." It's but a whisper. The man doesn't even look at Graciela as he says it. His eyes are focused on the ground.

I feel his fear all the way into my soul. I don't know what to say to help him.

"That's *my* job," Graciela's voice softens, but her smile remains chilly.

Orlando is moving around the pair with his GoPro out. It's low and not obvious, but I worry what Graciela will say if she sees it.

Tony is still. The detective knows when to pause and let a scene play out.

I'm right in the middle of this scenario and feel like I should address this. "Graciela, I'm so sorry. I backed into this piece and—"

"What are you supposed to be doing?" She doesn't even look at me, and I know she's not talking to me. Her focus is totally on the man-child trying to kneel once again in the wreckage of the art.

"He will punish me. He will—"

All of this is in Spanish, so Orlando has no idea what's being said, but Tony and I do. Do they know that? We'd been speaking to Graciela in English.

"Look at your phone, Alejandro. Focus on what you are

supposed to be doing right now." Graciela won't let the man go back onto his knees. "You need to check your phone."

Alejandro pulls out a smartphone from a pocket and looks down at it. "Check the newest statue in tribute to Oshun." He reads from it. "Near the fountain."

Graciela pats Alejandro on the back. "That is what you need to do." She pushes him forward.

Her negative energy makes my whole body tingle. What's going on here?

"I will take care of this mess. I will handle Jimagua."

She will handle the artist. *The tour guide?* This man fears someone. What did he call him? What was it? Luis.

"He's sleeping right now, anyway. He will never—" Graciela stops before she finishes her sentence. I'm about to ask her if she's talking about this man named Luis or the artist Jimagua, when she looks up and asks, "Have you been to the Wishing Wall yet?"

"Uh, no." Been a little busy. *And a little creeped out.*

"You should go now. We close soon."

We've been dismissed.

Graciela will handle the man, and, I think, the weird developing situation at hand.

But my feet are like concrete blocks. They aren't going anywhere. "Who is he?"

Graciela exhales like she's angry I asked. "Alejandro is the groundskeeper." Her voice has that air of exasperation. "He takes care of maintenance items, the landscaping."

"And the art?" I ask. "What's wrong with him?" I ask it in front of him, because, frankly, the man doesn't even look like he's with us anymore. He's reading his phone and mumbling the message repeatedly.

"He's not well," Graciela strokes the man's hair.

Which I also find creepy. He's the landscaper. But I guess they could be friends. They work together.

"We keep him around because"—Graciela shrugs—"well, to kick him out would be cruel. He couldn't survive, I fear. Jimagua is eccentric, but the talented one is not cruel."

The lady doth protest too much, me thinks. But I say nothing. The nausea roiling in my stomach tells me something is not right with this situation.

But what *is* right here? I'm standing in the middle of a place weirder than Alice's Wonderland, with evil eyes and Cuban flags flying and women praying for fertility. There's a man-child crying over a shattered piece of art, when this whole town is full of finer and more fabulous examples. Graciela appeared to be good-natured, but now I'm aware of her sharp tongue, firm grip, and her entitled air that tells me she's respected here. What did the Cheshire cat say? "We are all mad here."

"Would you like us to pay for the damage?" Tony enters the conversation.

"I'm sorry." The groundskeeper's body is shaking. "I'm sorry."

Graciela wraps her arms around the man, who has once again fallen to his knees among the chunks of broken clay. She seems to be hiding his face from us, but I can tell by the sound of his voice, he's crying. "I don't want him to be mad at me."

"Come with me," Graciela says, comforting him, but there's a sharp edge to her tone. "I will make it all right. I promise."

My desire to meet the famous artist vanishes. He must be a real ass. Despite what Graciela says.

Graciela stops and looks back at me. "When did she disappear?"

"When did who disappear?" Did I tell her about Izzy? Or is she talking about Teddy?

"Your sister."

"My sister." I roll my lips in, trying to remember when we discussed Izzy. "How did you know?"

"I overheard you talking to the other mother."

Did she? What do I have to lose? "Izzy came to Oshunvilla six days ago. She hasn't been seen since." I inhale. Hold my breath.

The groundskeeper's knees give, but Graciela catches him.

"I'm sorry about your sister," she says to me, the man-baby in her arms whimpering. "I have not seen her. Maybe you should look elsewhere."

My heart flutters. "Okay, I will. Thank you."

What Graciela doesn't know is I have no plans to leave and look elsewhere. I plan to find the Wishing Wall before Oshunvilla closes today. I plan to search for a wish by my sister. And I plan to leave a wish of my own.

"You are worried." Graciela looks at me. "Let me handle this, this situation." She points to the broken piece of art. "And then I will take you to security. We can look over surveillance video the day your sister came to Oshunvilla. We can see who she came with. And when she left. While I take care of Alejandro, you visit the Wishing Wall. It's your last chance before the wishes go up in flames."

Chapter Fifteen

Day One
4:30 P.M.
THIRTY-ONE AND A HALF HOURS LEFT

All paths in Oshunvilla lead to Oshun.

The earlier downpour made the path we're on slick. Fog dances around a giant statue with two faces. You can't miss *this* version of Oshun. First, she's tall. The tiled creation, at least four feet taller than me, looks half goddess, half sea creature. The fog only adds to the mystery. This Oshun, dressed in her yellow gown, has one face in profile, the other straight on.

She wears a sunflower hat with octopus legs extending outward from the top of the hat to the ground. Forty-eight hours ago, this weird piece of art would have freaked me out. Now, I'm merely noting how the statue looks like one of those alien creatures from Tom Cruise's *War of the Worlds*.

In one hand, Oshun holds an orange pumpkin and in the other, a white candle. The largest sunflower I've ever seen sits on her head like the most glorious Kentucky Derby hat, and long green stems protrude from the top of her head in four different places, curving up and out and finally toward the ground like tentacles, anchoring the statue in four different corners. Like a tent. I can't imagine how long it took the artist to make this version of Oshun. But I've literally forgotten to breathe while taking it all in.

Behind the giant statue looms the infamous Wishing Wall, a green mesh fence with wishes written on multicolored papers woven into holes in the mesh. Must be hundreds of them anchored with fabulously colored plastic ties. A rainbow of heartfelt desires.

"It's already four-thirty," Orlando says. "We'll never be able to go through all of these messages before they close."

Orlando needs food. He ate that Cuban bread and drank the coffee, but hours ago. We haven't had a real meal today. Eating hasn't been a priority. But eventually, we will all need fuel.

"Graciela said they take the messages down today and burn them." I don't have to add, "So I'm not leaving until I at least try."

"Why is it so important to find a message from Izzy?" Tony walks up next to me, staring at the wall, too. "Pretty safe to assume she's been here, based on witness accounts and the driver's reaction."

Tony, always the reasonable cop.

"I want to *prove* she was here, for one. I also want to know what she's been wishing for. Maybe that will help lead us to her." I'm a pain in the ass sometimes, but I have to do what I have to do. I came here to find my sister. This is what I can do right now.

"All right. Well, I missed a call from my source. Couldn't pick it up until I knew the groundskeeper didn't represent a threat."

Or Graciela. "Can you share?"

Tony squints at me. "I told you I haven't talked to him yet." He raises both shoulders and both hands like the question emoji.

"No, I mean can you share *who* your source is?"

He cocks his head at me like he used to when we were adversaries, him the homicide detective, me the nosy reporter.

"What if something happens to you and Orlando, and I need *a source* to help us get out of Cuba?" I'm a little aggravated Tony hasn't already thought of that. I must be hangry, too. *Get a hold of your emotions, Mari.*

"Good point." Orlando is on my side.

"Nothing is going to happen to me." Tony is on his phone, scrolling. "But, because you want to know"—he holds out his phone, open to a contact—"Tom Marshal."

"Thanks." I'm surprised he gave in so quickly.

"He's an undercover U.S. Marshal living here in Havana."

"Marshal is a marshal?" O asks.

"Funny." Tony rolls his eyes.

But I appreciate Orlando's humor. We need some comic relief right about now.

"This is Marshal's number." Tony air drops the contact to me.

Fugitive apprehension is a principal mission of the U.S. Marshal service. Tony really does want to haul Raúl's ass back to America and see him face justice. My heart swells at the thought. Pretty sure he wants that *for me.* "Where are you going to make the call?" I feel safe if I can see Tony.

"I'll be right over there." He points to a bench at the side of the giant Oshun sculpture. "Going to call him back. I'm hoping he's been able to track Izzy's phone location, and Teddy's, too. Maybe get us an address for the driver. Marshal's working on a couple of things."

"Got it." I'm impressed. I should share that with Tony,

but now isn't the time to tell him how much I appreciate him. Orlando is here and, well, Tony would think it unprofessional. "We're going to start looking at messages. We'll be here."

Tony nods and walks toward the bench.

I watch him go.

"Where do we start?" Orlando asks.

"I have no idea." Which is true. I'm a little intimidated by all the messages and the clock ticking on Oshunvilla's closing.

And on our chance to catch our ride back to America.

"If you want to leave a wish for Oshun, you pay for a piece of paper over there." A young woman, holding the hands of twin toddlers, has a piece of paper in her hands. She uses her head to gesture to the right.

An older woman, dressed in all white with yellow accents, sits on a stool, with a slew of items to sell around her. Paper. Pens. Flowers. Candles. Pumpkins.

"Write your message and use the fabric to tie it to the mesh of the wall. It worked for me."

She has twins, so I guess it did. "Thank you." I smile at her but say to O, "You got cash?" I doubt this lady in white will take American Express.

"I do."

O pays for two papers and fabric ties. I write my wish.

Find Izzy safe. Bring her home. Destroy Raúl.

Why waste words? I glance over at Orlando, who is also writing. I read: *Find Isabella.* My heart warms, because O uses his wish to find my sister. He's still writing. *Produce a documentary good enough to air on Netflix.* Okay. He's allowed a selfish wish, too. I smile at him when he catches me spying. "It will happen, O."

He shrugs. "We hang the wish anywhere?" he asks the woman selling the paper and fabric ties.

I repeat the question to her in Spanish.

The woman, dark-skinned with gray hair and sparkling

eyes, says, "You can leave your message on the far end of the wall. Messages are left in the order of the date they are written."

Excitement trickles through me. The wishes go in order? "I can't explain how helpful that is." I glance at the far wall from where we stand. It's less full. "We should post our wishes down there?" I point.

The woman nods and repeats, "The wishes are in the order of the date they were written."

My heart skips another beat. Orlando's smiling. He understands. This is how we'll find Izzy's wish before this crazy place closes. Izzy's wish should be near the left side of the wall, where the week's wishes would have begun, since we believe she came here six days ago.

To not look suspicious, I walk with Orlando, and we tie our wishes onto the mesh wall in an empty space at the end. I casually stroll down the wall toward the other end, stopping occasionally to read messages, trying to find if anyone dated their wishes.

Orlando walks in front of me, I'm sure capturing the wall with his hidden cameras.

A few do leave dates on their pieces of paper.

I'm getting closer, Izzy. I'm closer to finding you.

"Mari, I think I've found it."

My pulse surges.

Orlando is three steps ahead of me. How would he know a message is from Izzy? I wipe sweat off my brow. Tuck a strand of hair behind my ear. "Why do you think—"

"Guilt brought me here. Fears holds me hostage. Don't rescue me. I deserve to die. Don't rescue me," Orlando reads the message out loud. "It's Izzy."

My mouth goes dry. My body begins to tremble. Heat hits the back of my eyes. I'm sweating even more now.

"I recognize her handwriting," O says.

That's not all I recognize. "Read it again."

He does.

"She's using our secret sister code. Say something twice, it means the opposite." My heart flutters, making it hard to breathe.

O reads the message again. "Don't rescue me. I deserve to die. Don't rescue me. Holy fuck. You're right."

"Izzy knew I'd come after her. She wants me to rescue her."

"I'm all in. But where the sunflower and Oshun tentacles is she now?"

I smile. What would I do without O's humor keeping me from letting my anxiety take over? I spot three surveillance cameras pointed at the Wishing Wall. Why didn't I think of this sooner? My head is so scrambled with emotion, that's why. "We follow the video. Like Graciela said."

"Wha-?"

"Look around us, O." He moves his body in a circle. "There are surveillance cameras everywhere. This is a tourist attraction. They're monitoring everything everyone does. Like Disney or Universal Studios. There's got to be video of Izzy writing this and also of her arriving and leaving."

He snaps a finger. "If they don't erase it or burn it. Remember the hostel?"

"Well, Graciela offered. She must know."

"Let's go find the security office," O says. He's obviously excited.

I wave Tony over.

He nods and moves our way.

Maybe he's gotten somewhere, too.

Things are looking up. I touch the paper note left by my sister. I want to feel her DNA. *I'm closer to you, Izzy. I can feel it.* I pay for another piece of paper and write another wish. *Oshun, lead me to my sister. Lay out the clues so I can follow them. I surrender the power to you. I will follow. Amen.*

"I've got good news."

I jump.

Tony is behind me. His closeness makes every cell in my body wake up.

"My source got an address on the driver."

"Yes! I've got good news to share, too. We found Izzy's note on the Wishing Wall." *Ay Dios mio.* I feel all the emotion gathering behind my eyes again. I don't want to get all weepy in front of him. "We need to check out security footage. She's *got* to be on it. Maybe she'll be with the driver, Raúl—someone who can lead us to her."

He grabs my hand. "Perfect. I've got another lead we can follow afterward."

I'm lost for a moment, because I'm still focused on him grabbing my hand. A wave of sensation moves deep in my center.

"Marshal also found the last place Teddy's cell phone pinged."

"Here?" That would be my guess, anyway.

"About fifteen minutes outside of Oshunvilla, near Playa Hermosa."

Close to Raúl's home. My stomach tanks. All my ecstatic vibrations evaporate. *Of course.*

All roads on this mission lead to Raúl.

"Okay, let's check with security first. See if they can pull up video at the wall when we think Izzy visited Oshunvilla. Next, we'll go to where Teddy's phone last pinged and see how close it is to that asshole, Raúl. Remember the cell burned in his backyard? I wouldn't be surprised if Teddy's phone pinged right in the middle of Raúl's fire pit."

Chapter Sixteen

Day One
5:45 P.M.
LESS THAN THIRTY HOURS LEFT

One hour, fifteen minutes, and thirty seconds. That's how long we've been sitting in the cramped, non-airconditioned security office looking through surveillance video from six days ago. Apparently, hundreds of people visit Oshunvilla every day. Rain or shine, holiday or not. The room is tiny, one long desk, three chairs, two half empty coffee cups, and no windows. The air in the room hangs heavy, like a cape, smothering me.

Tony sits next to the head of security scrolling quickly through hours of tourists arriving and leaving. The head of security decided that would be our best bet in finding video of Isabella.

I'm surprised at how advanced their security system is. They've got at least twenty TV screens following movement in twenty different areas of Oshunvilla, including the entrance and exit, the Wishing Wall, Oshun's Fertility Fountain, and the main residence where Jimagua sleeps and works. I'm also surprised at their willingness to help us, simple tourists from America looking for my missing sister. At least, that's the story we're giving them. But true to her word, Graciela spoke to Jimagua, who gave the okay. Thought the artist slept all day. Well, it's evening now, even though the sun has yet to go down.

One man sits at the desk monitoring the TV screens. He's a big guy, probably in his fifties, strong but silent type. Only speaking when we ask him questions. A couple of walkie-talkies sit on the table, and I'm sure he has an undercover security force all over the grounds, waiting for word of who to escort out and why. I'm taking note of every detail.

"Stop the video."

Tony's urgency brings me back to the present. "What do you see?"

"That's the same car we came here in today, agree?"

Tony points to a cherry red, vintage Chevy. In America today, this kind of car would stick out. In Cuba, maybe not. Except, this car has been kept in pristine condition. Polished. Perfect. Like the one we got into at the hostel in Havana. This video was taken later in the same day Izzy came, almost the same time as now. The sun is setting, and there are few lights outside of Oshunvilla.

Orlando is standing behind Tony, his GoPro hidden in his baseball cap. Graciela may have convinced the artist to allow us to review security footage, but we decided not to push our luck, or show our hand, by pulling out video cameras or GoPros.

A young woman, could have been Izzy's age, walks out the gates of Oshunvilla. She's wearing casual clothes, shorts, and a tank top, with a Tampa Bay Rays baseball cap pulled down low. Sunglasses hide her eyes. A ponytail sticks through the back of the cap.

"Looks like Izzy," I say, but she could be any college-age brunette, really. "I don't recognize those clothes, but that doesn't mean anything. She does like the Rays."

Note to self: ask girls at hostel if Izzy wore a Rays hat the day they met her.

The girl stumbles, but I can't see anything on the ground for her to fall over. *Weird.* She puts her arms out to steady herself and walks toward the red Chevy.

"Why is she walking like a sloth? Is she drunk? Or maybe high?"

The head of security shrugs. He points to the time on the screen. "It's about six thirty p.m. We close at six, but sometimes tourists stay for a bit. Drivers wait to pick tourists up, same as every day. But I recognize this driver." He taps the screen next to the red Chevy.

Tony sits up in his seat. "You do?"

The man nods. "He's here often."

"And?" Tony leans in toward the guy.

"This driver drops off and picks up only younger women. Like this girl. They're always alone."

"Think that's weird?" I ask. *Cause I do.*

The security guard pauses, rubs his chin. His phone dings. He looks down at it then flips the phone over so we can't read the screen. "Most tourists show up in twosomes. Or in groups larger than that. This driver seems to find the ones who are here without partners."

Tony nods and glances my way.

We all understand. This driver likes young girls, unaccompanied and vulnerable. But why? Is he interested in sex or something more sinister?

"Okay, so we think this is Izzy," Tony says. "Where did she go after leaving here six days ago? We can't track her phone. I've tried. No pings. Nothing. Phone is either dead or—"

"Destroyed," I finish for him, thinking of Raúl's fire pit.

"Maybe the driver took her to the same place he takes other girls." Tony isn't looking at anyone, which makes me think he's talking out loud. "Maybe he's habitual."

Like a serial killer.

Chills hit me, and I shudder. "So, we go to where Teddy's phone pinged last." As soon as I say it, I glance at the security guard and wonder if I shouldn't have mentioned this.

Tony doesn't respond, which lets me know these are the kinds of details I need to keep to myself.

"Zoom in on the car, can you?" Tony changes the subject. "I'm trying to read the tag."

The security guard does as Tony asks.

"Same tag," Tony says. "It's a match. We need to talk to our driver friend again."

I glance at Orlando, but neither of us say anything. We both know Tony already has the driver's address. He got it from Mr. Marshal, the U.S. Marshal. This time, I'm keeping my reporter mouth shut and seeing where Tony goes with this. He's the detective.

"You know how we can find this driver?" Tony asks the security expert. "Like where he lives?"

Ah, trying to see what the guard knows about Angel.

"Not my job to track them when they leave. I make sure they don't do anything illegal or immoral while here."

Illegal or immoral. Interesting.

"Right," Tony says, keeping his tone flat, nonjudgmental.

Angel, the driver, has moved up to my number one suspect, and I want to go find him. Like now.

"Thank you. You've been quite helpful. Let's go back into Havana," I say to Tony, "and get something to eat at the hotel. I'm starving." I grab my stomach to pull off this lie.

Tony and Orlando know we're staying at Tony's farm tonight. But the security expert, who I'm sure reports to

Jimagua, doesn't know that. Why give him information he can use against us? Maybe he reports to a government watchdog, too.

"I'm glad we could help," the security guard says, standing. "Many girls come and go from Oshunvilla." He shrugs. "You are not the first to come looking for someone who is lost. I hope you find the girl you are looking for."

"My sister."

"Excuse me?"

"My sister." The security guard knows who we're looking for. I'd told him before, and I won't let him depersonalize her. "My baby sister, Izzy. That's who I'm looking for." I wait for a show of empathy.

The security guard turns back to the panel of TV screens and points to a line of about fifteen cars. "If you can't find a driver, you come see me. I will help you get back to Havana."

Kind of cold, but… "Thank you, and please tell the artist that we thank him, too."

The security guard nods and gestures to one of the TVs.

I walk closer and squint to make out a shadowy figure sitting up in a bed, looking down at his phone. How did I not notice that before? Because the room is mostly dark, the only light from a cell phone in the man's hand. I can't see features or even hair color. That intuitive feeling of something being off snakes down my spine. "Jimagua has been watching us?"

"The talented one watches everything."

I can't stop the fingers of fire, mixed with a little fear, shivering all the way down to my toes. I try to hide my reaction with a quick response. "Guess I would, too, if I had to protect my own wonderland." *This place is more weird than wonderful.* "Gracias," I speak to the camera above the largest TV, assuming Jimagua is watching us through some camera and can hear me.

The shadowy figure doesn't respond verbally. He doesn't

even move.

After an uncomfortable pause, Tony says, "All right. We got what we came for. Let's hit it."

We beat a quick path toward the door.

As we're exiting security, a flyer posted on the wall catches my eye. Big lettering, in Spanish, reads: DO NOT LET THIS MAN IN.

I grab Orlando's arm and gesture with my head to the flyer. I need him to get video of it.

Because the face on the flyer belongs to Raúl.

My heart races. I can think of only two reasons why Raúl would be unwelcome in Oshunvilla.

I ask the security guard, "This man"—I point—"what did he do?"

The security guard grunts. "He came here looking for a lost girl, too. But he threatened to tear the place apart until he found her. He accused the artist of doing something sinister. He's crazy. We had him arrested."

Raúl arrested!

He had to be searching for Izzy. Or looking for one of the other missing girls? Or covering his tracks?

"How long ago was that? Is he still in jail?" He can't be. I saw him leaving the address we had for him.

The security guard opens the final door for us. "Not my job to track them when they leave. I make sure they don't do anything illegal or immoral while here."

He's repeating the same line. Probably what the artist instructs him to say, when asked about people who come to Oshunvilla. And disappear.

We've been dismissed.

Outside, a handful of cars wait to pick up people left at Oshunvilla. Most of the drivers stand outside their cars, gesturing for those leaving to get in. There's only a smattering of tourists mingling.

Almost immediately, one driver stands out to me. His car isn't special. He looks like most of the other drivers, except for one thing: his perfectly white tennis shoes.

"Orlando, look." I nudge Tony, too. "The guy with the perfectly white shoes is back. We saw him at the altar this morning. And again, outside the hostel."

"Naw," Orlando says. "Can't be the same dude."

"It's the same dude," I insist. "Is he following us?" Nervous butterflies flutter around my stomach. "I'm afraid for us to go to the farm, Tony."

Tony nods but remains silent.

"Let's grab a ride into Havana and have dinner and take a different ride back to the farm," I suggest. "Like I told that security manager. So we can lose our tag. Or tags."

Tony's focus is on the government watchdog who got in his car and is now pulling out of the parking lot. "I didn't see any girls get in with him. Did you?"

I shake my head. "He wants us to know he's following us. Why else would he wait for us to see him, then leave."

Tony nods. "We're on someone's radar, for sure."

"Why?" I ask. "Think he knows I'm a reporter and you're a cop?"

"That, I don't know."

Another driver pulls up.

"Let's take this one." We get into the car silently. Except for Tony, who tells the driver, "Drop us off at the Hotel Nacional de Cuba."

Kind of an expensive choice for dinner, but okay. He's taking my advice, and we're going to Havana first. I've learned to trust him, and maybe he's learning to trust me.

I've learned something else at Oshunvilla today.

There is no one here in Cuba we can trust.

No one.

Except one another.

Chapter Seventeen

Day One
7:00 P.M.
TWENTY-NINE HOURS LEFT

HAVANA

The flashing disco lights smack the walls of this Havana nightclub, blood red turning into midnight blue, followed by evil green, all pulsating in beat with the DJ and my nervous heart. We retreated into this club off the main road near the Hotel Nacional de Cuba, hoping the flickering strobes would blind the watchdog in white shoes following us and allow Tony, Orlando, and me to slip through the crowd and out the back door.

But that isn't happening.

Alfonso, Mr. Perfect White Shoes, our constant tail since arriving in Cuba, follows us through the door and blocks the path toward the back of the club.

Like he knows the layout of the club. Like he knows our

plan.

My muscles coil. A cornered snake, I'm ready to strike.

How is it this scrawny, unassuming man keeps showing up where we are, as if he's got GPS trackers on all of us? Makes me want to do a full body check on myself.

The creepy guy walks to the bar and leans up against it. Bodies flood the floor, moving around us like incoming and outgoing tides. I catch his stare intermittently between dipping shoulders, twisting torsos, and bobbing heads. My spine straightens until it hurts.

He knows I see him, and he doesn't seem to care.

What is his end goal?

Does he know ours?

My stomach knots, and I search for Tony's hand. My fingers slip into his. But he tenses as my grip tightens. Orlando stands next to us, holding two heavy bags full of his camera and editing gear. Since we took a drive service here, he had no choice but to bring it with him. I'm sure those bags don't make him stand out... If he weren't my best friend, I'd distance myself from him.

Our goal is to lose this leech, so we can go back to Tony's family farm without him following. No guarantee Mr. White Shoes won't show up eventually, but we can't lead him there.

Orlando wants to send the video he's shot so far back to America.

Tony wants to check on his family.

I'm desperate to reach out to Teddy's mom and the girls from the hostel and ask if Izzy wore a Tampa Bay Rays hat on the day they met her.

The clock is ticking.

This day is almost done.

And this stranger is holding us up.

Glancing around the nightclub, I imagine Izzy in so many of these young girls. Izzy, the natural dancer, loved to go clubbing in Ybor City, Tampa. A salsa club located in the bottom floor of The Cuban Club had been her favorite. I'd go with her sometimes, nurse a sangria from a barstool, and curse my two left feet.

As I watch the flickering lights paint our stalker's shoes into a rainbow of colors, I focus on our options.

It's impossible to talk over the music driven by what looks like a barely over twenty-one-year-old DJ. I don't know if our pursuer can read lips, so I text both O and Tony.

How are we going to ditch him?

O texts back. *Want to send video back. In case my stuff gets taken.*

Tony responds. *Head to the bathroom. Find a stall. You can feed video back if you have WIFI, right?*

Right.

I look down at my phone. *I've got bars.*

Got em, too. From O.

We create a distraction. Once we do, you slip away.

What kind of a — I'm about to text "distraction" when Tony takes a hold of my arm, leans in, and whispers, "Let's dance."

Dance? I freeze. This is his idea of causing a distraction? Well, it will work when everyone in the club realizes I have concrete blocks for feet. Can Tony dance? I can't picture that.

He tugs my arm.

My feet move, even as my head is still stuck on the thought we're about to salsa on a dance floor full of naturals, to Cuban music played by a kid DJ in a funky Cuban club, with a government watchdog keeping tabs on us. *Surreal.*

But I follow him. He drags me in front of Alfonso, on purpose, I'm sure, trying to bait him.

I catch Alfonso's gaze again.

It sticks to me like glue. Mr. White Shoes pushes away from the bar and comes after us.

Orlando makes his way toward the bathroom on the other side of the bar.

My skin tingles. It's like I'm the *femme fatale* in a spy movie, trying to divert the attention of the hitman, while my colleague transfers important info back to the United States.

The higher frequency disco lights on the dance floor smack me back to reality. No one at the White House is waiting for O's video. He wants to send it back to cover our ass if we're arrested. That thought causes my heart to stutter step. I hope he gets a good enough signal. Not just to protect us, but I know how important this documentary is to O. He's still stung by what happened after we worked that serial killer story together in Tampa. After I got fired, and rehired, he said he wanted to quit local TV news. He needed to grow. He needs a powerful story to share with the world.

Well, he's got it. If he can find strong enough wifi.

I check out Mr. White Shoes. He's still on our tail as we move into the middle of the dance floor.

He stops short of joining us.

As Tony's fingers move to the indentation in my lower back, heat moves through my clothing. I'm very conscious of how close we are, despite the crowd dancing around us.

He twirls me into him.

Our bodies connect. Air rushes out of me. If I'd been anticipating that move, it never would have looked so natural. My body moved like a drunk person's, almost boneless.

My left arm falls over his shoulder, while my right hand moves into his outstretched palm.

He leans in and says, "Follow me."

"Salsa?" My pulse is rocking, because Tony is about to find out I don't know how to dance.

"Listen, it's easy." He must sense my apprehension. "I step forward, you back. On the beat. One, two, three."

"One, two, three. I know how to dance salsa. I'm Cuban."

But I don't. Why don't I admit that? Because I hate feeling vulnerable, and I'm about to embarrass myself. But maybe that's the distraction we need to create. If I make a fool of myself, it buys O time to transfer his video.

"You with me?"

Ay Dios mio. I'm so in my head, I'm not moving. Heat slaps my cheeks in time with the music changing.

Tony smiles. His eyes light up in the flashing interludes. And it's not a sarcastic smile. He's not laughing at me, I feel that. He's laughing at this awkward, unreal situation we've found ourselves in.

I pull him close. Electricity sparks when our cheeks meet. "I'm nervous."

"About the watchdog?

About being this close to you. "About dancing."

"Thought you were Cuban?"

I hear the smile in his voice. "Cuban American. Raised more American."

Tony pulls back enough for me to read his lips. "Trust me to lead?"

It's a question, not a demand. *I love that.* I nod.

He steps forward with his left foot. I step back, hesitate, and shift my weight onto my other foot. I'm looking at our feet, trying to see where he's heading, instead of relying on him to lead.

He leans in. "Close your eyes. Feel the music."

He has no idea how hard it is for a control freak like me to close my eyes and let someone else lead me on a crowded dance floor, where I know I'm being watched. My head is spinning, and my toes have gone numb. But I do it, and after a few times, we're getting the pattern of the one, two, three in better synchronicity.

That's when I let my mind drift. My fingers explore. His body is rock hard. Totally superficial thing, something I shouldn't be thinking about right now, but I've never had the chance to run my fingers over his body before. Like a lover, or a girlfriend, or a wife. But now, I have license to move my fingers from the center of his back, down his spine, to his waist.

When he leads me into a turn, I drag my hand over his hard shoulders. My fingers linger, even as we part and dance separately for a few beats.

I've always seen Tony as either a tough homicide cop or a protective patriarch of his family. Both versions of him attracted me, because they show strength. It's been a while since I've had a strong male figure in my life. Ten years to be exact. After Papi died, Abuela Bonita became head of the household.

I like strong. No, I *long* for strength. But it does bother me that Tony rarely smiles. Is he too serious? I don't know. How can one smile at a homicide scene? Or trailing a serial killer? Or taking care of your dying grandfather?

Maybe he needs more joyful moments in his life.

He twirls me around.

My two left feet trip over each other, and I'm going down.

He pulls me back to him, stopping an embarrassing fall.

Tony not only smiles; he laughs.

Even though I can't hear his laughter over the music, I catch the crinkle at the sides of his eyes. I savor the lift of his lips and the way his head falls back, for once unaware of his surroundings.

Once I've steadied myself, I throw my head back and laugh, too. If we're trying to cause a distraction, and our goal is to keep Mr. White Shoes' attention on us, the more we look like lovers, the more we convince him of the parts we've been playing, and the longer we keep him from noticing Orlando's absence.

Who am I kidding? And the longer I get to hold this

man I've longed to touch. Desire washes through me, a warm wave enveloping me. I throw both arms around Tony's neck, pulling him close for a full, body-on-body, press.

He hesitates.

I wonder what he'll do if I press my lips on his. Quickly. Lightly. Just enough for the static electricity to transfer.

He grins but shakes his head.

Like he knows what I'm thinking. *How does he know?* Does he like me the way I like him? I'm dying to know. If I kiss him, if I lean in and do it, if he pushes back, I can explain the kiss away. I'm playing my part as one of two lovers hoping to conceive by the grace of Oshun. *At least I'd know.*

He guides me into a series of turns. As if I'm not dizzy enough.

What kind of future could we have? We have things in common. Our culture. Our desire for justice. *We're both good dancers.* I laugh out loud at my own funny.

He cocks his head, one side of his mouth lifting a bit higher than the other.

I simply smile back and let him lead me into another spin.

Is it wrong that I'd like to spend the night with this man without any crisis? Without anything that needs fixing. No one who needs saving. One night swimming in the feeling of love.

I close my eyes.

He's pulling me into him, and we're rocking the one, two, three, easily now.

This could transfer to the bedroom. I'm pretty sure I'm blushing, surprised by where my thoughts pirouetted to. Guess I'll go there. All the way.

Oh Oshun, as my witness, if I ever get that chance to be with this man in the biblical sense, I will let my walls down. I will. I will. I will put my heart in his hands. I will trust this man.

Don't I already? Trust him?

"Hey, am I losing you?"

Ay Dios mio, I'd stopped moving, again. "No, no, I'm thinking."

Tony has stopped dancing, as well.

We're back to stiff and uncomfortable, in a sea of sexy, shimmying people.

"Thinking it's time to leave, right?"

Wrong. "Right." Might not be the right time to dive into romance. We have plans and a deadline. I shrug, but my heart is so heavy it's hard to lift my shoulders. "What's next?"

"We leave and hit El Malecón."

Cuba's Bayshore Boulevard, a five-mile-long stretch of roadway along the water near the Hotel Nacional de Cuba. Most nights, the walkway stays busy with both locals and tourists.

I nod, catching Orlando standing near the front door. Must mean he's transferred the video or couldn't get wifi and needs to try elsewhere.

I exhale. My romantic bubble burst. Time to get back to the action.

"What's the plan?"

"We mix with the crowd," Tony says, "and we lose the government watchdog in the sea of people enjoying a night out."

I nod but wonder if losing our tail will be that easy.

Chapter Eighteen

Day Two
9:00 A.M.
FIFTEEN HOURS LEFT

NEAR PLAYA HERMOSA

The three of us took that unexpected side trip into Havana last night. We ate dinner at the hotel, danced at the nightclub, hopefully pulled off lovers having fun. Especially because during those moments on the dance floor, I did have fun. Afterward, we walked down El Malecón, mingling on purpose in the night crowd of both locals and tourists.

Once we were convinced the watchdog with the white tennis shoes lost us, we grabbed another ride, making sure it wasn't from a government-run cab service, and arrived at Tony's farm safely.

But it was two in the morning before we got to bed. My room steamed with no air-conditioning, a fly landing repeatedly on my exposed leg, out of the covers, so the tiny fan on the single dresser could blast me with moving air. The insect had perfect timing, landing and taking off between each blast of air, as if jumping an invisible rope, making sleep next to impossible. I'm exhausted, my desire to find Izzy and get the hell out of this communist country the only fuel left in my tank.

We've come to this small town this morning, with less than fifteen hours left, because Teddy's cell phone last pinged at a car wash in a rural area outside of Playa Hermosa, not as close to Raúl's as I imagined. We couldn't find a name for the one-street town near the beach, but because it's so small, finding the car wash—easy.

"Let's ask the owners if the car wash has surveillance video."

I'm standing next to Tony, in front of The Avanza Car Wash, which is little more than a beat-up office building next to a large overhang two cars could drive under. There's a water hose, soap, and one of those round vacuum cleaners you roll around on wheels that has several vacuum heads you can use, one to get past those awkward angles and get under the seat and another, flatter head to sweep the dirt off the carpets. I'm not hopeful the owners invested in a surveillance system. Not much here to steal.

"Don't see any cameras on first glance," Tony says.

Wouldn't take long to check for cameras. Looks to be a mom-and-pop business, with a do-it-yourself atmosphere. I don't see anyone wandering around outside the office, offering to help us. Next to the white words AVANZA CAR WASH on the red roof, a telephone number in white: 7556006. "I guess we can call that number if no one's inside."

"I'll go check." Orlando has been shooting video of the car wash, even though we're not sure it's even important. "Maybe her phone fell out of the driver's car here? If someone's inside, I'll ask about a lost and found."

"Like a lost cell phone wouldn't be stolen by now."

"Not much of a car wash." Tony picks up a bucket with two sponges, hardened and missing chunks.

"Not much of a town." I glance down the main street. "Looks like El Lázaro is a cafeteria. It's open. Bet we could get coffee and some guava pastries there. Or at the bakery next door."

"You're thinking about food?" Tony walks through the empty car stalls to the other side of the car wash. Looking up for cameras, I'm assuming.

I follow him but continue my inspection of what Main Street has to offer. My stomach is eating itself at this point and that always makes me a little nauseous. "We haven't eaten breakfast."

A gray-haired butcher is hanging slabs of *carne fresca* from hooks in the open window beside a painting of a pink pig. Next to it, a medical clinic with a couple of people already at the door. On the other side of the street, a gas station with a single old-fashioned pump, the kind you might see in an old black-and-white movie. Finally, a medical office, if the picture of a big syringe on the door is any indication. No Bank of America. No McDonalds. No Target. No Starbucks.

"That looks like a bar across the street. El Gato Tuerto." *The one-eyed cat.*

Tony shades his eyes with a hand. "With a camera above the front door." He breaks into a grin. "Good eye, partner."

Joy rushes into my chest, lifting my spirits and easing my nausea a bit.

"Mari's gonna take your job, Detective." Orlando smacks me on the back firmly enough to make me bite the inside of my mouth.

"Thanks, buddy." I give O the side-eye.

Tony ruffles my hair. "She's already my partner."

My emotions bubble up like seltzer water in my stomach. He has no idea what those words mean to me.

"No one answered when I knocked at the car wash," Orlando says. "I guess it's the honor system here."

"Or you have to pay for the water to turn on." I point to a coin machine against the wall. "We've got that phone number we can call. Or we can check out the bar's surveillance footage."

It takes one hundred American dollars, in twenties, to convince the bar owner to let us go through archives of his surveillance video system. It's 9:00 a.m., so he either lives in the bar or he's up early doing accounting. Either way, he's friendly enough and tells us he added the camera after a bar fight rolled into the street one night and ended with a murder. "Mix alcohol and poverty and it often leads to violence." Lucky for us, they keep their video for a year. Meaning, they still have footage from the night Izzy disappeared and from the night Teddy left the hostel and never returned. We started with Izzy's night.

Detective work is so tedious. Hours of poring through video surveillance and such.

I decided to walk next door to get us café con leche at the cafeteria run by an eighty-year-old abuela named Florencita. She reminded me of my Abuela Bonita, with her orisha saints in an altar close by, her rosary around her neck, and funny stories on her tongue as she served up café, hot and sweet. The strong smell makes my stomach grumble.

Hitting the bakery for guava and cheese pastries, I leave a few flyers on tables, since I was able to copy them at the hostel, and tape one to the door, adding my cell number to the bottom.

I check out both the butcher and the medical clinic to ask questions and show flyers. The butcher was polite but when he didn't recognize Teddy, Arianna, or Izzy and had nothing to offer, he went back to breaking down a pig carcass into smaller, more manageable cuts of meat.

The teenager working the front desk of the medical clinic

had two people ahead of me. Once they'd been seated in the non-air-conditioned waiting room, with two fans blowing hot air around, she turned to me, red-cheeked, and said, "Can I help you?"

"I'm looking for my sister."

The young woman glanced behind and around me. "Did she check in already?"

"No." I show her a picture of Izzy on my smartphone. "She's not sick. She's missing."

The girl shifted in her seat. Just the slightest movement, but I caught it. Tony's been teaching me about body language and what it can say when words aren't being offered. I hold my breath and show her a different picture of Izzy from my cell phone. The one with Raúl.

She shakes her head. Almost too quickly. Did she even take a good look?

I pull out the flyer of Teddy. "Have you seen this girl?"

She curls her lips in and again shakes her head, but this time, her gaze flutters around the room instead of concentrating on the picture.

I don't give up. I bring out the flyer of Arianna. "What about this girl?"

The young woman glances over her shoulder at the sound of a door opening. Maybe she's worried about the doctor or boss coming out?

She whispers, "Girls like those girls, they don't hang out in this small town."

I show her a picture of Izzy, again. "This is my sister. *My sister.*"

She nods, dropping eye contact. "*Lo siento.*"

"You're sorry about what?"

"Did she travel to Oshunvilla? Your sister?"

My pulse zips. Now we're getting somewhere. "With a driver named Angel."

Her gaze lifts, catches mine.

My breath stops for a second. "Where can I find Angel?" We have an address for the driver, but I want to know if she knows. I'm learning from Tony.

"Don't go looking for trouble."

I throw both hands up. "Really? I'm trying to find my sister. She could be in danger."

The teenager's eyes widen. "If you can't find her easily, maybe she can't be found, and you should stop looking."

"What does that mean?" My right hand flies to cover my heart. "Is that a warning or a threat?"

A heavyset woman, older, walks out with a chart and calls a name. A patient in the waiting room rises. The woman, a nurse maybe, eyes us as she gestures for the patient to follow her back.

"You're here, because?" the teen at the desk says to me in a louder, professional tone.

I've been doing a lot of acting since arriving in Cuba, so I easily pick up on her distressed tone. "I'm here because I have a cough and a fever, and I'd like to be seen."

"Fill out these forms, please."

She hands them to me, and I fill out my name and phone number only, so she can call me if she's afraid to divulge too much information in front of coworkers. Which I can understand, because so far what the teenager has told me has me sizzling with confusion.

The nurse goes to the back with the patient.

We're alone at the front desk again. I hand the teen the form with my phone number on it.

"There are stories," she says in not a whisper, but almost.

I lean in. "What kind of stories?"

"They say at night, when everybody leaves Oshunvilla, the walls wail and the statues scream."

My hand covers my heart. "How can a statue scream?"

This isn't a Stephen King novel. "Who is *they*?"

She leans in, too, looks around, and whispers, "The wise women at our church. They keep their daughters away from Oshunvilla. They don't like what goes on there."

Heat hits the back of my neck, and the room spins a little. "If everybody leaves at night, how do they know what goes on there? How would anyone know the walls wail?" I grab the counter for support.

"Angel knows."

I bet he does.

"He's heard the screams. He's told me."

She knows Angel. I can tell by the fear in her eyes, and the way her skin pales, this young woman also believes what she's saying. What bull has Angel been feeding her? And why? To keep her out of his business at Oshunvilla? Or is he responsible for the screams and is one of those killers who like to talk to innocent people about what they do, without letting on they are the ones doing it.

"Checked in?" A woman in scrubs appears from I don't know where and gives the woman at the front desk a disapproving look. "You have others waiting."

I turn and look behind me. *Ay Dios mio.* There are a couple of people in line. Did they hear us?

"Thank you. I point to my cell number on the forms I handed her. I look deep into her eyes and tell her what I need to say without saying a word. "*Please call me. You know more.*"

I walk out of the medical clinic.

On my way to the bar, I pass Orlando outside, shooting more video. Tony, inside, fills me in. "You want the good news or the bad news first?"

"You always lead with the bad news. Don't you know that?" I wink at him, trying to keep things light after my weird and worrisome conversation with the teen at the medical clinic.

"All right, bad news first." Tony is sitting at the security office table with the bar owner and another man. "We checked the video for the day Izzy left the hostel and went to Oshunvilla. Nothing at the car wash."

"That's not necessarily bad news."

He keeps a poker face. "The good news is the surveillance camera clearly picks up both stalls where cars can be washed and vacuumed. Like I said, nothing on Izzy's night, but on the night Teddy left the hostel, our boy Angel washed and cleaned out the interior of his cherry vintage Chevy. It was late, too. Like ten p.m., right?" Tony glances at the bar owner.

The man grunts and nods, puffing on a thick cigar. The other man continues fast forwarding through footage.

"Okay," I say. "Let's talk this out. If the driver brought Teddy to this area, as her phone indicates because it last pinged here, then maybe he brought Izzy here, too. What did he do with the girls? Where are they now? No one I asked has seen them, although I heard some strange things about Oshunvilla at that medical clinic."

Tony tilts his head, eyebrows up.

"I'll fill you in later. Are our girls being held hostage in a home nearby? Maybe Angel's home? Because he's tied into all of this, in my opinion."

"Angel lives five miles from the car wash."

My mouth falls open.

"Had my sour—" Tony was probably about to say he had his source check but stopped himself in front of the bar owner. "My friend double-checked for me."

"Well," I say, "let's go pay Angel a visit. See if he's got company." *Like my sister.* "It's early enough. He may be home."

I thought it would be easier than this. I thought if I found Raúl, I would find Izzy. I really thought it would be that straightforward. At least now we've got a new lead.

Orlando rushes in the front door, nearly knocking me over. "Hey, can you go back to live video from the camera out front?"

The bar owner flips a switch. The live feed returns.

Orlando leans over Tony, still sitting at the table, and points to a man on video, standing in the shadows of one of the stalls in the car wash. "This guy showed up. But he's not washing his car. In fact, he didn't even park it in the stall."

"So?" I ask.

Tony stares at the screen, finishing off the café con leche I bought him. "Look at his shoes."

"I can't tell the color of the man's pants, much less his shoes. He's in shadow." But as I say it, a streak of sunlight crosses the man's feet. *He's wearing perfectly white tennis shoes.* "He's found us again."

"Obviously," Orlando says.

"How in the heck?" I ask, swallowing the knot forming in my throat. "How does he know *exactly* where we are all the time?" That question rolls around in my stomach like a wad of left-open safety pins.

"That's the first thing we need to figure out," Tony says. "Before he follows us to Angel's place."

"Or your family's farm."

The watchdog must know we're staying with Tony's loved ones. Will they get in trouble? I visualize Domingo and his dog, so hopeful for a better life. "I'll never forgive myself if something happens to your family."

Tony reaches over and squeezes my hand. "They have weapons."

But he knows what I mean—the government could take everything from them. Or make family members disappear.

I rub a hand over my chin. "Where did we first meet Mr. White Shoes? At the altar during the festival. That's when he started following us." Suddenly, it hits me how the watchdog may be tracking us. I grab my backpack. "I've got an idea."

Chapter Nineteen

Day Two
10:00 A.M.
FOURTEEN HOURS LEFT

NEAR PLAYA HERMOSA

Tony had the idea to park a street over and have Orlando walk toward the driver's house, to check if a car is in the driveway, and scout out how many people might be there, before we alert Angel we know he's here.

Sitting in Enrique's car, a street away from Angel's house, I dig through my backpack for...I'm not sure what. The government watchdog, Mr. White Shoes, is tracking us somehow.

I've pulled everything out. The back seat is covered with mints, a water bottle, powder for my face, lip gloss—I know—ridiculous under current circumstances, phone charger, rubber band for my hair, brush, wallet. Nothing unusual inside my bag. I shake my head, thinking maybe we need to check Orlando's gear bag while he's gone.

I can't figure out how this watchdog guy stays one step behind us. Literally. We go someplace. He shows up within the hour.

I turn my backpack upside down and shake it, my frustration evident in the strength with which I punish this innocent, inanimate object.

A small object, round and about the size of a quarter, falls out of a side pocket I didn't even know existed.

I recognize the silver and black item immediately.

"It's an AirTag. That's how he's doing it. He bumped me as he passed us leaving the altar. I remember being paranoid he heard us talk about the neighborhood watchdog system as he passed. Couldn't have been hard to slip this baby in the side pocket. I was so distracted and freaked out by his presence."

"Pretty smart. It's connected to his smartphone, and all he'd have to do is use his Find My Phone feature and it'll show him where the tag is. Anywhere in the world, if there are other Apple devices around so it can signal to the cloud," Tony adds.

"Even though the phones near the tag aren't his?" I ask.

"Even though the phones near the tag aren't his."

Both Tony and I have iPhones.

"It uses Bluetooth to connect to the Apple network worldwide. Think of how many people have phones, tablets, laptops with their Bluetooth on."

My Bluetooth is always on. "Should I throw it out the window? Stomp on it?" That would feel good.

"No," he says quickly. "Let's think about where we should leave it. We don't want him to realize we're on to him quite yet."

"I wonder if Orlando has a tag in his bag, too?"

"Tell him to check when he gets back in the car."

As if on cue, my phone goes off. It's O. "Hey, we found out how he's tracking us. You need to check—"

"Good. Our man Angel is home. He parked his car in the driveway, and I see him through a kitchen window."

My breath catches. "Izzy?"

Silence on the other end.

"O?"

"No signs of her. Or any girls. Looks like the dude lives alone. Grass isn't cut, no cute outdoor furniture signaling a wife or girlfriend. Nothing really in the back. A few tools near an old lawnmower that probably doesn't work anymore. The house has a couple of rooms where the windows are covered. Not by boards like at Raúl's, but I can't see in, so I can't rule out that they aren't in there."

Now I'm silent. But blood pounds in my ears. Another dead end? I put O on speakerphone, so Tony can hear. "O says Angel is home and in the house. No sign of Izzy. What do we do now?"

Tony keeps looking to his right and left. But he's a cop, so maybe it's habit, to constantly be looking for trouble. "We switch over to Plan B."

We'd decided if Angel was home, I'd call him, sticking to a script Tony and I thought out. The goal is to motivate Angel to leave the house so we can follow him, while Tony's source, the U.S. Marshal, already in a car one street over, moves in and searches the house. Orlando will stay behind to videotape anything they might find.

"Use this phone." Tony hands me a phone I've never seen before.

"A burner phone?"

"Something like that. Don't want anyone tracing the call back to you." Thank God Tony is always thinking like a detective.

"Keep Orlando on the phone. When Angel answers, have

him on speaker, so we can all hear." Tony turns his attention to me, his eyes narrowing. "Stick to the script, okay Marisol?"

Marisol. Hmmm.

I dial the number we got from the girls at the youth hostel. Three rings.

I shake my head, playing with the AirTag to dispel energy. "He's not going to answer."

"He's in the kitchen," Orlando says, still spying on him.

"Are you someplace safe, where he can't see you?" I ask O.

"Yup. He's walking out of the room. Wait. Can't see him—"

"*Ay Dios mio*, now wh—"

"*Diga me*," Angel answers. *Talk to me.*

So I do.

Chapter Twenty

"I know you did it," I accuse him.

Tony's plan: jump right in and put Angel on the defensive.

"Who the fuck is this?" Angel replies in Spanish.

I explain who I am, and how he picked Tony, O, and me up yesterday and took us to Oshunvilla. "You drove my sister to Oshunvilla, too. She hasn't been seen since."

"You crazy bitch. I don't know your sister."

I exhale. As a crime reporter in a big city, this isn't the first time I've been talked to this way. "I may be a bitch, but I am not crazy." I can see by Tony's clenched jaw he doesn't like Angel's words either. I mouth, "It's fine," to Tony. Then to Angel, "How can you say you don't know my sister when I haven't even told you her name yet."

He hangs up.

All the hairs on the back of my neck stand, and I squeeze the AirTag so hard I'm afraid I've broken it. It cuts my skin. I pitch the device onto the car's floor.

Then I call back and get his voicemail.

I don't like being ignored. I belt out a noise, something

between an Eastern owl's screech and an angry alligator's growl. I'm leaving a message. "We can do it this way if you want. I don't fucking care!" I hang up.

Tony's eyebrows shoot up. "Take a deep breath, Marisol."

"What devil is possessing you?" Orlando asks.

I forgot for a moment O is listening. He knows I don't use the F-word.

"Hey, he's walking out of the house."

Smart to have eyes and ears at Angel's place.

"Heading to his car," O says.

My phone rings.

Angel's number. My heart leaps as if energized by jumper cables. I answer, press speaker, and start talking before he has a chance to. "I've been tracking you. AirTag." Threw that in on the fly. "Following the clues you've left behind. I know who you've picked up, when, and where you took them. A few of the girls have not been seen since. I've been to the youth hostel in Havana. The girls there all say you picked up the missing girls. They say you have a deal with the hostel. The security person at Oshunvilla told us you target girls who are alone and vulnerable. They can identify you. Where are the missing girls, Angel? Where are they?" I say all of this in one breath, and now I'm breathless. I've gone off-script. Beads of sweat litter my forehead.

Tony is shaking his head staring at me like he's super disappointed, or maybe super freaked out at my unusual behavior, which makes my heart skip.

I've let my emotions get the best of me. I can't even look him in the eyes. I pause. Tony always says remaining calm while being disrespected or challenged is a superpower. One I obviously don't have.

Angel's breathing sounds ragged through the phone. Heavy. He says nothing.

"Where are the missing girls?" I barely whisper this time.

My throat is dry, the words scratch their way out. "Because if you don't tell me, I'm calling the police. Right now."

"Call them," Angel answers immediately, his voice low, controlled.

"I will." I sit back in the seat, stretching my cramping legs. "I will, and I'll show them the proof I have."

"Call them and *you* might disappear next."

My gaze catches Tony's. From the front seat, he gestures for me to keep going.

"What do you mean I might disappear next? Are you threatening me, Angel?"

"Are you recording this?"

"No." *But Tony is.*

"Police protect the killer."

My insides freeze. He said killer. Not kidnapper. Not sex trafficker. *Killer.*

My fear squeezes the air out of my lungs. I hold onto the seat in front of me. "Who said anything about a killer? The girls are missing."

"You have no idea."

His words trigger an adrenaline dump that makes me physically sick to my stomach. "That's why I'm asking. Do you have any of the girls with you?"

Silence.

"He's hung up, again," I say to alert Orlando it's okay to talk now.

"He's pulling out of his driveway. Going left," Orlando says. "You can pick him up when he turns onto that main street. Same car as before. Can't miss his fancy red Chevy."

"Got it." Tony takes the car out of park. "You lie down in the back seat, so it looks like I'm driving alone."

Orlando makes some noise, doing something we can't see. "I've got the Marshal's number. I'll text him now. We'll search the house if we can get in. I'll wait for him. I'm assuming he'll be armed."

"Yes," Tony says.

"Orlando, be careful." I lie back and throw an arm over my face. I'm still feeling nauseous, and the smell of fresh asphalt on the main street, mixed with the heat, is also giving me a headache. *Killer. He said killer. Is Izzy dead?*

"You also," O says.

"Let us know immediately if you find anything. Or anyone." My tongue feels thick and chalky. I feel around the floor of the back seat for my bottle of water. Tony makes a turn, and it slides into my fingers.

"Tony," O asks. "Searching Angel's house for the girls or other evidence makes sense. But following him? Why? You don't know where he's headed, or what he's planning."

"Exactly," Tony says. "But I do know one thing. Mari rattled him enough to get him to leave his house. He's going somewhere for a reason, and I'd bet everything I own he's going to cover his ass. Don't know what that means, but it's a lead we need to follow."

"If we're lucky," I say from the back seat. "He's going to lead us right to them." *Right to my Izzy.*

Right to the missing girls.

Chapter Twenty-One

Day Two
10:30 A.M.
THIRTEEN AND A HALF HOURS LEFT

NEAR PLAYA HERMOSA

As we follow Angel from a few cars behind, I revisit his words, letting them roll around in my head like clothes in a washing machine, hoping the tossing around of his statements will make what he meant clearer.

I'm stuck on his comment "police protect the killer." Not that the words confuse me. There's no doubt about what he said. It's just not what I expected or wanted to hear. *The police protect the killer.*

Who *is* the killer? Who has he killed, and why would the Cuban police protect a killer? Maybe the killer is a cop? Or a member of the government? Mr. Perfect White Shoes? Or maybe Angel is the killer, and he's throwing out a red herring to confuse us and lead us off track. If that's the case, following him may turn up something.

I still haven't ruled out Raúl. We haven't had time to go back to his house yet, but we intend to. Especially after I saw his face on a flyer at Oshunvilla, telling security he wasn't allowed in. I need to hear what's behind that. We know now not to bring the Cuban police with us if we go back.

I sigh. Lying down in the back seat disorients me. I can't see where we're going, can't see where Angel might be driving, can't even see Tony's face.

I'm lost like a lamb, and I've lost track of how long we've been on the road. I can tell we're getting into a rural area only because the drive grows increasingly bumpy. Gone is the stinky, new asphalt road. We're bouncing down a dirt road, kicking up dust I can see through the window. The tires keep dropping into potholes. My clothes stick to my skin, and I smell myself. *Nice. Not.*

We come to a stop.

"You can sit up now," Tony says.

"Where are we?"

"Back where we started."

"That's sounds like something the Cheshire Cat would say in *Alice in Wonderland*." A chuckle from the front seat. "What I mean is, we're back in the town with the car wash and bar. Angel parked in a parking lot close to the bar. He pulled a large bag out of his trunk and took off down a trail. Can't see him anymore. He's walked into some dense woods. I'm getting out. You stay here." The door slams.

"Uh, no." I rush out, too.

"Uh, yes." Tony is checking his weapon and unsnapping the holster.

Great. He's expecting trouble. "Tony, we're in this together."

He doesn't even look at me. "Don't have time to argue." He walks toward the trail entrance; a click of the car door lock tells me he knows I'm coming with him.

"Good." I'm right behind.

He stops. Looks back. "If you're coming, will you do what I ask you to do?" His hair is damp and curly around his forehead. His skin carries that sweat shine, and his eyes appear hooded and tired. It's been a couple of rough days. "Please. For your safety." He's walking again.

I appreciate the "please," and the warning, but we both know when I'm hot with emotion, I act before I speak. Something I need to work on, for sure.

"For *our* safety, Marisol."

Since he's looking ahead and not at me, I twist my azabache charm, three times to the left, three times to the right. I do it once again. I feel better, taking some of the edge off. Now maybe I can do what Tony's asked of me.

I amble after him, careful not to step on anything that might signal our approach. It's daylight, to our advantage, and there are no other people we pass or see in the woods.

We hear something first—the rhythmic sound of something plunging in and out of the ground. *Kwuh, Kwuh, Kwuh.* Pause. *Kwuh. Thud. Kwuh, Kwuh, Kwuh.* Pause. *Kwuh. Thud.*

Angel, shovel in hand, scoops earth from one area and throws it to the side. A big tarp sits next to him.

My body begins to tremble.

Is Angel *digging* a grave? Or *unearthing* a grave?

I can't bear to look at the tarp, fearing it covers my sister's dead body.

I squeeze Tony's arm, needing the connection to something strong.

He pulls me into him, hiding my head in the crook of his neck. I don't have to watch what this devil may be doing.

Time drips by, slow like honey. Finally, when my clothes are seeped with sweat, and my legs twitch with restlessness, I separate myself from Tony and take another look.

Angel had been digging a hole in the woods, but he's no longer digging; he's staring at the open hole in the ground. He throws down the shovel, drops to his knees, and throws his hands over his face. "What did she do with the body?"

The body. As in *dead* body. *Ay Dios mio, please not Izzy's.*

My stomach clenches. I lean over and vomit stomach acid that looks like coffee grinds. I squat down. Tony crouches next to me and gently gathers my hair away from my face.

I'm trying like hell not to make noise. Eventually, I stop heaving.

"She's going to blame me." Angel falls forward, still on his knees, his head resting in his hands on the ground. "She's going to kill me."

Much to my luck, Angel seems to be in his own private hell. Not looking around. Not suspicious of my gagging.

"Who is she?" I mouth the words to Tony.

He shrugs, his gaze glued on Angel, his hand resting on the gun holstered on his belt.

"The driver is afraid of her," I whisper. "Whoever she is."

Angel pushes himself to his feet, swipes his hands down his face. He rolls up his tarp, picks up his shovel, and drags his feet away from us, back down the trail. It's as if he's got the weight of a bunch of dead bodies on both shoulders.

Despite the heat and humidity, I'm rattled and chilled. "What do we do now?"

"We wait long enough for him to get back to the car. I'll go check out where he was digging, although I'm sure we won't find anything. He seemed disappointed. Like he didn't find—"

"The body he'd buried there," I finish his sentence. "He came here to dig up a body. It must be one of the girls." I theorize out loud. "Because we told him we were on to him."

I lay my head on Tony's shoulder. "He led us to where he knew a body had been buried."

"We assume." He strokes my hair, which calms me.

"He thinks *she* took the body somewhere. Who the hell is she? If we figure that out, we'll know where she might have taken—"

Tony stands and holds out his palm. "You wait here. After I check out the hole, we'll head back to the car."

I take his hand and let him pull me to my feet, fighting off more stomach spasms. "Angel threw out a new suspect. A woman. But a woman with no name and no known connection. We're still no closer to finding Izzy." And the clock continues to tick. It's now afternoon on Day Two. "The boat is leaving tomorrow at noon." We have about thirteen hours left.

"Text Orlando. Ask him if he's found anything. If they have nothing, we're diverting to the last place Izzy was seen alive. We'll meet back at the farm, that way we can get Enrique to take us and wait for us. There's something I need to take care of first. Won't take long, and I may not get another chance. Ask Orlando to make sure he's not followed."

I shudder, fearing we're putting Tony's family at risk each time we go back to the farm. But I can't change Tony's mind. He's on a mission, too. I respect that.

He doesn't have to say where we're going after the farm. I know where. I *feel* where. I'm scared of where.

My upset stomach tells me the artist's weird, wonderworld Oshunvilla is the last place we should go back to.

But maybe it's the only place left where we can pick up a trail that leads us to Izzy.

Chapter Twenty-Two

Day Two
1:30 P.M.
TEN AND A HALF HOURS LEFT

THE FAMILY FARM

Back at Tony's family farm, his one-armed cousin Maximo insists on giving Orlando and me a quick tour. I know why— he wants to give Tony a chance to talk with Esme again about Domingo. I don't want a tour because I need to find Izzy.

The invisible clock ticks constantly in my head, leaving little room to take in anything else.

But the yearning in Tony's eyes hits me hard. My heart stretches with the feel of it. He longs to make a difference in his Cuban family's life, but so far, Domingo is the only one who wants to come to the U.S. The two have talked about nothing else since we arrived in Cuba. Tony stays with his aunt and Domingo in the kitchen while she prepares the last of the chicken they killed and stripped in anticipation of our arrival. To convince her to let her son follow his dreams in America.

Sofrito bubbles in a pan on the stove, flooding the small kitchen with the aroma of garlic and onions. My mouth literally waters, but Esme is slow cooking the chicken for dinner, and I know better than to ask for a snack. Tony warned me how scarce food remains in this country, a real nutrient desert. Plus, you'd need a butcher knife to cut through the tension in this sweltering kitchen.

Freedom barks at Domingo's heels.

"Hey, I'll take Freedom on our tour," I offer. "He needs to expend a little energy."

I catch the gratitude in Tony's eyes.

Maximo takes us to the back side of the farm, an area we haven't seen yet.

Orlando videotapes as we walk, documenting a handful of elementary-school-aged kids chasing ducks through the yard, as well as family members harvesting corn and yucca from their fields.

Freedom pulls on his leash, barking as we approach a row of concrete pens occupied by the fattest pigs I've ever seen.

"We fatten 'em up good, don't we," Maximo says in Spanish. He must be reacting to the shocked look on my face. "Pick one."

"Ah, I'll leave that up to you," I say, fearing what's coming next. Tony's told me about the slaughter. Just a way of life here. But I'm not sure O will appreciate this depiction of rural Cuban life.

Most of Maximo's pigs are covered in dirt or mud, crowded into a space too small for their comfort, in my opinion. A younger family member I haven't met yet, in torn-up jean overalls and bare, dirty feet, grabs one of the fatter pigs by the back of his neck, like you would a dog or cat. The pig's skin pulls away from the meat of his neck, his front hooves scramble in the air, an unearthly squeal escaping.

Orlando stares at the pigpen in wide-eyed disgust. "What the *Charlotte's Web* is going on here?" he asks, videotaping the pig whining, despite his obvious revulsion. "They aren't going to slaughter this guy for dinner?"

"Not for tonight's dinner," Maximo says. "Takes a whole day to smoke pork. This fat boy is for tomorrow's feast." He holds his shoulders back, chin up. He's in charge of the family's pens and is obviously proud.

"Thought we'd be out of here by tomorrow." Orlando moves the GoPro from one end of the pen to the other.

"That's the plan." I shrug, shoulders heavy. "But nothing has gone as planned." And I have no idea what to expect next.

The younger cousin whips out a knife and rips through the pig's throat.

Just. Like. That.

Blood spurts out in a Las Vegas Bellagio Hotel water dance.

I jump back to avoid being sprayed.

O falls back, too. "We're not in Publix anymore."

Freedom pulls against his leash, visibly distressed at the animal's suffering. I hold tight.

The cousin drops the pig, and as soon as hooves hit the ground, the animal takes off, running in small circles, whelping and shrieking, banging against the side of the concrete pen, until, worn out, it collapses. Two deep breaths and the animal stiffens.

"I'm glad it's no longer suffering." *Ay Dios mio.*

"All that necessary?" O asks.

Maximo says in Spanish what equates to, "Circle of life, my friend."

I put a hand on Orlando's arm. He's never witnessed anything like this. "This *is* a different way of life. They will use every portion of this pig. They'll be eating it for days."

I'm repeating what Tony has told me. "What they don't eat, they'll feed to the other animals on the farm. Nothing will go to waste."

O pulls down his GoPro and pockets it. "I've lost my appetite." His whole body shudders. "I need to edit." He turns away. "And try again to feed the video back."

Orlando had said the wifi last night wasn't strong enough to feed back video the size he shot it in. We head back toward the farmhouse, leaving Maximo to deal with the rest of the slaughter. Freedom is pulling me, like he's ready to get back to the farmhouse, too. "Who are you afraid will take our video?"

"That government watchdog dude who keeps showing up where we go. I have a bad feeling about that man."

Mr. Perfect White Shoes. "Did you search your gear?"

"No AirTags."

"Good. Mine is on the side of a rural road. Couldn't keep it with us."

As we approach the back door leading into the kitchen, I hear voices. Tony's first. "It's what he wants."

"It's what I want!" Domingo's voice.

"He's a kid." That's Tony's aunt. "It's not what *I* want."

"I'm right here. It's what I want."

"There is nothing here for him!"

"I don't like the sound of Tony's voice," O says. "Time for me to divert."

Something crashes from within the kitchen; the sound is loud and unexpected, causing both of us to jump. Freedom barks wildly, jerking on his leash.

"He has a home here. He has food on the table. He has a family. He has love."

"He has no future."

Ouch. It's a bit primitive here, but I wouldn't say Domingo has no future.

"Stop talking about me like I'm not standing here!" The back door flies open and Domingo stumbles out, his feet moving faster than his body. He trips, but quickly rights himself. He gestures to Freedom. "Here, boy."

I let go of the leash.

Freedom hobbles over to Domingo on his three good legs.

He hugs his dog, burying his head in the dog's fur, rubbing his back with furious strokes. "I'm going to my room." The boy's voice cracks. He doesn't make eye contact.

My heart feels the tears he's trying to hide. His sadness wrenches me. He places Freedom's paws back on the ground and guides his pet around the side of the house, obviously heading to the front door, thus avoiding another confrontation with his mother and Tony.

Neither Orlando nor I say anything until he's disappeared.

"Well, I wanted to edit in Domingo's room." Orlando purses his lips, his eyebrows shooting up. "Maybe not."

"Domingo will run this farm one day." The aunt's voice, low but determined, rings loud enough to be heard past the screen door that slammed behind Domingo.

"He wants to come to America to get an education." Tony's voice isn't low. "He wants to be a doctor." It's escalating. "A doctor. Not a farmer."

"The Cuban government will pay for his education. He can be a doctor here."

"Like you?"

I know where this is going, and my nerves flutter waiting for it.

"You are a dentist, Esme."

Tony had told me this story about his aunt.

"You quit your practice to grow crops and let Maximo raise pigs here because that's more profitable. You don't use your medical degree, and you still have an empty refrigerator.

You still depend on me for help."

Ouch. I've never seen this fiery, passionate side of Tony. He's usually the calm, controlled homicide detective. Right now, his anger rolls out the back door like waves of heat lingering above hot streets on a tropical afternoon.

"I want to mentor him," Tony continues. "I will pay for him to get to Tampa. I will pay for his education. I will provide everything he needs."

"I will not send my son into a country that will eat him alive. And the United States is no longer what it used to be. It's dangerous. Things are expensive. Crazy criminals run your country."

"Stop. I'm here to help my family."

"You came to assert your power over the family using your American dollars."

I grab Orlando's arm. "Maybe I should interfere."

He shakes his head. "I'm out. I'll be editing in a corner. Where no one can find me."

"I pay for your food. I send medicine. I send cash every month. You have never complained."

"And you want my son in return for that? That's the cost of your help? The rest of my son's life?"

"It's what your son wants."

"Leave my kitchen."

Uh-oh.

Tony pushes his way past the screen door and stalks by me, not making eye contact. Heat hits my skin as he flies by.

Where is he going? I bet he doesn't even know. I must cool this situation down, but I'm not sure how. I follow him, taking long strides to keep up. "Don't be angry."

He stops mid-step, pivots, and glares at me with eyes hot as burning coals. "How long were you eavesdropping?"

I throw both hands up like he's arresting me. "Okay, not eavesdropping. Coming back to the house, and your voice carried all the way to the pigpens."

His jaw clenches. Without a word, he turns around and continues walking, but his pace downshifts.

I'm able to catch up with him. I grab his right arm and pull hard enough to stop him. I don't think, I walk around and throw my arms around him, drawing him to me and squeezing tightly.

His heart pounds against my chest. Or maybe that's my heart. I don't know. I let my hands fall down his back and rest there.

He stiffens, but he doesn't pull away.

We stay there, suspended, my head buried in his neck like Domingo buried his tears in his dog's fur. I yearn to tell Tony my feelings for him are changing. I want to look into his eyes and see if his are changing, too, but I'm afraid of rejection. I'm afraid of *his* rejection.

Gently, he digs into my arms, pulling us apart.

Tears form I don't want him to see, and I shift my gaze down. He's doing exactly what I feared he'd do. My chest aches like a bulldozer carved a hole into me, and I feel pain and emptiness at the same time.

"We can't do this." His voice shakes.

Why? But what I say is, "I want to hug you." I risk looking up at him, knowing he'll see hurt gazing back at him. "Only to support you like you did me." It wasn't even two hours ago that he drew me in to him and hid my face, my eyes from the horror of maybe seeing Izzy's decomposing body being pulled from the ground. I pull him back in to me, searching for that easy intimacy we'd shared not too long ago, before my heart found its way into my throat.

"Don't." His voice is softer, and this time he doesn't move away.

"I don't understand." He'd rubbed my head when I got nauseous. He *has* to have feelings for me.

"I don't want your pity."

"It's not my pity." I shift enough so I can see his face. "It's my support. We're partners."

"Don't." Now he looks away.

All the emotions bottle up in the knot visible in his throat. Why is this so hard?

"Please, Mari. Stop. We need to stay focused. Too much is at risk right now. I'm responsible for you and Orlando. My family, too. I need to keep my head right."

That hole in my chest widens, an expanding sinkhole, and the gap growing between us increases, too. I do as he wants and step away.

But we're locked in a stare.

Celia Cruz plays in the kitchen. Two teens are practicing salsa on the back patio, oblivious to us. To my left, a table of four relatives play dominoes on a table with three legs propped up on one side by cinder blocks. Tony's aunt is in the kitchen window, face full of flat lines, scrubbing dishes with fast and furious arm motions, like she's washing away her fury with water and soap.

"I'm going to talk to Domingo." Tony's statement pulls me back to him.

I put a hand on his chest to stop him. I want to say, "Talk to me. Please. Talk to *me*. I'm your partner. I'm the one you came on this dangerous mission for—to protect me. You did this for me, right? I'm the one hurting. I thought my sister's body would be uncovered today. I need a hug. I need your arms around me. I need a connection. I need you." But I can't say anything. Because I know, in this moment, what is most important to *Tony*. He wants to comfort Domingo.

I should let him.

So I do. But I also must remind him, "We have to meet the boat captain tonight at midnight. We need to go back to Oshunvilla before we leave." I sound like a nagging wife but,

"Izzy." My voice cracks.

Tony stops. His head drops. We stand in silence for a moment.

My pulse ticks faster.

Finally, he looks at me. "I'm sorry. I should have told you sooner. I just…I'm trying to convince Esme."

"I know."

"I got a hold of the captain. He's giving us another twenty-four. We'll go back to Oshunvilla in the morning. I—I have to—"

"Convince your family to come with you. I understand." My shoulders fall. Twenty-four more hours. So, thirty-four hours left. I'm a little irritated he didn't tell me sooner; I'm his partner. I'm going to tell him that. "I'm happy you got us an extension on time—" But when I look up, he's gone.

I stomp the ground. Don't care if it makes me look like a teenager. I throw my hands up to my head and take a frustrated spin. I want to scream.

When I stop, my gaze lands on a man-made shelter, half hidden by palms and other greenery. An altar. To Oshun. Tony's aunt had said she'd put the bags given to me by the Santera next to her altar out back.

I know what I must do next, especially now that I have time. I'm going to do exactly what the Santera told me to do. I'm not going to cry. I'm going to pray to Oshun.

I am not a victim of my own self-induced pain. I am not a victim of rejection, either. I may be a broken girl. But I am also a warrior. And I am going to get what I want. What I want is a chance to get to know Tony better. I need Oshun's help breaking down the concrete wall encasing Tony's heart.

Chapter Twenty-Three

Day Two
6:30 P.M.
THIRTY-FOUR HOURS LEFT

I pull all the ingredients out of the two grocery bags given to me by the Santera Josefina and spread the items out across the dirt floor, reading the instructions left by her.

First, you take a square of yellow or gold paper and write with graphite pencil five times the name of the person you want to care more about you.

I look around before I do it, blood rushing from my heart to my cheeks. I can't believe I'm doing this, and I really don't want anyone to see me. I'm not even sure what it is I want from Tony. All I know is I need more.

No one is paying attention to me. *Good.* I grab the pencil included in the bags and write: *Tony. Tony. Tony. Tony. Tony.*

How did the Santera know? This woman I've never even met knew I'd need to pray for Tony's wall to be broken down and for him to let me in. I can't wait to see her again and ask her about that.

Focus. Do this before anyone misses me, or worse, finds me in the process.

Next step. Take the pumpkin and wash it to remove all kinds of negative energy it may have collected. *Really?* Can a fruit collect negative energy? Whatever. *Trust the process. Don't waste time.*

I take a knife, also in the bag, and follow the next instruction: cut the top and make a lid then remove most of its inner mass. That takes a few minutes. I wipe my fingers, now gooey, on my damp clothes. Damp from sweat. I place the almost empty pumpkin on a plate and take the written piece of paper and place it inside the fruit, Tony's name facing up. Not sure why it has to be facing up, but okay.

Next, I throw on top of the paper five drops of calm balm, honey flavored. Followed by five teaspoons of brown sugar, five teaspoons of honey, and five shakes of ground cinnamon.

Then, I pour the pulp of the pumpkin, the slimly, mushy mass of seeds and strings I dug out, back in the pumpkin and put the lid back on. I take the honey and smear a little on my hands and massage the pumpkin, closing my eyes and visualizing the moment I shared with Tony in the nightclub, when we lost ourselves for a moment dancing and laughing and really enjoying each other. I'm supposed to visualize the relationship I want. So, this time when I picture Tony and me in our standoff, in my mind's eye, he doesn't fight me reaching out to him. He puts his arms around me and lets all the anger flow from his body into mine. My center heats as I accept his anger. I do it willingly, to ease his pain. We both have so much pain we're shouldering. His body relaxes, and I catch him when his knees give. This is all in my mind's eye.

I will take care of you. Like you take care of me. Let me. Please.

Keeping my eyes tightly shut, I take a deep breath. *This*

I what I want, Oshun. I want Tony to trust me the way I trust him. I want him to lean on me the way he's allowed me to lean on him. I want to be the vase that collects the broken flowers of his frustrations. I want to be his best friend. Maybe more?

I open my eyes and grab the altar. The ground is moving under me. Blinking a few times allows me to focus, and I read the next instruction.

Take a red ribbon and place it under the pumpkin and wrap it in the shape of a gift, by making a bow at the top.

Takes me three times, but I finally figure it out. The red ribbon she gave me really wasn't long enough.

I read on. Take two candles—the ones she gave me are both yellow and heart-shaped—and I smear both with honey. *Why honey, honey? It's so sticky and hard to get off.* I wipe my hands with some wipes, also in the bags, then I light both candles. Now I'm supposed to read from a prayer letter left for me by Josefina.

I glance behind me. The teens are still dancing salsa on the back porch area of the farmhouse. The old men are on to another game of dominoes. Esme no longer washes dishes in the kitchen window. Dinner must be ready. I need to hurry.

I recite: "Loving mother Oshun, here I am in front of you, your daughter, Marisol Alvarez. I'm asking for your blessing and thanking you for everything. Here I place before you the sacred gourd with the name of Tony Garcia and the permission of your guardian angel, so that you attract him to me with your honey and cinnamon. Let him come to me, calm as balm. That we unite as I tied the pumpkin with the red bow and may the aforementioned yellow precipitate our union. Thank you, Mother, for helping me."

I exhale, not knowing what I've done or what may come next. I only know I felt compelled to do it. And now that it's done, a thousand pounds lift off my shoulders, because I'm letting go. It's out of my hands.

"Oh," I add last minute because it's not in the script, "Please lead me to my sister, Izzy. I need her, too. I'm the only hope she may have."

"You must light the candles for five days, at the same time, and on the last day let them burn out."

I jump at Esme's voice. I assumed she'd be busy putting out dinner. I turn toward her. "I…I…I won't be here for five days."

She smiles. It's a gentle thing. "You might."

"If not?"

"I will light them for you."

The urge to have a good cry comes back. She would do that for me? "What happens after five days?"

"The pumpkin must be left to Oshun in the river."

What river? But I don't ask. "Does it work?" I really want to know if Esme believes.

"Not always," she says, walking toward me. "If it does not"—she grabs my hands in hers—"perhaps it's a sign from Oshun that this person is not an appropriate fit in your life." Esme's eyes are warm, as is her skin.

"What do you think?" *About Tony and me?*

She squeezes my hands. "It's not for me to say."

I sigh. "I've never met anyone quite like him." I break eye contact, the emotion in me so strong the tears heat behind my eyes, and my hands tremble. "He's so nurturing and kind and—"

"He wants to take my son away from me."

That stabs me in the chest. "No, he wants to offer your son different opportunities." I do understand what it feels like to think you'll never see someone you love again. It pulls your heart apart, till the muscle is nothing but strings of meat, like my Abuela Bonita's famous *ropa vieja* dinner. "He would never take Domingo away from you—"

"I won't let him go."

"What does Domingo want?"

She doesn't answer.

"Can Oshun help with this? Your indecision?" *And mine, too?*

Esme, dressed in a cotton dress, apron, and green Crocs, the kind Tony probably sent from America, looks at me like I'm her child. "I've made up my mind."

"I see." What else is there to say?

"But you don't agree?"

I shrug and look over at the altar of Oshun. "Not for me to say."

She smiles, and it reaches all the way into her wise old eyes. "I didn't know my son wanted to be a doctor."

That surprises me. "Maybe he feared telling you."

"Because I failed." Esme releases my hands and walks toward the altar, her back to me. "I trained to be a dentist."

I can't help but feel a connection to this woman. "We do what we have to do to survive."

"I never wanted to be a farmer."

I never wanted to be alone. "So, why would you force that fate on your son?"

She turns toward me, the late afternoon sun landing flat on her sad face. Water fills her eyes. "I don't want to lose him. His father left as soon as I got pregnant. Domingo is the man in my life."

I break her gaze. It's too much, the weight of those words meshed with her history. We are all wounded. "But maybe Domingo needs a man in his life, too." I say this because I believe it. "Maybe he needs Tony to show him how to be a man."

Esme clicks her tongue, making a noise that I can't quantify. "You do care about him."

My breath stalls. "Tony?"

"Yes."

"Why do you say that?"

"Because you want what's best for him."

"And for Domingo."

Esme hangs her head.

I watch the setting sun play with the natural highlights on the top of her head.

"I will pray on it." She looks up and pushes her shoulders back, as if resetting her thoughts and agenda. "Dinner is ready. I'm calling everyone to the house."

I nod, but reach out to stop her from leaving. We haven't had much chance to talk, like really talk, woman to woman. I may not get another chance. "How about a compromise?"

The softness in her gaze hardens.

I don't let it stop me. "Let Domingo go to America with Tony for six months. Then he comes back, and you talk about the future. It's a compromise all three of you can live with." I'm speaking for Tony, without really knowing what he would say.

"It's not that simple. I will pray on it."

"While you do that, will you say a prayer for us as well?"

"For?"

"We are going back to Oshunvilla tomorrow morning." *And I'm nervous about it.* "I want to go back tonight but—"

"You do not go to Oshunvilla at night."

I pause. "Why?"

"Everyone knows."

"Knows what? The place freaks me out. Even during the daytime."

"You don't like art?"

I envision Izzy's handwriting. Proof she'd been at Oshunvilla with a wish in her heart. "Izzy wrote a message on the Wishing Wall. Asking me to rescue her."

"From what?"

"I don't know. But that message is the last clue we have of her whereabouts. What do you make of it?"

"You think your sister is at Oshunvilla?"

"Or kidnapped from there." I shrug, a big move so Esme can see my confusion. "There's this ride-share driver who picked her up, took her to Oshunvilla, and they came to get her the same day. We followed him today. I thought he was digging up a body, but he didn't find anything. Out of the blue, he says, 'She'll kill me, too, if she finds out.' Or something like that. Scared me, so I don't remember word for word. He also said the police protect the killer. Not kidnapper. *Killer.* What the hell is going on at Oshunvilla? You've lived close by all your life. You must know. People must talk. Is it a human trafficking thing?" I'd been thinking about that lately. All the missing girls are college age, young, beautiful.

"The only real evil comes from those trying to control the artist."

"Jimagua?" The artist I still haven't met or seen. Even a picture of him.

"I can offer only this advice. If you want to find your missing sister, look for those who control the artist. For he is the one who brings not only the magic, but the money, two things people are willing to kill for. And die for."

Chapter Twenty-Four

Day Three
7:00 A.M.
TWENTY-TWO HOURS LEFT

TONY'S FAMILY FARM

Bang. Bang. Bang.

Someone is pounding on my door.

Bang. Bang. BANG.

Not my door. Too far away. The front door to the farmhouse?

I roll over, throw the thin excuse for a pillow over my head. Am I dreaming? When did I finally fall asleep? Last I remember, my restless legs had me rolling around trying to ease my apprehension. The young cousin I share the room with had finally gotten up and left.

Left me alone.

A beehive of various voices advance. Can't tell everything they're saying, but the buzzing includes different

Spanish phrases, "Open the door. Police. Do you have any weapons?"

Police!

I bolt out of bed, run to the window, and lift the black bedsheet covering the glass. I step back, let the sheet fall. My hand finds my heart. It's whacking against my chest like the mallet in one of those Whack-a-Mole arcade games.

The farm is being raided. By men in threatening uniforms.

What should I do?

A door breaks open. I jump. Front door. Not my door.

Call Tony. My phone's on the nightstand. I grab and unlock it.

Footsteps down the hallway.

I fly to the bedroom door. Lock it.

Gulping air. Still can't breathe.

A text comes in fast and furious. Five words.

Arrested. Run. Hide. Call source.

From Tony.

Pulsing blood rocks my temples.

I could hide under the bed, but they'll look there. Remember the movie *Taken*? The closet has no door. There's no bathroom. The window. That's it.

The door handle jiggles.

I go still.

"It's locked."

Not a voice I recognize. In Spanish.

Ringing fills my ears.

Boom. Boom. Boom. "Open up."

An order. Not a request.

I grab my backpack, throw the phone in, throw on my shorts, a tank, and my slide-in tennies.

What next?

A tap at my window. Do they have my room covered

from the outside, too?

"Mari," a voice calls from outside the window. A voice I *do* recognize.

I pull off the sheet covering the window and try to jerk it open, but it's stuck.

Boom. Boom. Boom. "We're coming in."

I can't fit through. "Domingo, help me."

We both pull on the glass. Tug it open wider.

I haul myself up like a gymnast on the uneven bars. Literally flip through the window, shortening my legs, banging my ankles as they whip over and through.

The sting of skin tearing follows.

Domingo catches me.

Freedom's angry bark fills my head.

"Get on."

I shoulder my backpack and jump on the scooter.

The bedroom door bursts open, but I don't look.

"Hold on!"

I throw my arms around the teen.

The scooter takes off at a surprising speed. Domingo must have rigged it with an upgraded motor. I lurch backward but clench my thighs around the seat.

"Where's Orlando?"

No answer.

Now that we're far enough away I doubt a bullet could catch us, I sneak a peek back.

Freedom hobbles after us on his three good legs. He'll never be fast enough. We'll have to leave him. My heart stretches for Domingo. He's helping me and risking the thing he loves most. *I'll remember that.*

Family members are gathered in the front yard. Esme, in a housedress, waves her hands. I can't hear her, but she must be yelling at them to let Tony go. His hands are behind him, cuffed I'm sure, being led out by two uniformed men. Cops?

Military? Can't tell. They're leading him to what looks like a small tank. What did he do?

Enter the country illegally.

We all did.

Punishable by prison.

Standing next to that tank, Mr. Perfect White Shoes, Alfonso. But this time, he has on boots. I can't breathe. Literally. Can. Not. Breathe.

Will Tony go to jail?

Dust from the farm kicks up into my face and I blink, hiding my head behind Domingo's.

Tony is being arrested. *Call source*—Mr. Marshal, the U.S. Marshal living undercover in Havana. Thank God, Tony airdropped me his number.

I reach into my backpack and fumble around until I find my phone, a struggle on the bumpy off-road ride.

I grip my phone so hard my fingers go pale. But I'm not losing this phone. It's my key to Tony's freedom. Still holding onto Domingo with one arm, I pull the phone around him so I can dial.

The U.S. Marshal answers on the first ring.

Breathless, I shout, "Tony's been arrested."

"Do you have a place to hide?" he replies.

Where should I go? Wherever Domingo takes me right now.

Then it hits me.

"I'm going back to Playa Hermosa, where we saw the Oshun festival. I'll text an address."

Oshunvilla will have to wait. First, I need to find Orlando and meet up with him, if he's not also taken into custody.

"No. Tell me an address."

I don't have it, but I tell him the name of the Santera's store. I need to talk to her. Maybe she knows where we can hide. She knew why we were here and saved us from the watchdog, Mr. Perfect White Shoes. She gave me instructions to pray to Oshun.

My reporter's instinct tells me she'll hide and protect us. And she'll know what we need to do next.

Chapter Twenty-Five

Day Three

Esme and Maximo's farm is so rural, we race down bumpy, dirt roads for what seems like forever, and don't see anyone.

My heart rate drops in increments the farther from the farm we get. I glance back occasionally, to make sure no one is following us.

I pull air into my lungs as we race toward Playa Hermosa—full speed.

My arms grip Domingo's middle, but finally, my muscles relax.

He hasn't spoken a word since we left his family, and his dog behind.

I rest my head against his back, but it takes me a second to realize I'm crying. The hot tears drip down my face like a showerhead leaking. I've been so scared, so focused on survival, my brain must have shut down the connection to my emotions. I'm fried. And now that I know we're safe, feeling rushes back in waves, flogging me, despite the warm air moving over me as we race forward.

Thoughts jolt my brain, whacking the sides of my head like the bumps we hit on the road.

Who told the Cuban government we were staying at Tony's family's farm? Raúl could have alerted the authorities after he fled his house. Maybe the driver, Angel? Or maybe Mr. Perfect White Shoes, the government watchdog?

It couldn't have been any of Tony's family. They wouldn't betray Tony, right? I really don't know them well enough to know.

Why raid the farm? *To take Tony into custody and make an example of him.*

Tony is a Cuban national. Born in Cuba. Now living in the United States. And he came back illegally, without the government's permission, on a secret mission. The message: don't mess with the government.

Where did they take him? How the Jesus, Mary, and Joseph am I, little ole me, how am I going to find him, much less get him back? How can the U.S. Marshal help if he's undercover?

Worry whips through me, making my heart skip beats. I know what it would do to Tony if his family suffered a doomed fate because of our mission. It would kill everything good in him, because he'd blame himself. He brought trouble to his family's doorstep.

And he came here to help me.

He'd also blame me.

I exhale and squeeze Domingo's center as we catch a little air going over a rise in the dirt road.

"We're almost to the main road," Domingo says.

Translation: *We're almost to asphalt and a less bumpy ride.*

That's not what I'm worried about. I want to get to the Santera's store and safety. I want to find Orlando safe. I want to rescue Tony. I want my team back. *I want my people back.* I realize that's what I've been longing for. *I need my village.* We've been pillaged.

My shoulders shake from the weight of what happened this morning. I wonder if Domingo knows I'm losing it.

The scent of burning oil whiffs up my nose. The kid keeps pushing the scooter at a pace I'm sure challenges the motor.

We merge onto a paved road, entering a small town with homes and businesses on each side, and about a dozen cars on the road. We take our place in the right lane, which I'm assuming, like in America, is the slow lane. We won't be able to keep up with most of the cars, although most are older Fifties models, so maybe.

To my surprise, we do zoom past the cars. We make a few turns, and now we're driving down the middle of a two-lane highway, where the traffic to our right is going one way, and the traffic to our left is going a different way.

"Hold on!" Domingo yells. He jerks the scooter to the left and takes a side road, swerving to the right. We're on the sidewalk, zipping past businesses, mostly closed due to the early hour. When the side road ends, Domingo cuts sharply to the right to merge back onto the main road, and the scooter leans so far over, he uses his foot against the street to make sure we don't fall over.

I imagine smoke flying from his cheap, hand-me-down tennis shoes as he pushes us upright again.

I'm gaining respect for this kid.

Domingo whips his head around, glancing behind us.

What's up? I look back.

A cherry-colored Chevy is fast approaching.

Angel, the driver? Or the government watchdog? Someone is getting too close. Following us? Since when?

My heart tap-dances. This is not going to be fun.

The main road curves left, but Domingo keeps going

straight. We're off-roading again, heading from the main highway onto a dirt trail. Not even a road. Now I know he thinks we're being followed.

The dirt road thins, and small trees with long limbs smack me. I'm swimming in green leaves, the coolness coming with sharp stings as the leaves brush my skin. I'm afraid we'll smash into a tree trunk too thick to bend. My breath catches in my throat.

The first indication we've been hit is the sound of something large crashing into us.

The scooter tips, going full speed. We're airborne, and I'm lifted off the scooter. I cling to my backpack, not wanting to lose it.

I hit the ground, rolling like I learned in self-defense class, my body bending, dirt shooting up my nose, my mouth, and into my eyes.

I roll a few times before something stops me. Something large like a log.

I hear brakes squealing. A car stopping.

I roll over, push up to my feet, adrenaline fueling me, numbing any pain. The scooter's to my right. Not damaged, but on its side. Domingo's running toward it. Picks it up.

The sound of tires screeching makes me turn.

The car that hit us is turning around. To come back at us? My stomach freefalls. *Of course.* The driver, who I can't make out, thanks to the sun hitting the windshield and blacking out the glass, is going to run us over. I know it. My cortisol dump confirms it.

Domingo has the scooter upright and gestures to me.

I don't think I can make it.

Then, the car's tires spin in the dirt. It seems like minutes, probably only seconds, before the Chevy lurches forward heading not for Domingo and the scooter, but straight for me.

I stop breathing.

Brace myself for impact.

Boom.

Another car crashes into it, coming from the direction we'd come from.

My scream takes flight as the car coming toward me leaves the ground and shoots up and over me, landing behind me, rolling to the right. Missing me.

Two cars following us?

"Get on! We've got to get out of here." Domingo's voice jerks me back to reality.

I run toward the scooter, hearing Spanish expletives, followed by gunfire.

I throw my leg over, wrap my arms around Domingo.

The wheels spin. Dust erupts like a volcano around us. I can't see.

The wheels find traction, and we're off.

I'm squeezing Domingo's center like my life depends on it.

As we're taking off, I hear my name, followed by a rapid assault of gunfire.

No doubt about it now.

Someone is trying to stop us from finding Izzy or maybe from finding the other missing girls. And they're willing to silence us any way necessary.

Arrest us.

Run over us with a car.

Or bring us down with a barrage of bullets.

Chapter Twenty-Six

Day Three

Domingo slows as we enter Playa Hermosa. No need for speed now—after we escaped the car that tried to run us over, we faced no other threat. The second car that crashed into the Chevy took off immediately. I never saw the driver.

We pull up to the general store on the main road of the beach town. My mouth waters, and I realize, not only am I hungry and thirsty, I haven't even brushed my teeth yet. I've been on the run since my eyes opened. I left everything, except my backpack, behind at the farm. Do I even have money to buy a drink?

Domingo stops in front of the store, puts one foot on the ground, but doesn't turn the scooter off.

"I'm going back," he says.

I don't unravel my arms glued around him. "I'm sorry?"

"I have to go back for Freedom."

I can't see his eyes, since I'm still behind him, so I don't know if he's crying, but I feel his tense muscles vibrate. I swallow, knowing better than to argue with the kid.

When you love someone or something, you go back for them. Or search for them. You don't leave them, even if it means you do stupid things, like go back to a farm being raided by men who have guns and big tanklike vehicles. Who am I to judge? I entered this country illegally to search for Izzy. "Okay. Please look for Orlando, too." I pull out my phone and dial O's cell, but it goes right to voicemail. Not a good sign. "I can't get ahold of him."

"If the *policía* arrested your friend, I'll find out where they took him."

I nod, throwing one leg off the scooter. "What's your number?"

Domingo tells me, and I text him mine, so we can keep in touch.

"If he's at the farm, I'll bring him here."

I secure the backpack. "Domingo."

The kid blinks a couple of times before making eye contact.

I want to hug him. "When you find Freedom, I'd like you to come back. With your dog. You'll be safer here."

He looks away, silent.

"You're with us now, right?" It's what Tony wanted. "You're coming to America?" Convincing him is what I can do for Tony, in his absence.

"I'll find your friend and make sure he meets you here."

Domingo must be changing his mind about coming to America. "Thank you." Have the raid and the attempt on our lives convinced him *we* are not *safe*?

"Be careful," he says. "You can't trust anyone here."

I glance into the general store. Josefina, hair hidden in her white turban, is working the counter, checking someone out. I don't think the Santera has noticed me yet. "I can trust her," I say more to myself.

"Can you?"

"I don't know."

"Don't believe everything you see. My mamá tells me some things are shells of what they used to be. Or what they're supposed to be."

That does sound like something Esme would say. "What did she mean?"

Domingo's eyes widen, and his grip on the bike tightens. "Gotta go." He lifts his foot and guns the bike, raising a layer of dirt as he takes off.

I swipe at the dust, coughing. When the air clears, I walk in a circle, taking in the street around me. Today, no dishes clang at Casa Del Chocolate, just a few customers sipping what I imagine is café con leche or strong shots of Cuban espresso. Only one vintage car drives down the main road, and far fewer folks walk by me.

A quieter energy fills the air today.

I search the street for the neighborhood watchdog who's been trailing me. The AirTag is gone, and I don't see him anywhere. My reporter senses are no longer tingling. Maybe I can relax for a moment.

Breathe.

The front door to the store rings. A woman, dressed in a typical Cuban housedress, light cotton and non-formfitting, flutters by me, her arms full of a couple of bags. She doesn't make eye contact. Josefina is no longer at the counter, and the store appears empty.

Paranoia skips across my flesh, hundreds of millipede legs moving at once.

The flashing OPEN sign stops blinking.

Did Josefina close the store because she saw me? I'm going in, anyway. Frankly, I have nowhere else to go.

People passing on the street stare at me. I must look lost.

Confused. *Vulnerable.*

I hate being vulnerable. I hate being alone.

A burst of *screw this* fires through me. I turn the handle and push at the front door, and it opens easily. "Josefina?"

No answer.

Stale air in the room makes me think I imagined her earlier.

All is quiet, except for the rush of blood flying past my eardrums.

A cool hand slides over my mouth.

I freeze.

An arm snakes around my waist.

I grab at it, pierce flesh with my nails.

Someone pulls me away from the door, away from the glass windows.

I scream, but a large, calloused hand presses down over my mouth, muffling my voice.

"Be quiet." A whispered order. "Come with me."

Chapter Twenty-Seven

Day Three
10:00 A.M.
NINETEEN HOURS LEFT

GÜIRA DE MELENA

Orlando and I sit in a backroom lanai, in a home about an hour away from Playa Hermosa and the Santera's store, continuing our discussion about what just transpired. "Why didn't you jump out after the accident and let me know you and Enrique were in the second car?"

"You jumped on that scooter, and Domingo took off like you all were running from the devil."

"Maybe we were." The screened-in back porch is empty, except for a beat-up futon in the sofa position, a glass table with rusted iron legs, and a wooden rocking chair, no seat cushions.

"I knew where you'd go," O says.

I'm rocking almost violently. "You knew I'd go to the

Santera's store?"

"Where else would you run?" Orlando, sitting on the futon, shrugs. "Made sense to me. Josefina wants to help us but needs to keep it on the down-low. She doesn't want trouble. So that's why I—"

"Why you covered my mouth, dragged me through the store, and kidnapped me here?"

"I needed to get you out of her store quietly. I needed to bring you here, where Josefina said she'd meet us."

I throw heat bombs with my eyes.

"All's well that ends well."

"Quoting Shakespeare, O?"

"You're not the only one who got an A in English lit."

I laugh at our banter. The physical release helps assuage my anxiety.

"It's good to hear the sound of happiness again in your abuela's home." Josefina enters from the kitchen, waddling in white, carrying a tray holding two small espresso coffee cups and a large plate full of bread. All thoughts of brushing my teeth before I eat vanish when I smell the strong aroma of espresso with sugar and see the melted butter drip off a slice of still warm Cuban bread. A low, long rumble erupts from my stomach. "Where did you come from? When Orlando dragged me out of your store and threw me in Enrique's car, I didn't see you."

"I brought my husband's car here."

"Happiness might be taking it a bit far, Josefina," Orlando says staring at the food, too.

They're on a first name basis? "Wait. What?" I stop rocking. "My *abuela's* home?" I glance around, the back porch taking on a whole new meaning. Excitement floods my body.

"Where are we, by the way?" Orlando's eyes follow the tray.

"Güira de Melena," Josefina says, placing it on the glass table.

I bet that bread is soft in the center. I lick my lips at what else she's brought. "*Mariquitas*." I sigh, already tasting the garlic and salt, even before I grab one of the crunchy golden plantain chips and place it on my tongue.

"I thought you might be hungry," Josefina says, smiling at me, a twinkle in her dark brown eyes.

The flavors twirl on my tongue as I chew, and it's delightful, like dancing salsa under a midnight moon. My mind spins with Josefina's new revelation. "We're in my abuela's house in her hometown." My back straightens. "Her birthplace?"

Josefina nods.

I walk to the patio screen and stare out into the backyard. "The garden she planted before she left." My heart swells with satisfaction that at least I'll be able to complete this task, do this one last thing for my abuela.

The garden is divided into six rectangular areas. A variety of plants are growing in the dirt. "It's still flourishing. Who took care of it all these years?"

"Your abuela's husband entrusted my husband with this house before they fled Cuba. She had only one wish: keep the garden alive and keep it feeding the mouths of our family's loved ones. Your abuela has—" She stops on the word has. "*Had* been sending me seeds with relatives who traveled from Tampa. Corn, tomatoes, lettuce, potatoes. Much of what we eat grows here."

I turn back to my abuela's happy place. "What did Abuela love to grow most?"

"Happiness."

My heart inflates, and heat hits the back of my eyes, because this is true. My abuela is the one person who planted seeds of happiness in my soul and watered those seeds with love and reliability. My hand finds its way to my heart. I could always count on her. I turn away from the garden. "I have her ashes with me." My voice cracks.

The Santera nods. "I know she wanted to be buried here, child." Her eyes water, too. "My husband is the Babalawo who came to Tampa to visit you on my calling."

I picture the Babalawo sitting in a similar rocking chair on the lanai of his sister's West Tampa home, with the low beat of drums in the background, tall, lush tropical plants covering the porch from floor to ceiling, isolating us from prying neighborhood eyes.

"He is the one you talked to in West Tampa the night the killer gunned down the deputy."

"I remember." I shudder, recalling what he'd said to me that night, months ago. "*Child, you must lean on your orisha and stand on your own two feet or these questions you ask will crush someone you love dearly. This is what I see.*" Did he prophesize Abuela Bonita's death? "Did I kill Abuela Bonita by not heeding his words?" Guilt strangles me, and I can barely get the thoughts out.

"No child. No." The Santera moves in and gathers me to her.

I melt into her, thankful for the comfort. "Why didn't Abuela Bonita tell me about this connection?" I step back so I can look her in the eyes. "Why didn't she tell me about you?"

"She spent her whole life trying to protect you from the dark side of life."

"You're not part of the dark side." But a vision of that plastic heart sitting on the altar, next to a severed goat's head, flies eating at the eyeballs, comes full motion-picture into my mind. I can even hear the missing person's flyer flapping in the wind, whipping a wishful plea: *Find me. Find me. Find me.*

I shake my head to clear it. "I will spread her ashes as she wished." That's why I wouldn't let the backpack go.

"No rush. You both can stay here until you are ready to… leave."

"Think the bad guys will find us here?" Orlando asks.

The Santera drops her head, not even asking who Orlando thinks the bad guys are.

Not a good sign.

"Do what you came to do quickly. Time may not be on your side."

"We already missed our boat." Orlando glances my way. "The forty-eight-hour deadline came and went while we were running for our lives."

"Tony got a hold of our captain. He's waiting one more day. Well, we have about, I don't know, about eighteen or nineteen hours left. But Tony is MIA. I have no idea how to get in touch with the boat captain. Do you? I don't even know how to get back to that marina." Why didn't I take pictures or take notes?

"We'll figure it out once we get Tony back."

If we get Tony back.

I could kick myself for not getting the captain's cell like I insisted on getting the marshal's. "I'll call Mr. Marshal." I dial the number I've tried several times already. "No answer. I've texted him, too, but had to keep it vague."

The Santera points to the food. "Before anything, you both eat. You look pale." She hands a piece of bread to Orlando, who takes it without question. "I'm going back to the store. Everything must go on as normal. I'm there every day." She pulls a dark key out of her pocket. "Come and go as you need. There is water in the kitchen but not much else. Except what's growing out back. I pray this will be a safe place for you."

But she can't guarantee it. I hear that unspoken sentence. We're on our own, but not quite yet. I envelop the Santera in my arms. She's soft like love should be. Warm and forgiving. Total acceptance. Abuela Bonita's arms were bony, her fingers cold on my skin, but I felt the same rush of acceptance with her. "Thank you for everything." I don't want to let go.

"I knew your grandmother at your age." Josefina pulls back and takes my face in both of her plump hands. "I promised her I would take care of her garden. You, my dear, are the most beautiful thing she's ever grown." She kisses my forehead.

Gratitude clogs my throat until it aches.

The cool, calm energy swirls out of the room with Josefina's flowing white skirt.

Once she's gone, I turn to Orlando. "Back to work."

Orlando stops chewing and gives me a *here we go again* look. "We doing your wall thing again?"

I nod, my mouth full of bread and butter. I soften it with a sip of cool espresso. *Damn, it's strong.*

"We need tape," O says.

"Let me run up to Target," I joke.

He doesn't laugh.

I pull out duct tape from my backpack, sitting next to the rocking chair. "I took this from the farm. I came prepared."

"All right, all right, all right. Where do we start?"

"Begin at the beginning." My *Alice in Wonderland* quote for the day, inspired by the weirdness of Oshunvilla. "With my missing sis, Isabella Alvarez."

Chapter Twenty-Eight

Day Three

Missing girl #1: ISABELLA ALVAREZ

I write my sister's name on a piece of paper, a yellow wrapper from a Pulparindo, a hot and salted pulp candy popular in Cuba. I found a box in the kitchen, and Orlando ate enough for me to use the packaging. Can't waste anything here.

I tear off a piece of duct tape and use it to stick my sister's name to the clean cement wall.

"What else you got, Detective Alvarez?" Orlando is rocking in the chair now, sucking on the candy, watching me. He's finished his espresso and all the Cuban bread.

I don't blame him. Who knows when we'll eat again. "Here's what else I've got. Plastic soda bottle at Raúl's house. Izzy drinks Fresca, but I bet most Cubans don't even know what that is." I write Fresca underneath her name.

"You also got that message she left on the Wishing Wall."

"Got it." I write Izzy's message on the rest of that candy wrapper and tape it next to her name. Had she been kidnapped by Raúl, or did she come to Cuba of her own free will, but now wants to leave? "She knew I'd come looking for her. So I'm going to figure she came here under some duress. Maybe not kidnapped. Maybe confused and scared by Raúl showing up after all the years he'd lived in Cuba."

"That's why she used your secret sister code?"

"I'm not sure. Also, we need to ask the security officer for different surveillance video of the Wishing Wall the day Izzy visited. He showed us only video from outside of Oshunvilla. On purpose? I'm sure they still have video near the Wishing Wall from that day. That video might tell us who was with her. Maybe one of the other missing girls?"

"Izzy went to Oshunvilla to look for Arianna." Orlando now has his GoPro out, and he's videotaping our conversation and the creation of our investigative wall.

"Agreed. She was looking for the American college girl she'd befriended at the hostel."

Missing girl #2: ARIANNA JOHNSTON

I use another candy wrapper and a marker I had in my backpack and write her name on it. I put it up next to the envelope addressed to me. I pull out the missing flyer of her I found at Raúl's house. "Who brought this flyer to Raúl's house? Was it made by Izzy? What is their relationship, that Izzy would go looking for her? Does Arianna have family looking for her, too?"

"Maybe Raúl brought the missing person flyer to the house."

I gawk at Orlando. "If he did, why?"

"Maybe he kidnapped her and needed to gather evidence

that might fuck him.'"

I cringe at the word he chose. "All right. It's possible Arianna was the girl with the fake nails locked in Raúl's guest room." I write that with a question mark at the end.

"How did they meet?"

"Who? Arianna and Raúl?"

"No. Izzy and Arianna."

"Oshunvilla? The hostel? Raúl?" I write those three words under Arianna's name.

"What's the connection?"

"Did Izzy meet Arianna and introduce her to Raúl? Or did Arianna know Raúl, and that's how Izzy met her?"

"Or did they meet in Raúl's locked room with boarded up windows when they both became Raúl's prisoners?"

I remember the bunk beds in the room. I shake off the horrible thoughts entering my head. "Arianna took the same private driver as Izzy from the hostel to Oshunvilla." I pull out the UGA keychain I found stuffed into the seat of Angel's car and tape it next to Arianna's name. "The missing flyer showed Arianna in a Georgia T-shirt. That's a connection. Did Arianna know Teddy, who's also from Georgia?"

Missing girl #3 TEDDY MEYERS (Frederica)

I write Teddy Meyers on another candy wrapper and tape it up next to Arianna's wrapper. "We know Teddy Meyers is a friend of the girls we met at the hostel staying there when she disappeared. Her friends said she had a relationship with a guy named Raúlito. Coincidence? Lots of Raúl's in Cuba. Add *ito* to the name, and it's like adding a term of endearment."

Orlando shakes his head. "No freaking way. It's our Raúl."

"I agree. Where did that murderer disappear to? We

need to go back and find him."

"Mari, concentrate. We're on Teddy."

"Right." I inhale, exhale, and count to ten. That usually clears my head of unwanted tangents. "Teddy took the same driver to Oshunvilla that Izzy took. Let's assume the same one as Arianna, too." I write the name "Angel the driver" on a scrap of paper from the depths of my backpack. Tape it next in line. Next to Izzy, Arianna, and Teddy's wrappers. "Teddy and Arianna have ties to Georgia. Teddy has a mom, but no dad and no siblings. But she does have a friend, Mandy. Which leads us to—"

Missing girl #4: MANDY PEACHER

One wrapper left. I write Mandy's name on it. "Arianna's mom is looking for Mandy, too, because Mandy is a product of the foster care system and aged out with no real family to help her. When I googled her, I found nothing on Mandy Peacher. Not even on social media."

"Where are you going with this, Mari?" Orlando has the last of the chips in his mouth.

My stomach growls. I'm still hungry, but what I want more than food is a whiteboard to write on. *Screw it.* I'll write on the cement wall with my black magic marker. "What do all these missing girls have in common?" I write on the wall:

1: College students or in early twenties like Izzy

2: Staying at the same hostel in Havana

3: Raúl?

4: The same private driver—Angel

5: Visited Oshunvilla

6: Traveling alone or with other young girls

7: Had little to no family to look for them

I write in bold, capitalized letters: **BROKEN GIRLS.** "The missing girls are also broken girls. That's why they were targeted."

When O's gaze meets mine, I realize he's thinking the same thing I am and not saying it.

We may have stumbled onto the trail of another serial killer. How screwed up is that?

"We need to go back to the last place these girls were all seen alive," O says.

"We need to go back to Oshunvilla. I want to go back tonight, though. Especially now that the boat captain gave us a time extension."

"Night? Didn't someone you interviewed say the walls wail and the statues scream? I mean what the—"

"Don't say it."

He lifts his shoulders in a whatever shrug.

"We go at night because I want to find the artist. Apparently, he sleeps all day and works at night. Plus, it will be closed, so we can really explore without worrying about people watching us."

"Except security."

"When we were in security before, Tony watched surveillance video, but I checked out their system and cameras. We can sneak in, through the security office. I've thought this through."

He nods. "Okay, well, gotta change batteries, get my gear ready. Got plenty of time."

"We go back when the sun sets." I smile and make my way to the screen where I can look out on Abuela Bonita's beautiful garden. "Can you text Enrique and make sure he can take us? Also, check on Tony. Do they know where he's been taken? For how long? And the rest of the family—"

"Will find out what I can."

"I have something to do before we leave." Something I

must take care of, in case anything goes wrong at Oshunvilla tonight. "I have a promise to fulfill." One that will break my heart. But I can't avoid it any longer.

I reach into my backpack and take out the urn holding Abuela Bonita's ashes. My hands are shaking.

Orlando stops rocking but says nothing.

I close my eyes and think back to the Sunday afternoons, when Izzy and I would help Abuela Bonita in her small garden behind her modest West Tampa home.

Orlando gets up and leaves the room, his footsteps light like he's trying not to disturb me, trying to respect this moment.

As soon as I make out the door closing, I hear Izzy's laughter tinkle in my memory. She knew how much I hated to get my expensive, salon-dipped nails dirty. She also knew I'd never tell Abuela Bonita no. Abuela had started the ritual right after Mamá died. Pick the ripe vegetables or plant new ones on Sunday afternoons, right after we changed from church, weather permitting. I'd throw on shorts, pull my long hair into a twist tie, and kneel in the grass surrounding the garden out back.

Izzy had no problem getting dirty. She'd plunge her hands into the soil and do everything Abuela asked her to. This love of the earth and fresh food bonded them. I joined only because I never wanted to disappoint Abuela and because during these hours Abuela persuaded Izzy to talk about her life. After Mamá's murder, Izzy withdrew from us. Well, if I'm honest with myself, her emotional retreat began the night Mamá found Raúl in her bedroom. I'd heard them fighting, then having sex. Even a pillow over my head couldn't silence their passion for each other. I hadn't told Mamá—she'd woken up to the noise—but Izzy never believed it wasn't me. I never did like Raúl, the West Tampa King, the gangster. So I understood her misconception.

But in Abuela's garden, for some reason, we were able to bury our bad feelings and plant only laughter or good tears; sprinkle heartfelt stories of our week like fertilizer, growing love again in the infertile soil of our uncomfortable distance after Mamá's murder.

Oh, the nails I broke in Abuela's garden. My Mondays usually included a stop by the salon, where my girl would dig out the dirt from my cuticles and apply fresh paint to my chipped nails.

Izzy would grab my hands over dinner on the Monday nights she joined us. She'd say nothing, but wink. Some days, she'd laugh at my attempts at perfection. I lived for those moments, hearing Izzy chuckle, even if her amusement came at my expense.

She had—my breathe catches. I shake off the thought, like the flakes of dirt I'd find in my hair. No, no, she *has* the most lyrical ring to her joy. The sound, when I hear it again, will be like water to my dehydrated happiness.

I sit with these images, Abuela on her hands and knees instructing Izzy on the signs a tomato is ripe, or how to tell which still needed time on the vine.

In my mind, Izzy's eyes sparkled as she asked me to dig deep and help her pull out a thick, stubborn yucca stem. Unearthing Abuela's favorite allowed us to grow and entwine again, like sister cassava roots.

Warm tears drip down my cheeks. I blink until the garden comes into focus.

Maybe fate led me here. Maybe God or Oshun. But here I am, standing feet away from where my abuela tended garden as a young girl. Her peaceful place. Where she told me she wanted her body to be buried.

It's time to let my abuela go, by returning her ashes to the earth.

I wish I could share this important moment with my Izzy.

Chapter Twenty-Nine

Day Three
7 P.M.
TEN HOURS LEFT

OSHUNVILLA

Orlando and I arrive at Oshunvilla on foot. Enrique dropped us off close enough we could walk the rest of the way, but far enough away security wouldn't hear an approaching car engine. A flat, dirt-covered field near the main road to the west of Oshunvilla became the perfect place for Enrique to park his ride, turn off the lights, and wait for us to return. He'd be in no one's sight, off the main road and off Oshunvilla's security camera radar.

Enrique promised he wouldn't leave us here.

He also promised that his family remained at the farm, okay. The police wanted only Tony. Well, and Orlando and me. But we'd escaped. I also know now we are wanted outlaws.

A barely visible waxing crescent moon replaces the rare, black moon of two nights ago, shining, but not nearly enough to light our path. My iPhone flashlight does that.

The night is steamy with heat brushing my skin in damp strokes, along with invisible insects nipping at me, probably mosquitoes or sand fleas, or both.

I'm in my same pants, socks, and tennis shoes, hoping they're enough to avoid being eaten alive. Perspiration drips down the back of my neck, weaving a wet finger along the curve of my spine.

A flash of heat lightning illuminates a cumulonimbus cloud, but I don't think it's going to storm. Rain, maybe. If we do get a quick downpour, hopefully we'll be inside by then.

"We're here." Orlando stops.

I press off the flashlight app and look up.

We've come to the back entrance of Oshunvilla. A camera, pointing away from us, hangs above the opening in the gate where employees enter, and drivers drop off deliveries.

I nudge O with my elbow.

He looks up, too.

The camera moves our way.

We find a dark nook, flatten ourselves against the wall, hiding in the skinny shadow created by a tall, shelflike unit. Even the cement feels hot, like it's been licked by flames.

Above and to my right, a giant mosaic sculpture towers over the entranceway. Spotlights illuminate it in the dark night, like the entrance to an amusement park. Is it made in the artist's image? The statue sits on top of the wall, arms open wide as if welcoming staff and others into his kingdom. But I fear this is no Mickey Mouse. The artist wears a bright yellow hat, his full red lips standing out below it. Otherwise, he's dressed in black, his mosaic arms made of pale white tiles. *Interesting.* On each side of him, large hearts made of red tiles and Spanish words translate to, ENTER WITH LOVE.

Behind the mosaic head, the crescent moon peeks out from between patches of towering thunderstorm clouds. The clouds shimmy over the celestial sliver, rendering the world temporarily dark and silent.

Except for the rumble of thunder.

And the whirring of insects.

One buzzes past my ear. I don't swat it away; afraid any movement will be picked up by the security camera.

The moving lens passes by us and moves away to scan the other side again.

O grabs my hand, and he pulls me toward the opening in the fence. There must be some employees who arrive this time of night, because the gate is open.

The door into the security office, though, remains closed. Probably locked. I look around but don't see any other way into Oshunvilla. This area is fenced off from the actual grounds and the artist's home.

Rocks pop on the uneven ground. Someone's approaching from our left.

O grabs me, and we duck behind a dumpster. My stomach turns at the aroma—rotten food mixed with dirty toilet paper. I turn away, pinching my nose with my free hand.

O drops my other hand and peers around the dumpster.

A door squeals as it's ripped open. A man speaking Spanish shouts questions about being dragged in on his night off and being hungry.

So, there's more than one person in security tonight. *Good to know.* But they also may be short-staffed. Also good to know.

O darts out from behind the dumpster. He manages to stop the door into the security office with his foot. It's dark, but the light above the door makes it easy for me to see his wild gesture. I don't even have time to check if security cameras are pointed our way.

I bolt.

He opens the door slowly, to avoid a creaky noise, enough for us to get in. Then he controls the close.

The door shuts without making a sound.

I exhale.

More Spanish in the room in front of us.

A crackle of a walkie-talkie. "New piece in place."

A low moan. Then a girl's garbled voice… *"Help me"*? I turn to Orlando to see if he heard it, too, but it's too dark in our corner to see each other's features.

"Got ties in place." The voice on the walkie-talkie sounds male.

"Still wet?" someone in the main security office asks.

"Not going anywhere," walkie-talkie man responds.

Another low moan creeps through the walkie-talkie.

My stomach clenches. It *is* a girl's voice in distress.

"Shut her up," the person in the office here growls.

A gasp and then nothing.

Only crackling.

A few seconds later, from the walkie-talkie, "Done."

What the hell are they talking about? Who is moaning, and why did they say still wet?

I reach for O's hand, needing to squeeze something so I don't gasp. I'm breathing so hard I'm sure the men in the other room can hear my heart thumping against my chest and my slow, labored attempts to inhale oxygen.

"Got food?" That sounds like the guy who entered the office.

He's thinking about eating? After hearing that? *Psycho.*

"In the kitchen. Bring me something if you're going."

A door opens and closes.

The crackle of the walkie-talkie returns. "Hey, we got a problem."

Silence. Then, "What kind of problem?"

"Come check it out."

"Can't leave."

"Now."

"Right." Sounds in the office make me think someone is moving around, maybe cleaning up or gathering things? "Hey Saul, gotta check out a problem. Get your ass back here."

If we're lucky, and the one guard leaves before the other comes back, we may have thirty seconds to a minute where no one is in the security office, and we can pass through.

All we need is thirty seconds. We've been in this office before and know where the door into Oshunvilla is.

Another door slams, this one significantly louder than the last.

We tiptoe through the office, careful not to touch anything, careful not to make a sound. I'm looking at the door leading into the main building, waiting for the new guard to come back.

He doesn't.

We exit the security office into Oshunvilla's grounds.

Bright lights. *Ay Dios mio.*

We duck into a shadow again, unsure where the security cameras are pointing, but knowing they are there. They're everywhere. *This won't be easy.*

"Where to now?" Orlando asks.

"The artist's home."

"Know which way?"

"Yep. The tour lady pointed it out to me."

"After you."

If I'm right, young girls walked into Oshunvilla and never came out. Or if they did, they got into a car and disappeared, never to be seen again. One may even have been buried not too far away.

Do I really want to do this? No. But, I don't have a choice.

I cannot leave Cuba until I meet the artist Jimagua. I need to look into his eyes as I ask him if he has anything to do with the disappearance of my sister and the other missing girls. Mostly, I need to look for Izzy.

The sky lights up with leather belt-like straps of heat lighting snapping across the sky. A clash of thunder follows, no longer in the distance.

It's going to storm, after all. *Of course it is.*

I reach for the azabache charm and twist three times to the left, three to the right. "I wish Tony was with us."

Orlando pushes me forward. "We stay together. No matter what happens, we do not separate."

"Don't worry." I grab his hand, and at that very moment the thunder ends, it's replaced with the wail of a child.

Broken and in pain.

Chapter Thirty

Day Three

"Follow that sound," I whisper to Orlando.

"You mean follow the creepy kid's voice?"

I nod, and we make our way through Oshunvilla, which is mostly dark, except for ground guidelights highlighting the path, like those you'd see on the aisle of an airplane during an emergency exit. Because its dark, we don't need to hide. *Yet.*

O strides in front of me. He turns so I can hear his whisper. "Isn't this a little like walking into the dark basement where the guy with the chainsaw is hiding? After you realize the lights don't work, and you've misplaced your cell phone so you can't call for help?"

"Funny," I speak softly. My hand, gripping his, sticks to his skin. "The kid may be in trouble." I'm whispering, because this tourist trap, once ablaze with excited voices in many languages, sits in eerie silence.

Except for the intermittent rumble of thunder.

And the recurrent wails of the wounded we can't see.

"Sounds like a *kid* crying." I shiver in the humidity. *The walls wail.* That's what the girl in the medical clinic told me. *The statues cry and the walls wail.* Now I can confirm that. "I'm glad I told the U.S. Marshal where we were going. In case we—"

"Disappear." Orlando freezes. "You hear that?"

"Yes." I squeeze his hand, thankful he's with me. "Sounds like a scream."

The statues cry? Maybe she should have said scream.

"Could be Izzy." I glance around. No signs of anyone, not even security. But cameras are everywhere. Evil eyes watching. I can't see them in the dark. Hopefully the cameras can't see us, either.

"Stop." Orlando glances back at me. "We'd recognize her voice."

He's right. Anyway, what would be the chance? I need to get the hell out of my head and stay calm and composed. Focus on finding the artist. I have a million questions for him.

"Can't tell where it came from."

I nod, checking out a giant evil eye painted on a wall we're passing. Could a camera be hiding in the pupil? "Main house is over there." Jimagua's studio sits in the center of the compound. It's a three-story concrete building, the only one with lights on inside. "Let's start there." The lights are coming from the third story, where the silhouette of an adult is visible. We're too far away to see details, but he's sitting with his back to us, painting a statue in front of him. *The artist sleeps all day and works all night.*

"We've got to get closer." I pull at Orlando. In my effort to move quickly, I trip over a mound of something. A mound? Looks like it's been recently overturned. My heart stalls. I envision the driver, on hands and knees, digging vigorously at the ground as if looking for a body. "What the hell is this?"

Orlando puts a finger to his lips.

The hair on my neck tingles.

I spin around, sensing someone behind me.

Another streak of lightning zips across the night sky, like skeletal bones reaching out to grab something.

In that flash, I'm staring into startled wide eyes embedded in a white-tiled face.

Bright red lips purse as if under duress.

Thunder rolls.

Another streak of light. Black tiles flow down the sides of the statue's face. *Long hair with a Farrah flip.*

"What are you doing?" I sense the urgency in O's whisper. "Art shopping?

"Looks like a college student." *Looks like my sister.*

It's so quiet I hear him exhale. He moves closer because it's dark again. "Doesn't look like Izzy. You're seeing what you want to see." He strides around the statue. "I'm seeing huge eyes, bleeding. What the fuck?"

I squint. Red tears, made of tiny tiles, drop down the statue's face. I touch it. Not wet, but cool, due to the tile pieces covering the plaster.

"Skinny body with a pumpkin head and man-sized hands," O continues.

I'm zeroing in on one weird detail. "A hole." Lightning illuminates Oshunvilla again. Only for a second, but long enough to see— "There's a hole in the middle of the lips. Look." I step closer. I want to stick a finger in, but it goes dark again. Fear freezes my finger.

Why the hole?

"Pay attention!" a new voice pierces the night.

A snap. Sounds like a belt. I cringe as if hit by it.

"Focus. Do your work." The voice is loud enough to be heard from the artist's third-story room.

Another flash of light, followed by a rumble, and for a

brief second, I swear another person moves past the third-story window. "Did you see that?" I whisper.

"See what?"

The rain starts, Mother Nature adding water to those tears dripping down the statue's face.

I don't repeat myself. Can't see through the fat droplets falling now, anyway.

"Let's get closer." I lurch forward, anxious to see what else is in that room on the third floor. Also anxious to find shelter from the rain.

I plow into a piece of art, hard and unyielding. I bite my lip to keep from yelling.

Orlando tugs me, and I follow, limping, my clothes and shoes soggy.

We get to the artist's house and stand under an awning over a side door. A tiled heart surrounds the third-story window where the artist still works in silhouette. He's backlit. Iron bars cover the window. Like anyone could climb up there and enter.

"You okay?" Orlando asks and gestures at the same time to a security camera on the artist's home.

It's on the second story above the front door. We're good for now. "How are we supposed to get up there?"

"Front door."

A blue light hanging over the front door shines down onto a tiled octopus, mouth wide open where the door is. Steel bars make teeth. "This place looks like a prison."

"More like a madhouse. Someone wants to keep everyone away from the artist. Or"—Orlando leans in, probably so he can be heard above the rain—"they want to keep the artist inside creating new masterpieces, so the town makes money."

"Or both. Either way it's creepy—"

"As fuck."

The windows on the first and second floors have bars

across them, too. We're not getting in unless we knock and take our chances he'll answer, and then be understanding to our mission. Which I doubt. Standing under the awning keeps me at an awkward angle. I no longer see the artist, but hear mumblings of conversation, muted by the rain. Until—

"Don't make me do it."

That's a young boy's voice.

"Don't make me."

The kid's voice escalates, so full of fear and terror it lifts the hair on my skin. My heart flutters like a caged butterfly's. How many people are up there? Why would a child be up this late? "What do we do now?" I whisper under the rain, hoping he can read my lips.

"Trying the back door." Orlando points to his left. "I'll go. You stay here."

"What happened to 'we don't separate?'" I slide against the wall, careful to stay hidden in the dark as long as possible. My fingers crawl against the house, sliding easily due to the downpour, picking up where the tiles end and paint begins, finding some comfort in the changing landscape under my fingers. Anything to take my mind off the terrifying fact I'm in an R.L. Stine fantasyland in a thunderstorm, knowing the monsters are about to show themselves, and I can barely see to run.

Orlando climbs up a few stairs off the back porch of the artist's home. His feet are light. I barely hear him.

Of course, it's pouring.

Blood pounds at my temples, throbbing in my ears.

I take a chance and step back, jumping behind another statue of a woman. Why so many of them? Oshun. Fertility. *Right.*

Two things happen at once.

Orlando tugs on the back door.

The lights in the third-story room flick on full force.

The artist chisels at a statue.

My breath hitches. Acid rises into my throat. I grip the statue I'm hiding behind. Wipe the water from my eyes.

"What are you doing?" A woman's voice, again.

The artist jumps up, brings his hands to his head, as if protecting himself. "Stop. I'm working." His loud voice booms over us, deep as the thunder.

My heart jumps through my chest. Who is he talking to? I don't see anyone else.

The statue in the third-floor window moves.

Or did it?

"Run!" Orlando grabs my arm and pulls.

Why does O want to run?

"Back door's locked. Backtrack. Security's patrolling. We'll get caught."

He jerks me forward. I struggle to keep my feet under me.

The rain isn't letting up, large droplets splatting against my eyes like they're windows.

Long strides. Must keep up with Orlando. He's yanking me. I'm sucking in air. And water.

My feet slosh against the ground.

Our grip is slippery.

My hand slides.

I lose him.

It's dark as the night we entered Cuba.

Inky dark.

My lungs burn. I'm pushing forward. Hair in my face.

Boom. I slam into something hard.

Plaster.

It cracks.

Falls.

I follow it down.

It moans.

What?
Was that me moaning?
I push off the plaster statue.
"This way!" O yells.
A hand grabs my ankle.
Someone caught me.
I kick. Kick. Kick.
It's hard.
The statue?
The statue!
Ay Dios mio.
The statue came alive.
I scream.

Chapter Thirty-One

Day Three

OSHUNVILLA

Sizeable drops of rain smack my skin. The drone of the downpour drowns out my hearing, except for a mosquito's buzz as it lands on my face. My hands are stuck beneath my body. I can't move them fast enough. I'm stung.

"Holy shit on a stick!"

I flinch at Orlando's voice.

"Get up!"

I can't tell where he is.

My limbs move like thick sludge. I push myself to my knees. Try to stand but, "Get it off me!"

In the pause that follows, a woman screams, the sound so sharp it could break glass.

"We gotta get the fuck out of here." Orlando's hands dig under my armpits. Pain shoots through me as he jerks me up. But a wet hand still holds my ankle hostage.

"The statue," I puff out the words, heart racing, fingers

tingling. "It's got me."

"The statue?"

Doesn't he see it? No, because he's staring into my eyes.

I squint back at the artist's house. The light in the third-story workshop is still on, the statue still there. *Still.* Not moving. *I imagined it.*

"Let's go," Orlando yells.

But *this* statue *is* alive and it's holding me hostage. "Let go!" I kick against the hand. Again. I'm shaking my leg. Can't O feel me doing this? "It's got my foot."

"It?" He looks down. "Holy fucked-up shit!" He takes a knee.

I do, too.

He pulls at skinny fingers that feel pruned against my skin, trying to pry them away from my ankle.

It's not working. I'm locked in a death grip. I'm not getting away.

The light in the workshop window shuts off.

I kick wildly.

"Stop!" a high-pitched voice yells from the plaster.

"She's in the plaster!"

Orlando stands and grabs a nearby piece of art, a vase. "This might hurt."

I throw up an arm in case he accidentally hits me.

The vase cracks open some part of the plaster.

A hysterical scream erupts next to me. My eyes struggle to adjust to the turbulent darkness. Still, the fingers grip my ankle like an iron fist. The person is grabbing me like their life depends on it.

Another crack.

I shake my leg again. Gently this time. "You can let go. We won't leave you."

It sounds like Orlando rips away a big chunk and pulls more plaster away from the woman. Another ear-shattering screech pierces the night.

"Is it Izzy?" *Oh God, maybe that's why this statue wouldn't let go. It's Izzy!*

"No."

My hope crashes down like that vase, shattering.

O grunts as he swoops a girl up into his arms. He stumbles past me. "We gotta get her outta here." He's carrying the young woman, who looks as if she's passed out. He lurches along like a big monster running off with his limp victim.

"What about Izzy?" Mud squishes between my fingers as I push off the ground, praying for traction. I stumble forward, staggering toward the security office. *Stupid? Maybe.* But it's the only exit I know will be open right now.

"We don't even know Izzy's here. We'll come back to look. We need more people. We—" Orlando stops speaking, breathless.

"But what if Izzy is entombed here, too?" In the artist's office or maybe some other place. The Fertility Fountain? The statue of Oshun with octopus legs?

"We'll never find her in the dark."

I slam into a piece of artwork painted black. I spin around it as troubled thoughts twirl like a tornado in my head.

O's right. Oshunvilla is too big. It's too dark. The storm is right over us. And we need to save this girl. Maybe she can lead us to Izzy.

A low, guttural growl stops me.

I whip around.

Like a werewolf out of *Twilight*, a dog is streaking my way. I expect it to take flight any sec—

"Mari, bust your ass!"

I turn and dash toward Orlando. I visualize Bella from *Twilight*, freed from her human restraints, flying as a vampire. *Manifest superhuman powers, Mari.* Don't look back. Don't think. Just do. *Save the girl. Save yourself. So you can save*

Izzy.

Orlando stands in the open doorway to the security office, and I sprint up the stairs.

The dog is almost at the bottom. I push O in and slam the door. Lock it. Seconds. I've bought seconds. "Security?"

O points to a sticky note pressed onto the main security TV.

In Spanish it reads, "Smoking." We caught a break.

Barking and scratching come from the door. "The dog will alert someone." Like the smoking guard, who may be close by.

The girl slumps against Orlando, her face planted in the crook of his neck. It's obvious he's having trouble holding her up.

"Let's get out of here." Adrenaline kicks in.

O cradles the limp body of the girl and pushes his way out the back door.

I follow him, locating the security camera we saw earlier. We pause for it to pass, and carefully move in the shadows past its range, then, when it's safe, we walk out of the gate. Before it closes, a thought hits me—I'm coming back to continue looking for Izzy and need to get back in. I take a pebble off the ground and shove it in the area where the bolt comes out of, wedging it in, so the bolt can't come out. I gently close the gate. Test it. It opens.

I pray it will still work when I need to reenter.

The dog has stopped barking.

Does that mean he realizes the threat is no longer in the office?

Or does it mean a security guard came and quieted it?

I take off after Orlando, fueled by sheer fright.

Chaptere Thirty-Two

Day Three
8 P.M.
NINE HOURS LEFT

OUTSIDE OF OSHUNVILLA

The first thing I realize when we arrive at the open field where Enrique parked: he's not in the car and all four tires are flat.

Someone has taken our driver and sabotaged his car.

We aren't leaving. We're—

"Fuuuuuck!"

"Yes, we are." I can't believe I'm not more panicked. It's like I've swallowed a Xanax or taken a gummy, and it's finally kicked in. Maybe I'm exhausted by the constant adrenaline dump that is my life right now.

I twist my azabache charm, three times to the left and three to the right. "Why isn't it working?" I ask myself. 'Cause our luck has been awful, and I do NOT feel protected.

Orlando lays the girl down on the ground. Her body hits

with a thud.

She must be heavy. Like my heart. "What do we do now?"

"Got your phone?" O is still winded.

"Yes."

"Call the marshal."

"Good idea." He's the one person we can trust to come get us. I squint, letting my eyes adjust to the dark again so I can dial.

Headlights burst through the dark, blinding me. I fumble the phone, drop it, my heart slamming into my chest.

"Who is it?" Orlando pushes me behind him and calls, "What do you want?"

"My phone." I try stepping in front of O to look for it.

He pushes me back. "Show yourself."

The bright lights drop back to normal headlights, and a man steps out of the driver's side door.

"Angel," Orlando and I say at the same time.

"I knew it." I knew the ride share driver, who tried digging up a body that wasn't there, had to be involved in all this somehow. "How did you know we were here? Are you working with the watchdog guy?"

"What?" Angel's tone makes me think he isn't.

"Where's my sister?"

"The driver doesn't know."

My back straightens like a pole inserted itself into my spine. The ground shifts under me. I haven't heard that voice in years. But I will *never* forget it. The sound of it triggers a memory: my mamá's gasp as she realized she'd been shot. Her bending over, hands covering her stomach, blood pumping out, bubbling in spurts through her fingers. Her dropping to the ground right outside of our front door. My vision goes red. I spit out, "I've been looking for you, Raúl. Finally showing your face, you coward!"

"Mari!"

"What, Orlando?" I throw my arms up as if being approached by a cop. "Raúl's going to shoot me, too? I don't care." In this moment I really don't. My stomach rumbles, acid rises in my throat. I'm about to vomit. "You and Angel are working together." I drop my hands and go for my azabache charm. Twist. Twist. Twist. Muscle memory. "I should have put two and two together but—"

"You know nothing," Raúl says. "I would not work with this pig." Raúl's voice remains steady. "If I didn't need him, I would have ripped his heart out already. For what he did to Izzy."

"Where is she?"

"I'm looking for her, too."

"Really, Raúl? If so, why aren't you in Oshunvilla, tearing the place apart trying to find my sister?"

"I already have. I told her to stay away from this place. Fucking horror house. But she went behind my back. I've come here twice and couldn't find her. Last time, security kicked me out. Said I harassed the tourists and staff, and I couldn't come back. They even called the police."

Which explains his picture on a flyer in the security office. That's the Raúl I remember—always pushing boundaries and getting in trouble.

"Which is why I need Angel. He knows how to sneak in. He knows more."

"Where's Enrique?" O asks.

Raúl opens the passenger side back door and pulls Enrique out.

"*Lo siento. Lo siento.*" Enrique's hands are up in an apology. "I'm sorry, Mari. I didn't tell them you were in Oshunvilla. They already knew."

Security cameras everywhere. "It's okay." Word must have traveled fast. "Are you okay?" I ask in Spanish. It's too dark to see if he's been beaten up, or tied up, or something worse.

"He's fine."

"Well, excuse me, Raúl, if I don't believe you. I'd like to see for myself. Let him go."

"He's a free man." Raúl shrugs. "But it's a long walk back to Havana."

"You slashed our tires."

"I needed to talk to you. We need to look for Izzy together. I knew you would come with me only if I gave you no choice."

A moan from the ground. *The girl*. I can't tell if she's moving. The weakness of her wail indicates she's in pain and not doing well. "We need to get this girl to a doctor."

Angel, the driver, finally speaks. "Sometimes they use fentanyl."

"Fentanyl?" I stare down at the black blob on the ground. I didn't even have time to notice her hair color, what she's wearing, if she has shoes on. Nothing. I don't know her name, if she has a sister who's looking for her, a mother who's putting up missing girl posters, a father whose heart is broken. We've been running for our lives since police raided the farm. And we aren't safe yet. "Who is *they*, Angel?"

"Get in the car," Raúl barks out the order.

"You really think I'm going anywhere with you?" I point to Oshunvilla. "You can take the girl and get her help. I'm going back to look for Izzy." But my stomach knots as I say it. It's dark. Wet. And there's a dog outside security waiting for me. I wouldn't get far, and I know it. I need a bigger team, along with Angel's knowledge of Oshunvilla. I need to know how we can get around without being caught. "You killed my mother. If I had a gun right now, I'd—" I drop the next words as Raúl pulls a gun from his waistband and points it at me. Every nerve in my body goes on high alert.

"Get in the car, Marisol. The healer can help this girl.

We'll discuss our next move."

"I've got Narcan in the car," Angel says. "That will keep her alive until we get to the healer. Get her in the back."

The rolling thunder and the slapping of falling rain isn't enough to cover the hammering of my heart.

O looks at me. I exhale. We've been through so much together. "O?"

He squats and gently scoops up the girl. She's a rag doll, head flopping back, arm rolling out of his grip. Standing in the car's headlights, his silhouette looks like Superman carrying Lois Lane.

The young woman has long blond hair. She's wearing a simple sundress. She doesn't have shoes on. Her right arm dangles, and that's when I catch the tattoo. My heart flutters.

"I know who this girl is." I step closer, reaching out to touch it, a small, orange peach inked onto her inner wrist. "It's Mandy Peacher." The foster girl from Georgia. "We have to keep her alive."

If the artist kidnapped Izzy, Mandy may know. She may be able to lead us directly to my sister, so we don't have to search every statue.

I fall to the ground and feel around for my smartphone.

"Marisol!" Raúl bellows at me.

"My phone." I'm not leaving without my lifeline to Tony and to the marshal. And to the boat captain, who may be the only person who can get us out of this country undetected.

The engine roars to life.

Got it! I jump up and squeeze myself in the back seat next to Orlando. Enrique is on the other side of O.

Mandy Preacher's body lies across them.

Her white, cold, feet flop onto my lap.

Chapter Thirty-Three

ON THE ROAD

Angel flies down the two-lane highway leading away from Oshunvilla. The roads are full of potholes and irregularities. I'm bracing myself by gripping the leather upholstery of the front seat with both hands, fingernails digging in.

But I can't take my gaze off the bare, wrinkled, dirty feet of Mandy Peacher. At least I think it's her. Her feet flop up and down against my thighs as we bounce over ruts and depressions. The chipped pink paint on her toes tells me she's been captive for a while. She's got a peach tattoo on her ankle, as well as her wrist. And a hemangioma across a portion of her face, almost like someone slapped her and left a reddish imprint across her cheek. Shivers snake down my back.

Her toes are discolored. Like she's dead.

Acid burns my throat. Her skin, as I touch that peach tattoo, is cold and clammy.

I go cold, too.

Raúl shoves an injector at Orlando.

"Stick her?" O looks horrified, like it's a heroin needle off the streets.

"I can't do it. My hands are full. Take off the red cap."

O does.

I'm shaking and glad it's not me doing it.

"Yellow end against her thigh."

O presses the injector into her skin.

"Press the top. Hold it down."

"This will save her?" Is this croaky voice mine?

"Narcan reverses an overdose," Angel answers, his gaze on the road.

I use my flashlight on my smartphone to guide him. Orlando presses it against her thigh. A click.

I'm waiting for the body to jump. Or her eyes to pop open like Bella's at the end of *Twilight*. Maybe a scream. A moan. Something.

Nothing.

"She's breathing." Orlando has his other palm on Mandy's chest, above her breasts. "It's shallow, but—"

"We bought that girl time." Angel speeds down the dimly lit highway.

"We're going to the hospital?" I ask, wondering what in the world we'd say to an ER doctor.

"No." Raúl looks back at me, and although I can't see all his facial features in the dark, I feel the intense energy he's putting off. "We're going to the Santera."

"I'm sorry?"

"Josefina," he says.

I freeze. How the hell does Raúl know Josefina? Playa Hermosa is a small town, but... I'm not leading these two evil assholes to our safe house, which obviously is no longer safe. Who else knows? Alfonso, the government watchdog, does he know, too? Wait, Josefina doesn't live at the safe house. She brought us there to keep us safe.

Where exactly is Raúl taking us?

"Head to Playa Hermosa," Raúl orders.

Chapter Thirty-Four

Day Three

"You know where the…the Santera Josefina lives?" Orlando's voice cracks.

O must be thinking the same thing—we have no safe place to go. No safe place to hide. Despite the fact Raúl and Angel haven't killed us, and despite the fact they saved one of the missing girls, I still think they're involved in the weird world of Oshunvilla. I don't know exactly how, yet.

"Everyone knows Josefina," Angel says. "She's the town healer."

Raúl glances back at me. "How do *you* know her?"

I'm not going to tell Raúl the Santera used to be my Abuela Bonita's friend, or that she took Orlando and me to my abuela's old home where I spread her ashes. I will *never* get that personal with the man who killed my mamá. I will never forgive him or trust him. But right now, I do need him, so I'll play the game. I lean forward, looking over the seat.

Raúl's got his gun laying on his lap. His finger is on the trigger, but the gun isn't pointed back at us. It's aimed at Angel. "Why are you threatening Angel?" That's probably why he had O do the injection.

"I told you I'm working with him. But he will continue to cooperate only if he knows I will shoot him, and he knows I have a way to save his life after this night is over." He turns to look at me.

We stare at each other. Even in this dark, humid, sticky-seat Chevy, I feel the cool blast of icy hate coming from him. "How do you know Angel? Why do you need to aim a gun at him to get him to cooperate? What does he know about Izzy? Was he the last person to see her alive? How can you keep him alive after tonight?"

"You ask too many questions," Raúl says.

"Angel?" I ask the driver, although I bet he won't answer unless Raúl tells him to. He doesn't. After an uncomfortable pause, I ask Raúl, "How long will it take to get to Playa Hermosa?"

"You still interviewing me?"

"I'm trying to find out what happened to Izzy. If you don't know where she is, and you're forcing Angel to help you at gunpoint, I'd like to know why. Fill in the details, so we *can* work together. Like you wanted."

"Isabella disappeared after visiting Oshunvilla, right before you showed up at my house. She'd been trying to help a few girls she'd met at a hostel in Havana. They'd go out together. I don't know, I guess she missed having girlfriends."

You weren't enough for her. I want to say it, but sparring with Raúl right now won't get me information. I rein in my hate. "Why did she want to help them?"

"Lost souls, she called them. I told her they were likely spoiled, entitled Americans. But she called them broken."

I sit forward, my fingernails digging into the leather. "What broke them?"

"Fucked-up families. One had a boyfriend dump her."

"Teddy Meyers," I say her name. Wait for a reaction from Raúl. Did he know her? Was she one of the broken girls he kept in a locked room?

"One of the girls, don't remember her name, had money problems. Izzy asked if she could stay with us for a while. Before long, another one began sleeping at the house. I told Isabella I wasn't running a sorority house."

That might explain the bunk beds and the initials on the wall. Maybe even why Teddy said she wanted to meet Raúlito.

"I thought it would make Izzy happy." Raúl looks away from me.

In his silence, I feel his love for my sister.

"What happened to them? The girls who bunked at your place?" I envision the fire pit and bleach and torn up flooring. I exchange a glance with Orlando.

O nods.

It's a slight movement, but I understand what it means. The camera in his hat is recording Raúl's words.

I'm breathless with this opportunity to capture a confession. I bite my lip, anxious to go in for the kill, be direct, and ask Raúl if he murdered any of the missing girls, but my reporter's intuition tells me we'll get there if I let him talk at his own pace. We have time before we get into Playa Hermosa. Raúl may be holding Angel at gunpoint, but I consider him my captive audience.

"Izzy and the girls would go to Oshunvilla. Like it was some magic place that could cure them. I warned them to stay out of that—" He doesn't elaborate.

"And they all go missing," I say. I inhale and count to five. When I exhale, Orlando kicks me gently. He's so attuned to my energy; he probably knows I'm about to go somewhere I shouldn't. *Here goes nothing. Or maybe everything.* "Raúl, we found a burned-up cell phone in your fire pit. With torn up flooring and bleach. Did you kill Izzy?"

Chapter Thirty-Five

On the road to Playa Hermosa

Raúl flips around in his seat and glares at me.

"Wouldn't be the first time you got away with murder." I push his buttons on purpose. He's a thirty-five-year-old man now. He no longer looks scared or victimized.

"I didn't kill Izzy. I love your sister. I waited a decade to be with her again."

What he says does make sense. If that's true, why would he wait ten years to get Izzy back with him, only to kill her? Because he's an intense, emotion-driven man who has no boundaries. *Or had none.* "Why the bleach?"

His eyes never leave mine, while giving me the silent treatment.

"Stop it, Raúl." I'm no longer a scared teenager, either. "We have too long of a history to play this game. If you didn't kill Izzy, you know the clock is ticking on her life. So, answer my question, and we can work together to find her. Why the bleach in your backyard?"

Orlando adjusts in the seat next to me, moving so his ball cap points at Raúl's face.

"When the girls went missing, I knew if police found out they'd been staying with me, they'd assume I killed them."

"Or they'd use you as a scapegoat," Angel interrupts, finally speaking on his own accord. "Make people *believe* you killed them."

"That's why I got rid of evidence of them."

My stomach is no longer somersaulting. It's churning like concrete blocks rolling around inside me. 'Cause I'm not sure I believe Raúl. Why should I? "Or maybe you did kill them and called Angel here to help you. He seems to know a few things about burying bodies." I hold my breath, waiting for Raúl to snap and point the gun at me.

He doesn't. Instead, Raúl answers in a calm voice. "I tracked Izzy the same way you did."

"How do you know how I tracked her?"

"When I came home, after you'd been in my house uninvited, the piece of paper with Angel's number on it was gone. Luckily, I'd already called him and had it in my phone. Too much of a coincidence that you're here in Cuba right after Izzy goes missing. But I knew she wasn't with you. You wouldn't have come to my home if you had her. You came to my home because you were looking for her. I went back to speak to Angel again. The first time we spoke, he denied driving Izzy. This time, I brought my gun and convinced him to talk to me."

"Same with us," I say. "We"—I point to Orlando—"we saw him try to dig up a body. I thought it might be, it might be…" I can't say her name.

Raúl turns slowly to look at Angel. He raises the gun.

"Not, not your girl," Angel's hand comes up. As if his

flesh and small bones would protect him from a bullet. "I've told you what I know about your girl."

"The body wasn't there," I say, not wanting Raúl to kill the man in control of the car. I direct my next comment to Angel, "Now tell me what you know about my sister."

"I brought Izzy to Oshunvilla," Angel's voice is light, breathy, nervous. "She stayed all day, and I picked her up as it closed."

Which surveillance video confirms.

"But I took her back."

"What?" That's new info. "To Oshunvilla?"

"When the drugs start kicking in—"

"What?" That roils my stomach once more. "Izzy took Fentanyl. Knowingly?"

"I don't know."

It's beginning to make sense. "Girls come to Oshunvilla looking for help with their problems, praying it's as easy as writing a wish and pinning it to a wall. Then you, the Angel of Death, pick them up, slip them some drugs, and bring them back. How do you do it, Angel? Offer them something to drink? Use a syringe or *injector*? Was that really Narcan we gave Mandy? Or Fentanyl?"

"Not me. *They* use different drugs on different girls," Angel argues. "They are already drugged when they leave. I wait till the drugs kick in and take them back through a back entrance."

The one O and I entered earlier.

Anger shoots through me, fireworks reaching all the way to my fingertips. I bang my hand on Angel's back seat.

"I get paid after I bring them back. I don't know what happens after that."

Rage rushes like an out-of-control brush fire. "You do know what happens."

"I know now."

"Bullshit."

"You dropped Izzy off days ago, right?" Orlando asks, kicking me to calm me down, I'm sure.

Indignation washes over me, only enlarging my internal fire. "She's probably dead by now, you asshole." My hand swings, smacking the back of Angel's seat, wishing it was the back of his head. "You let my sister die."

"*No mas*," the big man with skull earrings whispers.

"No more? No more what? No more killing?" I can't breathe. It's hot. Mandy Peacher's body smells like sweat and mold. Orlando's body odor is pungent after all that running in the heat. I smell myself, too. I've got to get air. I roll the window halfway down.

"I promised Angel if he told you the truth I wouldn't shoot him, and you'd get him out of Cuba," Raúl says. "Alive."

The fresh night air isn't helping. "Well, let me call our private jet. Tell them to fuel up." I'm still sickened by the blends of acrid odors and half-truths. "If that's the case, why do you still need to point that gun at him?" We don't need another body.

"The gun?" Raúl continues, "My insurance. I don't trust easily."

Well, now that's a statement I believe.

"They'll kill me if I tell the secrets of Oshunvilla," Angels says.

"Who is *they*? *They* have my sister."

"You can take Angel back on the boat you came in on," Raúl says.

I'm silent, facing the half open window. I'm not confirming anything.

Orlando nudges me. He shows me his phone.

Had to take off. Government is on to you and me. You're on your own. Stay away from Oshunvilla.

I figure out the time the text came in. Hours ago. Enrique

has the man's number but it's too late to try to stop the boat captain from leaving without us.

Well, I'm not going to tell Raúl our boat is gone. If I do, we'll never get info from Angel that might lead us to Izzy and other missing girls. So, I do something a journalist should never do. Something I'm not proud of. "Okay, we'll get you on the boat with us, Angel." I lie.

Orlando remains silent.

"Tell me everything you know that might help me find Izzy when we get back to Oshunvilla. Don't stall. The police probably already know you're involved."

"You still don't get it," Angel says, sounding like a man who knows it's useless, and he's given up any hope of survival.

"Get what?"

"They'll kill me if I talk. They'll kill *all* of us. Oshunvilla makes them a lot of money."

The half dead girl lying across our laps begins to convulse, awful spasms that jerk her body like a horror movie creature.

"She's not going to make it if we don't get help." Enrique, who's been silent, jumps in. "I know where to find Josefina right now. We will go there. Hold her tongue down."

I'm not sure which house he'll lead us to. I pray we have a power player there once we arrive. I'd given the U.S. Marshal Josefina's home address, as well as the address for our safe house, Abuela Bonita's childhood home. I need him to update me on Tony's situation and his efforts to get Tony released. My heart aches. I mean, it literally aches to the point of real pain. It seems like days since I've seen Tony, not hours. I hope he's being treated okay, wherever he is. Or has he been thrown into one of those bare, rock-walled prison cells his grandfather had to endure, with bugs crawling over him, no place to use the bathroom, no air-conditioning, no comforts at all. I fear the Cuban Government is punishing him for coming back.

With the boat captain gone, I'm praying that when we arrive, the marshal will be there, and he'll have an idea of not only how we can leave the island, but get back to Oshunvilla first and make one last search for Izzy. She *has* to be there. If not, then where?

Send me a sign, Abuela Bonita. Send me a signal that everything is going to work out.

Through the open window, a gnat flies into my right eye. I jerk back from the rushing air, fingers finding my eyelid, tugging at it, hoping to force the bug out. In my haste, my wrist hits the glass. I'm going to have a good little bruise.

"*Conyo!* Roll the window up," Raúl barks out the order.

Now that's the Raúl I remember. The demanding asshole. The bug isn't out. But I do as he asks.

It isn't until I blink the gnat away, and I sit back, I realize my sudden movement at the window must have caught my azabache bracelet, the one Tony gave me as a gift. *It's gone!* Ripped off by the window when I jerked back?

Tears smack my bottom eyelids. I lose my breath. It's a superstition, but I feel unexpectedly unprotected.

I look back through the dark window. There's no way I'll be able to find the black charm on the black roadway in the black of night.

I feel like I've lost a piece of Tony. The bracelet was his first gesture of friendship—it symbolizes the moment I started to trust him, because I realized he saw the real me. And accepted me, superstitions and all.

My wrist is bare.

My heart stripped naked.

Not exactly the signal I was looking for from Abuela.

Chapter Thirty-Six

Day Three
ALMOST MIDNIGHT
LESS THAN SEVEN HOURS LEFT

PLAYA HERMOSA

As I walk into the Santera's house, I'm rubbing my bare wrist, still thinking about the fact I asked for a sign and got one.

A bad one.

I enter first, holding the door open for Orlando, who's carrying Mandy. The young woman's head rests against O's chest, her arms and legs flopping over his arms, like she's barely awake or aware.

I tense my muscles, but it doesn't stop the shivers.

The house is mostly dark, only a light on in the back part of the house. It reeks like a dungeon, despite three fans running in the living room where we enter. The hum of those fans is all I hear, until the slap of house slippers escalates from down the dimly lit hallway.

It's almost midnight, and Josefina appears in a typical Cuban woman's housedress-slash-nightgown. Her hair is covered in a white wrap, and her face is devoid of makeup, as she walks into a space lit by moonlight streaming through the window.

"I've been worried." Josefina's gaze lands on Mandy. Her jaw tightens. She looks behind me, seeing Raúl and Angel. Her eyes widen, her gaze shifts back to me.

"Mandy Peacher," I whisper. "Found her in Oshunvilla. Almost dead. Raúl gave her Narcan. Angel drove us here." I say no more, wanting Josefina to fill in some blanks for me. Like how she knows Raúl and Angel, and what she thinks of both.

Josefina drops her gaze. Her chest rises and falls, twice, like she's trying to calm her nerves. She motions for Orlando to move down the hall. "Raúl and you"—she points to Angel— "you follow, too." She waves the two men past her, and they follow Orlando. "Last room on the right. Place her on the bed. I will be right there."

As she passes me, she places a firm, if fragile, hand on my shoulder. "You stay."

"Okay." She must have a good reason.

"I must go to the backyard and gather the necessary items. I have a surprise for you. But when you see it, make no noise. We must work silently to not draw attention from the neighbors."

"Or those who watch us," I whisper, thinking of Mr. White Shoes.

"Enrique," Josefina calls to Tony's relative.

I flip around. I totally forgot he was with us. "You hide the car and meet me out back. I need your help."

He nods and slips out the front door.

Okay, Josefina knows Enrique, too. Remember, this is a small town, and she's the known healer. Makes sense everyone would know her, and she, everyone.

The sound of her slapping slippers recedes as she walks down the hall, but this time she enters the door on the left. Maybe there's a back door leading to her backyard through that room?

I know what's out back—a Santeria altar and items needed to help Mandy Peacher.

Suddenly, I'm surrounded by silence. What is my surprise? I literally have no idea.

A door opens.

Josefina moves toward me. As she walks by, I catch her gaze and slight smile. But she says nothing, just walks into the kitchen and out a sliding glass door into the backyard, and disappears.

I'm not sure what to do next but I do know I'm incredibly thirsty. I make my way slowly through the kitchen, careful to use my hands around corners to guide me, so I don't run into anything or make any unnecessary noise.

I open their small fridge, praying to find one bottle of water, but the fridge is empty. That makes me sad. This is a resource desert out here. And that leaves me longing for the comforts of America.

A hand from behind me pushes the fridge closed.

I jump.

"Don't speak."

My breath catches.

I recognize that voice. I spin around, throw my arms around the body in front of me; my arms slip around his neck so naturally. I press my cheek against his chest.

"Tony, you're here." Tears well up, and I bite my lip to keep from crying. I've come to grips with the fact my feelings for this man are growing. I squeeze him. Hard. I don't want to let him go.

At the same time, his arms wrap around me.

A strange sound forces its way out of me.

Tony doesn't say a thing. He pulls me in tighter. His hand finds my hair, and he strokes my head.

That unusual physical display of affection from him makes me weepy. "Oh God, there's so much to tell you."

I feel the emotion in his silence. His Adam's apple bobs like he's fighting back tears, too.

Tony doesn't like public displays of emotion. But we're alone. We are never alone. I want to stay this way for a long time, entwined with him. But I know him well enough to know this physical intimacy, during such a dangerous time, will make him push back soon. Get back to the job. Now is not the time to admit feelings or explore our sexual attraction. "How did you get out?"

"Long story." His voice cracks.

"I know, but—" I literally need to keep him talking. Or whispering. I need to hear his voice, to make sure this is real. I don't want him to pull away. He smells like aftershave. Clean, like he showered here and put on new clothes. "How?"

He exhales.

Even his breath smells clean.

"My marshal friend paid to allow me to escape."

"Meaning?"

"Meaning he has prison guards on his payroll. They turned their backs when I ran during a trip from the prison to court. I jumped out of the van at a certain point, where I was told a motorcycle and driver would be waiting." He flinches, as if remembering a pain he endured along the way.

"Like out of a James Bond movie." But I'm really thinking he's lucky to be out and still alive.

"We need to get out of the country tomorrow. If they find me—"

I gulp. He doesn't have to finish that sentence—I know what will happen if the Cuban police find him, the escapee from America. The man who outsmarted them. "Tony..." My chest tightens so quickly it takes my breath away. I don't want to be the one who has to tell him our escape plan is no more. I lick my dry lips. No saliva to even wet them. "The boat captain left us."

His body stiffens. "The marshal has a plan B." He's still holding me. His chin rests on the top of my head. "We will leave at dawn tomorrow."

"Dawn. Tomorrow," I repeat, giving myself time to think. I need to get back to Oshunvilla to see if Izzy is there. I have no idea how long it will take to find her. "What time is it?"

"Around midnight."

I bury my head in his chest. I have a new deadline. *Six hours.* "I have to go back for Izzy."

His shoulders fall. "I know." But his tone doesn't sound angry.

"We were so close. I thought I might have seen her in the artist's window, but I couldn't be sure. And then I stumbled onto this statue, and it was alive and now we have Mandy and—"

"It's okay." He pulls back enough for me to gaze into his eyes and lifts my chin with a finger. "We have hours before we have to be at the meeting place."

"The meeting place," I echo. Right now, I'd follow him anywhere. After I find Izzy. "That sounds mysterious. Also, dangerous."

He doesn't respond.

"You said *we*."

"Yes, we."

I strain to see what he means, by the look in his eyes. But it's too dark. I reach for his face, placing my palm on his skin. He's heated. Almost feverish.

The arm around my waist tightens, and I feel his arousal. Heat hits my center, and I stretch up so he can kiss me. It feels so natural. So right. So—

"If you two leave, you're on your own."

A new voice.

Tony jerks away from me like a high school boy caught kissing me in my bedroom. By my dad.

My hand flies to my heart. "You scared me."

"I can't wait for you." A new voice speaks with that military authority.

The seal is broken and a deep well opens in my chest, filling quickly with fear and sadness. "I have to go back for my sister," I say, as if out of body.

Tony pulls me back into a hug. "You are not going alone. I'm going with you."

In this moment, I really love him for standing by me. For understanding.

"Before you go, you must hear from this girl you brought back." That voice belongs to Josefina. I strain to see her in the dark room. Her voice hardens. "And both of you need to know the horror that awaits you when you return to Oshunvilla tonight. Mandy's information might be what keeps you alive."

Chapter Thirty-Seven

Day Four
AFTER MIDNIGHT
SIX HOURS TILL EXTRACTION

PLAYA HERMOSA

"Jimagua looks for broken girls." Mandy Peacher's southern twang shakes, much like her trembling, pale limbs. She can't sit up, so we've gathered around her in the back. I sit next to her bed, in a rickety rocking chair Tony dragged in. He stands behind me, his energy and body heat reassuring, a replacement for my missing azabache charm.

Orlando videotapes from the corner, using both his camera and GoPro. Josefina sits on the side of the bed, stroking the girl's skin with a brush she keeps dipping into a wooden bowl full of a light liquid. Whatever the mixture is, Mandy's pores absorb it immediately.

I find that strange.

Raúl and Angel lean against the doorframe.

Enrique has left to make espresso in the kitchen.

Time ticks, the imaginary clock never out of my thoughts. "How does the artist pick which girls he wants?" As the reporter, I can't help but take the lead.

Mandy swallows and moves her lips, but when she speaks it sounds like gravel fills her mouth.

Josefina stops caressing her and reaches for a cup of water on the nightstand. "Drink."

Mandy's hands quake and some of the water spills over the rim, onto the bedsheet.

Josefina takes the paper cup from her, holds it until Mandy signals she's ingested enough, then hands the container to Raúl. "Please get her some more. Enrique will know what water to use. Maybe a little espresso, too, please."

I remain silent but am blown away by the familiarity between Josefina and Raúl. She doesn't act like he's the devil. And he follows her orders without question. When we're alone, I'll remember to ask her how she knows him, and what she thinks of him.

"The woman who people call Granny," Mandy croaks, finally finding her voice, "she talks to the girls who enter. She talked to me. She was nice."

"The tour guide?" I ask. "Graciela?"

Mandy shrugs.

"The one missing teeth and smoking a cigar? She wore pigtails and yellow bows."

"That could be her, I guess." Mandy adjusted in the bed, a low moan escaping as she moved. "She asks questions. You think she's trying to help you." She closes her eyes, and her voice changes, almost like she's channeling the woman known as Granny. "What are you here for, dear? What do you seek? Love? Of course you do. Let me take you to the artist's Wishing Wall. People come from all over the world, Paris, Shanghai, Sydney." Her whole body shudders. When

Mandy speaks again, it's with that sweet southern drawl. "She got me a piece of paper and a pen to write my wish on. She told me it would stay up for a week and then be burned in a ceremony to the Orisha Oshun. Have you heard of her?"

Mandy's looking right at me, and I nod.

"Granny said that's when I could expect my wish to come true."

"What did you wish for, Mandy?" This is important, although I imagine most of these broken girls probably wished for the same thing. "Love?" Isn't that what we all wish for?

"A family."

Tears wet my eyes. Mandy Peacher and I have something in common. We're alone in this world. She's a product of the foster care system. I'm a product of violence. Both of us seek the connection of unconditional love you're supposed to get from a family. "That's what you wrote on your piece of paper? I want a family?"

"Yes."

"And the granny, she read it?"

Mandy nods, tears sliding down her cheeks. She exhales in a long breath and turns her face away from us.

I understand. Some emotions are too much to bear, and it takes too much effort to hide the pain etched into your features. "That's how the old woman knew you'd be a good target." I shake my head and blow out a breath. Girls like Mandy didn't get any breaks. I reach out and touch her arm. "And then?"

Her body stills at my touch.

I remove my hand, aware of the abuse she must have endured at another's hands. "I'm sorry."

Mandy turns back toward me, but her gaze looks unfocused, like she's looking through me. "You don't have a family? Who are you here with? Surely someone would miss you." Her voice breaks on the last two words. She's channeling the granny again.

Shivers fly through me, from the back of my neck all the way to my toes. Trauma has broken this young woman. She'll need serious therapy. "She was trying to find out if someone would come looking for you if you disappeared."

"You wouldn't believe how many of us are out here," Mandy whispers. "Or in there."

"How many of *you*?" Tony asks, his hand finding my shoulder like it's the most natural thing. "What do you mean?"

"I mean, you have no idea how many broken girls there are in the world. With no one to care if we ever come back."

Her words widen the crack in my heart. Who would care if I never made it back to America alive? Really? My two best friends, Orlando and Tony, are here with me. My abuela is dead. Mother, father gone. Sister missing. I have coworkers I hang out with, but who would really care? Sadness shakes my center until it morphs into a low, throbbing pain.

"Did the granny drug you?" Tony asks, squeezing my shoulder like he senses my hurt intensifying.

"I don't know." Mandy licks her dry, cracked lips. It doesn't help. She's still bleeding in the right corner, where the skin has been ripped. "Wait." Her tiny hand rises, still trembling. "She showed me where to get water. From a fountain near the Wishing Wall. I did drink from it. When I began to feel fuzzy, I decided to leave. The granny was so kind. She saw I wasn't feeling well and led me to a driver who'd take me back to the hostel, but when I woke up, I was, I was—"

In that moment of silence, I feel my pulse pounding in my temple. We're about to get to the real horror of Oshunvilla.

"I was chained to the wall in a cell in a dungeon."

A dungeon. Is that where we'll find Izzy?

"I wasn't alone. My friend Teddy and a girl from the hostel, Arianna, were also in the dungeon. The granny would bring us food. She'd also"—Mandy's whole body quaked—"stick us with needles."

"Fentanyl?" Tony asked.

Mandy shrugged. "Whatever it was, it kept us weak and sleepy, out of it. We couldn't even get up to pee."

I wrinkle my nose, imagining the smell, urine on stone floors, the aroma of ammonia circling around a windowless room full of human cages. A real-life house of horrors. My heart swells with compassion for this young woman. But anger burns me as I think of Mandy and Izzy being abused.

"I still smell the urine." Mandy shudders at the same time I do. "My skin broke out in a rash from my wet clothes rubbing my thighs. Eventually, we all craved the needle. It meant escape. If only for a while."

To want drugs to numb the pain and fear. "I saw the artist working on one of his creations."

"We are all his creations," Mandy whispers. "When it was my turn, Granny allowed me to shower. She withheld the needle, so I was able to walk, clean myself. She gave me a robe, I think, something to wear, but I remember little at this point, except that I craved the juice. I wanted to sleep, forget about everything."

"What happened next?" I ask slowly, keeping my voice low and my tone soft, empathetic. Mandy is describing a living hell, but we need more details. "I think I saw my sister in the window tonight. Where the artist works."

Tony squeezes my shoulder again. He didn't know that. But he does know how hard this is for me, too. If that were Izzy, she could be dead by now.

"Is it possible I saw my sister being encased in tiles and plaster? Does he entomb the missing girls in pieces of art up in that workshop?" I think I saw that statue move. "While they are alive?"

"To die on display." Mandy's gaze lands hard on me. Tears well up and fall over her lashes. "He chained me to the floor in his workshop. I had to stand in front of him for days." She looks away again, facing the wall. "I had a steel stand to lean on. Eventually, he tied me to it when I was too weak to stand up on my own. At least Granny gave me the needle. Not enough to make me sleep, but enough to make the pain and humiliation go away.

"I faded in and out. He'd smack me if I fell asleep. He had moods. He could…could be mean like that, pinching me and describing in detail how he'd keep me alive only long enough to make me his latest artwork. That I'd have enough air to breath, but the final dose would be enough to kill me. But I wouldn't die overnight once he placed me out in Oshunvilla. I'd live beyond the sunrise. He'd tape my mouth so I could moan but not scream."

That's why people hear screams at night. Also, why her lips are bleeding—tape over her mouth. She or O must have ripped it off at some point.

"He seemed to enjoy it when I cried. I begged for him to let me go. But he'd keep making the plastic shell like a machine, building it up around me, covering it with tile. Sometimes he'd talk like a child, cry as he was working, begging Granny to let him stop. On those days, he'd call her Adora. And she'd make him dinner, brush his hair, treat him like a child, but she wouldn't let him stop."

I glance back at Tony and whisper, "Adora?"

O catches my attention. He's recording this. What a story to share. What a documentary he'll have to sell. He mouths, "*What the fuck?*"

"Sometimes when the granny wasn't there, he'd ramble about his mother and his sister and their family, and how he was never appreciated for his talent. How he sacrificed broken girls to his mother to win her love and make up for his past mistake. Something he did was so bad his mother would never forgive him."

"What did he do?" Tony asks.

"He didn't say. I bet he wanted to, but he'd talk himself out of it. He'd fight with himself, convince himself to not tell me what he'd done, why he had to keep making sacrifices of young women to not only his mother but also to Oshun."

"We found you already outside. Still alive."

"Alive, but partially paralyzed. He belted me into the steel stand like a rag doll. I couldn't move, barely speak, but I could hear everything, see everything through the mesh he placed in the statue where it covered my eyes."

"Could have given her Rohypnol or Ketamine. Maybe even GHB," Tony says to me. "Some have a paralytic effect and can last up to twelve hours. But most make you forget."

"I remember bits and pieces. I spent a whole day watching people walk by me. Most would stop and take pictures. Some would even touch me, compliment how pretty the tile designs were. I'd scream at them, 'Help me. Get me out of here. Don't leave me here.' But no one would react. After screaming at people all day, I finally realized my words could only be heard in my head. My mouth wasn't even moving."

"Mandy." My whole body aches for this poor girl. "That must have been terrifying."

"I knew I was going to die. I knew by the time the sun set, another drug would kick in. I don't know what it's called, but the artist walked me through what would happen. He's a biochemist, did you know that? Studied in Havana, because the government made him. He created a time-release drug to kill you by making your blood pressure drop until you pass out and your heart stops beating. But it's slow-acting. He promised me it wouldn't hurt in the end. It would be like falling asleep." Her eyes fluttered and then shut. "He smiled at me when he said it." Her body convulsed as if she was seeing that smile in her mind's eye. "But he also knew making us spend a whole day alive, knowing we were dying in plain sight, with no way to alert anyone to help us, he knew that was a living hell."

I can think of nothing to say.

"Right before closing that day"—she opens her eyes and looks right at Orlando, right into his camera—"a family stopped to take a picture. They were speaking Spanish, but I understood a little. Granny had told them I was the latest creation, and they wanted to post to Instagram. They had a little girl, maybe ten or eleven, autistic, I think. She sensed me in there. I know she did. And her dog, couldn't tell what type, but I heard it bark. The dog sensed me, too. The little girl told her mother the statue is alive. Hope surged through me. This little girl was going to save me. I was going to get out of my casket and live."

I slide forward in my chair, desperate to hear what happened next.

But Josefina, wiping Mandy's forehead with a rag now, tells her it's time to rest.

Doesn't matter—I know what happened next. I'm the one who ran into her as a statue and knocked her over, breaking the plaster and allowing her hand to grab me. Must have been after the paralytic wore off, but before her blood pressure dove so low it would kill her. The Narcan must reverse the effects like it does with opioids.

"Jimagua is a serial killer." It hits me hard, the realization there could be hundreds of girls like Mandy stuck in Oshunvilla. Hundreds, if you counted all the statues. "But if young women die encased in the plaster and tiled tombs, anchored somewhere in the labyrinth of his twisted world of art, wouldn't we smell decaying flesh?"

"Mari!" Orlando cringes.

"I gotta ask, right? We need to figure this out together. With Mandy's help, we can save the others. There are others still alive in that dungeon, right?"

"There were others. They'd come, get chained up, and one by one they'd disappear. Then one night, a week ago, Teddy had been unchained. It was her time to disappear. I didn't know what was about to happen at that point. A new girl was dragged in, and she fought Granny when she tried to stick her with the needle. Granny chained her, but not before Teddy managed to escape through the open door. She crawled out while Granny was wrestling the American girl—"

"Izzy," I whisper, heat hitting my center.

"Yes, that's what she said her name was. This new girl, Izzy, allowed Teddy time to escape. Is Teddy alive?" Mandy's gaze fired for the first time with a light that looked like hope. "Is—"

"I had already dropped Izzy off in the back, waiting to get paid, when that Teddy girl came running out," Angel interrupts, walking into the room, head down, not meeting anyone's gaze. "I know you don't believe me, but I had no idea what was happening to the girls. I got paid to bring them back if they managed to leave Oshunvilla before passing out. It was my job to drive them around till the drugs kicked in and bring them back when they were unconscious. I assumed maybe it was a sex thing?"

"Like that would make it okay?" Rage boils to the surface, spewing out in my hot words. "You're a liar. You had to know girls disappear and new pieces of art appear. Statues in the shape of young women!" I'm on my feet now, and as I stand, the room spins. Tony puts a hand out to settle me. Or stop me from advancing on Angel.

Raúl is back, and he steps between Angel and me. I push him away and stare at Angel with a passion that says *you better tell me the truth*. "What happened to Teddy? Is she the girl you were trying to dig up?"

He meets my gaze. "I put her in my car, with the intention of helping her. As we drove away, she told me about being chained to the wall, about girls disappearing and never coming back." His voice escalates and squeaks like he's having trouble getting the truth out. "I made the decision to hide her, but she passed out in the back seat, and when I checked on her, she was dead."

I envision Angel as I saw him before, on his knees, using his hands like shovels, digging at the earth in a fear-induced frenzy. "So you buried her?"

His gaze darts around the room. Who is he looking for?

"Why are you scared?" I ask him.

Angel leans in. "The police protect the artist. Oshunvilla brings in so much money."

"Who else knew Teddy had died?" Tony jumps in.

I follow up with, "This isn't your fault, Angel. Who else knew where you buried her?" I'm playing good cop. "That's what we need to know. We need to talk to them."

"Ms. Gonzalez. The old lady. I told her."

"Granny?" O says from the back of the room. "The granny with the braids scares you?"

"She runs Oshunvilla. She manages everyone there, including the artist. She cornered me. Said she had proof I left with the Teddy girl. That she was alive when she left."

I'm beginning to understand.

"Surveillance video," Orlando says from behind the camera. "She had you on video, leaving with Teddy."

"She threatened to turn me in to the police." Sweat droplets are beading on Angel's forehead. "They would have jailed me for her murder. Made me the bad guy."

"You're fucking kidding me, right?" Tony comes in with the bad cop questions. And the curse words he rarely uses. "There's an art museum made up of dead bodies right under their noses, but the cops will arrest you for murdering one girl? An autopsy would have proven she died of an overdose. I'm not buying your story."

It did sound nonsensical.

"Like I told you"—Angel's cheeks are red, his fists balled at his side—"Oshunvilla brings in money…so much cash—"

"It's worth killing for," I finish for him. "The local authorities are in on it."

The driver doesn't answer. He doesn't need to.

We all know. We're on the same page now. "Maybe the old lady took the body so no one would find it? Or so the artist could entomb her, too?" I ask.

"Her name is Teddy," Mandy whispers. But her voice is loud enough to make the room go quiet. "She was my friend. She has a name."

I swallow and turn toward Tony. "I'm going back for Izzy. He'll have to finish entombing her now. If he hasn't already killed her." Saying those words makes my skin turn clammy. "He knows we're on to him. I can't leave without—"

"I know." Tony looks deep into my eyes. "I have the location where the marshal wants us to meet that flight in a few hours. If we leave now, maybe—"

Maybe nothing. "I'm not leaving Cuba without Izzy." *Dead or alive.*

"I'm going to give this to you straight." Tony moves to the center of the room. "The Cuban government is on to all of us." His gaze finds mine again. "You fear the artist. I fear the cops looking for all of us now. I fear the prison we'll end up in if caught. I fear the life I love disappearing forever." He puts his hand on his gun belt, showing his weapon for all to see. "We have one shot at this. My friend, the marshal, is leaving, too. Things are too hot. Even he's not safe here anymore."

Raúl nods. I wonder if that asshole thinks he's going with us. *Uh, no. Over my dead body.*

"We'll be leaving by an unregistered airplane flown in from the United States, by an undercover agent friend of ours who's a pilot and a Cuban American. The pilot will fly under radar, into Cuban airspace, risking their life to get us out. The Cuban defense will shoot down the plane if it's discovered."

I gaze at Josefina, who is still stroking Mandy. Mandy's gaze is anchored on Tony. "Don't leave me here, please."

"If we don't make it to the meeting place, the marshal can't wait. He may not be able to come back for us, either." Tony scans the room as he talks, making sure everyone hears and understands the consequences of the decision each is about to make. "Mandy, you will stay here, and the marshal will take you with him. I'll give the rest of you the exact location. The plane is scheduled to land and take off within minutes. We have a 6:30 a.m. deadline. You can stay and go with my friend, the marshal, when he leaves in the next hour. Or, you can go back to Oshunvilla and help us find Izzy." Tony is now looking directly at Orlando, who is still recording. "And maybe we have a chance to rescue any other missing girls we might find there."

Orlando nods.

"But understand this. Whoever leaves this safe house now is on their own in Cuba. Who is willing to help Mari and me? Who has the *cojones*?"

Chapter Thirty-Eight

OSHUNVILLA

We've been walking through the artist's home, lights out, trying to avoid security cameras, hoping to find some stairs, an elevator, or a walkway to take us to the higher floor where I saw the artist working on a statue that looked horrifyingly like my sister.

Angel knew a back way to get in and which door the artist usually leaves unlocked. This, from a man who told me he knew nothing about what happened to the girls once he brought them back. *Right.* But the driver's presence has been key so far. We need him.

Tony leads the way, followed by Orlando with one GoPro on his head gear and another on his chest. Raúl is with us, too, but Enrique stayed back at the car, with it running, waiting for us to leave and make the mad dash to meet our 6:30 a.m. deadline. He estimates the escape location is about forty-five minutes away.

It's 3:00 am. That gives us two hours.

My limbs feel heavy, my eyes dry, my body weak from lack of carbs and water. At this point, I'm putting one foot in front of the other. A blast of cool air hits the skin of ankles. "Let's check in here." Call it my reporter's intuition. I want to check out what's causing the chill that's assaulting my ankles.

Tony grabs me before I can open the door. "If we find Izzy in here, it might be a trap."

"If the artist knows of our connection to Izzy, if it *is* Izzy, he'd expect us to come back for her, I agree."

"I've got my weapon."

"I'll stay out here, near the steps, in case anyone comes," Raúl says. "I'll either stop them or warn you."

Don't want to know what Raúl means by *stop them.* Tony places his hand on my lower back and gently pushes me forward. I keep one hand on the wall to guide me through the mosaic mansion. Even the walls feel cool and bumpy like everything here is tiled. Or entombed.

I can't stop the dread washing over me.

Angel enters the artist's studio first.

I follow and open the flashlight app on my smartphone.

Jimagua's workplace looks exactly like I'd imagine an artist's workshop should look. A large table sits in the center of the room with paint all over it, both in paint tubes and smeared across the table like someone finger-painted the tabletop. Paint brushes are scattered across it, a half empty water bottle, an empty coffee cup, a couple of dirty rags, and dozens of tiles are stacked around a red chair. One large butcher knife is clean.

I swallow and continue looking around.

On the opposite wall are tools that look like they belong

in a farmer's barn or a garage: screwdrivers, hacksaws, measuring devices, steel cutters. Tools used to cut tile and plaster. *Or bones and flesh?*

Various sized boxes fill a tall shelf against the wall. The containers are labeled and contain bits and pieces of random tiles in a variety of colors and shapes and sizes. Almost like a teacher's cabinet in elementary school, where students can play art with various scraps being reused.

I grab Tony's clammy hand. I've never felt his skin this way.

He pulls away and points to the statue we've been looking for.

I wonder what he's thinking. Is he sick to his stomach, too? Scared?

It's dark, but I run my phone's flashlight over the statue's features. The artwork does look amazingly like Izzy. Dark hair flipped back like the Farrah Fawcett hairdo made with dark tiles. But I saw a statue like this before, earlier tonight. So maybe the artist has a type.

I walk up to the statue, place my hands on the cool, tiled cheeks, look into the eyes, but I detect nothing behind the mesh. Still, I lean in and whisper, "Izzy? Are you in there?"

A gasp, followed by the low rumble of crying, the kind of sobbing that starts deep in the cavern of your chest, erupts into a sound almost unrecognizable. "Mari?"

The voice cracks. It's so low, I think for a moment I'm imagining it, wishing Izzy's voice into existence.

Then the voice my heart recognizes whispers, "I'm chained to the floor. Can't move."

Her words are breathless.

This is what I came to Cuba for—to find and save my sister. My whole body is trembling. "How do I get you out of this?" I'm afraid my fingers will fail me, because my hands are shaking violently.

"Jimagua carries the keys."

My hope dives. My stomach follows. I've found her, but I'm still helpless to save her. "Where is he?"

"Don't. Know." More whimpering.

I turn to Tony. "I thought the artist works all night. He should be here."

"Maybe he caught on to us being here earlier," Orlando says. "When you ran into Mandy, you did scream and cause a—"

"You. Saved. Mandy?" Izzy whispered her words, stretched out like she needs new breath to release them.

My focus lasers back in on her. "And we'll save you, too." I want to grab a hacksaw, break her out of this nightmare. I turn to Tony. "Do you think the artist went to bed? We need the key to break Izzy out."

"Izzy, It's Detective Garcia." Tony moves in behind me, gently takes my phone, and turns the flashlight app off. "Did you know Mari and Orlando were here? Did the artist?"

"No. No."

She's having trouble breathing. Her words are slow, slurred, her intake of air, labored.

"He, he works…night. Got upset…earlier. Yelled for Adora."

I glance back at Tony at the mention of Adora, but I can't read his eyes.

"He left. Get. Me. Out. Can't. Breathe."

Izzy's tone is escalating, her growing anxiety apparent in the thinning of her voice.

"Do you think the artist left?" I'm asking Tony and Izzy. "Because of us? Or Adora? I could hear them arguing earlier tonight. It sounded like she may have been beating him. Maybe he's on the run now?"

"No," Tony says. "He's here."

"In this room? Right now?"

We all go silent.

That's when I catch the rasping that is my sister trying to suck in air.

"Maybe he's watching us."

Is Tony trying to scare me? But I remember Jimagua watching us in the security office the other day. *Jimagua watches everything.*

Now my heart batters my ribs, making it hard to breathe normally. Looking around the room, my eyes have adjusted, but I still can't see what's in the corners or behind furniture. "Think he's hiding?"

"No," both Tony and Orlando say at the same time.

"Should we turn on the light? To make sure?"

"Don't leave me, Mari. Don't—"

"I won't. I promise."

Tony sighs. "We're going to have to split up."

"No!" My heart stops. I reach for his hand. Grab it. No intention of letting go this time. He's not leaving us here in the dark.

"We don't have time to wait for him to come to us. Where does he sleep, Isabella?"

"Don't know."

I should be glad she hasn't visited the killer's bedroom.

"I know where he sleeps," Angel says. "I will show you."

That makes me snap. "This, from the man who has no idea what's going on here. You are such a liar."

"Stop, Mari." Tony squeezes my hand. "We need to focus on freeing Izzy, or all this is for nothing."

"Want to die...with your...forgiveness."

Izzy's words chill me. "We can talk about this later."

"May not...be...later."

I can't believe I'm having to talk to my baby sister through plaster and tile. Frustration is strangling me. I've gotta do something. "Look on that wall, Tony." I point. "There's got to be some tool that we can use to cut her out of this plaster. Like, right now. Something we can use to cut off the ties to the floor. Something! We don't need the damn artist."

"Forgive me...for not telling...about Mom's murder." Izzy's voice is growing weaker, the segment of words coming at greater intervals.

But I hear every word. I ball my fists until my nails dig into my palms. "I don't want to talk about this right now. We don't have time."

"Forgive her," Tony whispers in my ear. "That's what she needs right now. If you don't forgive her, you'll regret it, especially if she doesn't make it."

"Don't say that." I turn and smack his shoulder.

"Breathe, Mari." He pulls me in to him.

I'm surprised and, in this state, struggle, because... because that's what I do. I fight. I've had to be a fighter for so long.

"Inhale," he whispers in my ear. "Exhale. Let. It. Go."

I'm uncomfortable in this vulnerable state. Despite my efforts to wiggle out of his hold, he won't let go.

"Forgiveness is what heals."

His words knock the wind out of me. My body shakes and tears flow and not because I decided to let them go. I break away from him and throw myself at the statue, wrap my arms around the plaster and tiles. I embrace my entombed sister. "I'm sorry. I'm sorry, too. I feel like you ran to Raúl and Cuba because you were afraid of me judging you. I made you run. Forgive *me* for *that*."

"If I live—"

"You will."

"I...love...you...Mari."

My knees go weak. Izzy hasn't told me she loves me in a decade. "Tony, we need to free her."

She's dying. We're too late.

"Tony, you have to search for the artist. We need those keys."

"Okay, we'll go." Tony grabs Angel by the arm. "You're coming with me, Angel."

"Free…my…friends." Izzy's words are almost unrecognizable now.

"You know where he keeps the others?" Tony asks Angel.

He nods, not making eye contact.

"You show me Jimagua's room. After that, you grab Raúl and go check for other missing girls. We're running out of time."

"Raúl?" Izzy whispers.

I say nothing, not wanting to slow down this rescue because Izzy wants to reunite with Raúl. I can't bear that right now, and I'm thankful he stayed in the hall to play lookout.

"You want me to go with you, Tony?" O asks.

"No, I want you to go with Angel and Raúl, make sure they go looking for others, and videotape everything. We may not be able to save them all."

"I'm staying with you, Izzy." I'm looking around the room, realizing we'll be alone soon. "I'll try some of those tools. Start sawing you out—"

"Take this." Tony hands me his weapon, the one he taught me how to shoot. I take it, glad he didn't argue with me, even though lines of concern etch across his face.

My hands still shake.

"If you need to use it, don't hesitate, Mari."

I open my mouth to speak, but the reply is frozen in my tightening throat. I wanted to kill Raúl, but could I take another person's life? Someone I don't even know?

Could I pull the trigger to save my sister's life? To save my own?

Would that make me a hero? Or a murderer?

Chapter Thirty-Nine

Day Four
3:30 A.M.
THREE HOURS TILL EXTRACTION

OSHUNVILLA

"Let me have the gun." Izzy must read my hesitation.

The sight of my shaky hands probably makes her panicky, too, since I'm holding a loaded gun I only recently learned how to use.

I lay the weapon down on the artist's table, barrel facing away from us both. I stare at Izzy like she's lost her mind. "You're in a Cleopatra sarcophagus. How am I supposed to give you the gun?"

"Saw."

Her voice grows weaker. Raspier.

"Tools."

I go over to the wall full of metal objects. A saw is a good idea.

"Okay. I'll saw an opening where your hands are. Large enough to get the gun through. That way you can protect yourself if Jimagua comes back. He won't expect *you* to have a gun."

I remember what Izzy wrote on the Wishing Wall: *I should die here.*

I hold my breath, realizing I have no idea what torture my sister's endured at the hands of an artistic madman or at the hands of Raúl. Maybe she does want to die. And I would be handing her a way to check out and end her pain.

But it would only increase mine.

"Maybe I should hold the gun."

"Mari."

"I can hide and—"

"Please."

Tears flood my eyes. What the hell am I doing, standing here like a shaking leaf, my fears paralyzing me? Time is ticking, for real, and I'm stuck in mental quicksand, unable to move.

"Help me."

The way those two words crack, smacks me into action. I flip the flashlight app on my phone and bolt over to the wall. I grab a saw large enough to slice through plaster and maybe even cut tile.

Back at Izzy's side, I slide the light over the casket-like creation. "Tap if you can. I need to know where your hands are."

Her breathing becomes more labored, like she's trying to move. "Can't."

"Try."

Tears cloud my vision. *Get yourself together, Mari. No time to panic.*

A slight scratch.

"Here." I tap the outside but realize Izzy can't lean over

and see where I'm pointing. "It's here."

Luckily, the artist didn't cover all the plaster with tile. It would be easier to break through plaster here, but it won't work without an opening. I need a hammer and chisel. Or maybe a drill. *No, that would be dangerous.* Especially with my shaky hands.

I rush back to the wall, searching with my smartphone light. "Got a chisel. Now I need a hammer."

A door slams.

I jump. Turn off the light.

Freeze in place.

Izzy whimpers.

"Sshhhhh." I hope she hears me and—

The whimpering stops.

I wait for footsteps.

An angry voice.

An indication I've run out of time.

Nothing follows.

I allow myself to exhale.

An insect buzzes and lands on my cheek. I press the bug into my flesh but not before it stings me. I want to curse but say nothing.

Sweat drips down the sides of my face. I can't even wipe it away.

Izzy whimpers again.

My heart aches for her. She must be freaking terrified.

I gulp and decide to continue my search. I find a hammer at the end of the table, near the wall of weapons. "Got it." I need Izzy to know I'm making progress. To ease her anxiety.

And mine.

"Hurry."

I'm back at her side. I prop the phone against that coffee cup on the artist's table, flashlight stream pointing at Izzy's artistic tomb.

I take the chisel and place it against the plaster and hit it with the hammer. Again and again and again. I stop and wait to see if the noise has awakened any problems or summoned any person.

Like the person who made noise in the hallway a few moments ago.

The wind is battering a tree branch against the window. *Th-wack. Th-wack. Th-wack.* The fact I can hear that, and nothing else, gives me license to continue. "Izzy, you okay?"

A low moan.

Ay Dios mio. "Stay awake. Stay with me."

She doesn't answer.

I hit the chisel. Harder. Hit. Repeat. Hit. Repeat. Hit. Repeat.

I'm crying as I do it, but holding all sound in.

My arms ache from the effort.

The plaster breaks. I move the chisel and hit again.

More plaster falls away.

"I've got it. I've got it." I continue to work, creating a hole large enough to reach in. I touch my sister's flesh. Her skin feels like chilled salmon. She's not moving. My fingers crawl up her fingers to her wrist. *Metal. I feel metal.* She's chained to something. I can't figure out what it is, but I know we're going to need those keys.

Please, Tony, get here quickly.

Izzy's fingers move against mine.

I gasp. "Isabella."

She moves two fingers until they entwine with mine.

I lay my head against her plaster body and let it all out. All the anger, all the frustration, all the hate. It's loud and messy, and I don't freaking care.

"I'm so sorry, Izzy. I'm so sorry. How did we get here? Don't answer. Don't waste your precious breath. Just know I forgive you. I love you. I will get you out of here. We'll start over. Forget the past. I don't even care what happened."

A door slams.

I stiffen.

This time, footsteps follow.

"It's Tony," I whisper to Izzy. "He's coming."

But I don't know if it's Tony, and I can't take the chance.

I run back to the table, grab the gun, and release the safety. "Izzy, can you hear me?"

"Yes." Barely audible, but there.

"I can hide with the gun, or I can give it to you. Can you even hold it?"

"Yes."

She sucks in air. "I want to kill him."

I know what it took for her to form those words and speak loudly. My sister needs revenge. And boy, can I relate to that feeling still buried deep in my soul. I slip the gun through the hole I created and work it slowly into her fingers so she can grasp it. "The safety is off, Izzy."

I guide her finger to the trigger. "If you pull, it will go off. Can you hold it?"

"Yes. Hide."

Fear rockets through me. "Don't shoot Tony." I have to say it, because those footsteps could be Tony's. I'd die if he died. "Don't shoot if you can't see or tell who it is."

"Yes." A hoarse reply.

The footsteps are louder, closer, and they approach with purpose.

Izzy will pull that trigger. She's always had more courage.

I find a place to hide. Quietly settle in.

Sweat wets my skin. Anxiety runs like blood through my veins.

Who is going to open that door?

Is someone about to die?

Chapter Forty

Day Four

I'm hiding in the perfect place, in an armoire full of smocks, a variety of colors and lengths, most long enough for me to hide behind. The furniture piece, handmade I think, is deep enough for me to get into a fetal position and surround myself with fabric that cloaks me, while still being able to close the door.

Izzy has the loaded gun, and no one would suspect it. The room is dark, so the hole I made, big enough for her to raise her hand and point the nozzle through the opening, should be hard to see.

My heart thrashes against my ribs.

The door to the workshop creaks open.

The squeaky sound is *Halloween Horror Nights* scary to me. It's *Psycho* and *Halloween* and *Nightmare on Elm Street* terrifying.

Someone enters the room.

I can't see who it is.

I can't control what happens next.

Nothing freaks me out more than not being in control.

Footsteps approach. The floor is tiled, so the person can't hide their presence or their direction. Doesn't seem like they're even trying to.

The branches no longer spank the windows. So now I'm able to pick up the smacking sound. It sounds like house slippers slapping the cool tiled floor. Approaching my side of the room.

I imagine the Santera and her slippers. How I wish Josefina were here. I'd ask her what to do, and I'd trust her intuition. The drag and pull sound of sloppy shoes convinces me it's not Tony who entered. Plus, he'd call out for me. I'd throw open the doors and run to him, throw my arms around his neck, and bury my face in that safe crook between his head and shoulder. The sound of the steps approaching convinces me it's a woman.

The footsteps get closer.

They stop.

Right outside the armoire. *I think*.

I hold my breath till my lungs burn.

Someone jerks the door open. "Come out."

My body tightens at the command. I've heard the intonation only once, but I'll never forget it. Despite the dizzying rate of my drumming heart, my muscles lock. I can't move.

"Don't force me to pull you out."

A hand jerks the smocks off the hangers, chucking them onto the floor.

I feel naked. My protection gone.

The lights in the room blind me. I blink, try to focus.

"Come out, Marisol Alvarez."

She remembers my name. "Ay Dios mio."

How did she know I was hiding here? She came right to me.

I exhale, take a quick second to pray. I pray for myself. I pray for Izzy, and I pray for Tony and Orlando. I pray for all the missing girls.

I push myself up. Some of my joints pop but, still hunched over, I step out of my hiding place.

In full light, I can't say I'm surprised to see who's staring at me. "Graciela Gonzalez." The one who calls herself *The Granny.*

She doesn't answer, but the way her eyes narrow and her lips rise, tell me I'm right. She appears in control of both her emotions and this situation.

I'm surprised by her appearance, though. Graciela still looks elderly, maybe in her seventies, but she's no longer slouched like she has severe osteoporosis. Her gray hair, once held away from her face in two childlike ponytails, is pulled back into a tight bun. Pulled so hard, it makes her eyes slant, and her lips look like she's had a facelift. She'd previously worn round framed glasses, smudged with ash, a thick cigar between her teeth.

She's not wearing the glasses she'd worn the first time we met. And now, her gaze is laser focused. No joy in them, like before. No warmth, either. And she lacks the infectious grin I connected with the first time.

She's like a completely different person.

This version of The Granny has ditched the colorful clothing and now wears a black housedress and no makeup.

And she's carrying a new accessory.

A handgun.

"How did you know I was here?" I point to the armoire. Graciela smiles and gestures to a security camera.

There are cameras everywhere. Too many to hide from.

The air in my lungs takes off like a plane. "You were

watching the whole time." I drop my head. Jimagua could have been watching with her. Maybe he's going after the guys right now. Maybe he saw Tony coming and surprised him. Even hurt him. My heart buzzes with fear. I look up. Grab her gaze again. "Who else is watching?"

The older woman doesn't drop my gaze. Instead, she holds it. "You should have left the artist alone."

Reporter's intuition kicks in. I'm missing something. Something very important.

Lives depend on what I do next. I feel it. So, I do what I always do when I need answers, but have only questions. I start pushing buttons. See which gets a reaction. "I'd like to speak to Adora."

The old woman's jaw tightens.

Bingo. I smile inwardly. I figured the name would be a tender spot. *Keep pushing.* "Jimagua's mother. She runs this show."

The woman's shoulders hike. Her eyes go cold. But she doesn't take my bait.

She's good.

I hold my silence. That's my strength. I will wait. I always do and eventually, even the strongest of mind and body will talk to me. Because everyone has a story. And everyone wants to be heard. If you can be still enough and patient enough, the truth will come out.

"Jimagua's mother is dead."

The way the old woman drills me with a challenging look makes me question her words. But I've seen the place where Adora is buried. The wariness reflected in Graciela's gaze tells me she feels a threat from me, even though I still have no freaking idea what the real threat is.

My pulse pounds in my temples. I'm exhausted, but I will continue to push.

She has a gun, and what I'm doing could end up getting

me shot.

But I won't leave Izzy, and I won't die a coward. "Adora is not dead. Jimagua told me so." I hate lying but—

"Oh, he did, did he?" Graciela doesn't even hesitate in her response—her tone is confident.

I take a step back.

We fall into silence.

Graciela continues to point the gun at me. I wonder what Izzy must be thinking. Can she see us through the mesh covering the holes where her eyes are? I hope she doesn't shoot. I'm standing right behind Graciela, and a bullet might go through her and hit me.

"I will tell you the real story, Ms. Reporter."

She knows I'm a reporter. "I already know the real story." *But I don't.*

"It's time you know Jimagua's story."

"How do *you* know Jimagua's story?"

"I knew Adora before Jimagua came into the world."

Usually I love hearing people's backstories, but right now, I can't focus on anything but freeing Izzy and the time we have left to do it. "Graciela, I don't understand—" I stop, because her eyes flare with anger, and her finger twitches near that trigger.

"Adora didn't understand, either. She prayed every day to Oshun for a baby girl. Every day she made offerings, honey and cinnamon, orange seeds, too. She lit yellow candles and allowed only fresh sunflowers on her altar to Oshun. She tended to her relationship with the goddess. And it worked. She got pregnant, eventually learned she carried twins.

"Her doctor in Havana confirmed she carried twins, one a female. Her pregnancy became the saving grace for her troubled marriage. They were both happy. Until the children were born."

I'm drawn into Graciela's tale, and the melancholy way

in which she's weaving the words. Like she's feeling all the emotions herself. I already know the answer, and should remain quiet, but I can't stop myself from asking, "What happened to the baby girl?"

"The baby girl came into the world stillborn. She never had a chance."

I've heard this story before. From Graciela, herself, at the Fertility Fountain, but my reporter's intuition tells me to let her talk. That she's about to disclose more. "What do you mean by that?"

"Jimagua killed her." Contempt taints Graciela's voice.

"Stop!"

I turn toward a new voice.

"S...t...o...p." It comes out this time like a low, extended growl.

A man slumps in the doorway, thin, weak like he needs the doorframe to hold him up. He wears a smock covered in...I don't know...splashes of paint, plaster, stuff artist's work with. His hair is atop his head in a loose bun, and his facial hair looks like it hasn't been trimmed for weeks. His shoulders slump like a man defeated.

"I did not kill her." The man is holding the doorframe. "Stop saying that."

"You sucked the nutrients out of your sister, Jimagua, and left her with not enough to live."

So, this is the world-famous artist. His pale skin and weary eyes lead me to believe Graciela sucks the life out of him. Like a thirsty vampire. And that the artist never does see the light of day.

"I had a rare disease." His tight voice stretches thin, like a hurt child defending himself.

"Like a vampire." Graciela speaks with palpable hatred.

Her words stab me, because I was thinking the same thing. About *her*.

"I spend every day making up for it," Jimagua fires back.

"You were supposed to stop the other men before they set the girls free. We already lost one."

"Maybe it's time to set the girls free."

That spurs Graciela's fury. She waves the gun. "Where is Luis?"

I flinch, wanting to duck behind something, but I'm too terrified to move.

"Where is Luis? I want to talk to him, Jimagua."

Luis? The guy the groundskeeper was afraid of. The poor man had been trembling, much like—a thought cuts through all others.

"No," comes a weak response.

"Get the men before they free the girls. You know that is what Luis wants."

Jimagua shakes his head, but I feel his fear. I also fear his retreat. If he leaves, Graciela's attention would be back on me.

"You are no better than Papi," Jimagua says, again leaning against the doorframe like he can barely stand. "Only difference, he beat me with his fists. You, with your demands and expectations. I'm done."

Graciela screams and sprints across the room, backhanding Jimagua with the butt of her gun.

He rocks back, squealing.

"Find Luis." She raises her hand to strike him again.

Jimagua puts up both hands and backs away. He's visibly quivering, his voice shifting down. "Luis will be mad at me. I don't want Luis to be mad at me."

I've heard that voice before, from the skinny man on his knees in Oshunvilla, picking up the pieces of art I'd accidentally shattered. My hand flies to my heart. "I need your keys to free my sister," I say and point to that mosaic masterpiece he'd almost finished. "Jimagua, will you help me set *this* girl free?"

"Don't say a word." Graciela whips around and points the gun at my head.

I study the artist's hands. And there they are: the clues I've been looking for. Letters tattooed onto fingers. P-E-R-D- I can't see the rest, but I don't need to. Those tattoos are unique to one person. Or maybe two. I'm taking a chance, but I think I'm no longer talking to Jimagua. "Alejandro, can you help me?" The shift was subtle, but there.

"You!" Shock rocks Graciela's voice. She knows I know. "Why am I wasting my time on you?" She flicks off the safety. Her finger moves toward the trigger.

"You pull that trigger, and I kill the artist."

Tony's voice!

My detective has moved up behind the artist. Tony has pulled the frail man into a choke hold, a weapon pointed right at his head. Tony always carries a second gun. Habits of a homicide detective.

"And then," Tony says quite convincingly to Graciela, "I will kill you."

Chapter Forty-One

Day Four

"Put the gun down," Tony reiterates, his voice low and steady. I sense the edge. He's a detective, but he doesn't carry a gun because he *likes* to kill. But he will.

Graciela's gaze holds mine, her finger still resting next to the trigger. "I should let you die."

My heart flutters, but I don't think Graciela is talking to me—I think she's talking to Jimagua.

"I should let you join your baby sister, but I can't."

"My sister lives on inside me." The artist's gaze doesn't appear to be landing on anyone. It's as if he's talking to himself. Or another part of himself. His personality may have shifted again. "She talks to me. Did you know that?"

"I can't do this alone, Jimagua." Graciela's voice softens, like she's now an adoring mother, not a manipulative tour guide or secret protector. "It's been us against the world. It's not too late. We can fix this problem. We continue as we've been told to. Together. We have each other, my son."

It hits me like the butt of Graciela's gun hit Jimagua's head.

I'm in a madhouse of multiple personalities. That's what Oshunvilla is.

Graciela is also Adora. Graciela controls the artist like a dictator and controls the operations of Oshunvilla. The other personality, Adora, worships Jimagua and may be codependent on him as her only living child. Or maybe this nice side of her is an act for us, and behind closed doors she tortures him and forces him to kill for her. Either way, Adora is still alive and pulling the strings. The two monsters are one and the same.

"I don't wanna, Mamá." As his voice changes, Jimagua's stature folds, his shoulders curve in, and I feel his whole spirit shrink.

This must be another personality. Maybe the little boy I heard crying out earlier? Maybe this is the child artist still entombed in an adult body, reliving his childhood trauma repeatedly with Adora?

Graciela knew so much about Jimagua's life because she's been with him since his birth. If Graciela *is* also Adora the mother, who is buried at the Fertility Fountain?

"Jimagua." The way the older woman says his name this time makes my back go straight. This is Graciela speaking again. How quickly can personalities change? Or is this all an act?

"Bring me Luis. I want to talk to him."

"No. No, I won't. I—"

I gulp, wipe sweat away from my eyes, and say, "I don't want to talk to Luis. I want to talk to Alejandro." The groundskeeper is the weakest of the personalities I've met so far. And the one I hope will help me.

"I told you to shut up!" Graciela aims for my head. "Now, I will silence you."

I can't move.

A gun goes off. The loud bang makes me jump, my heart almost leaping out of my chest. I freeze. Wait for the pain to rip through me. Wait for the blood to gush out. I feel nothing. Maybe it's the body's way of numbing me before the pain arrives.

Stars swirl in my peripheral vision. Pain must be ready to flood me. The room spins. I want to sit down.

A thud.

Wait.

It's not me who hit the ground. It's not me hit, at all. It's not me! It's Graciela—Adora—whoever she is in this moment. She's hit the floor, the gun flying from her fingers and spinning across the tiled floor.

"Mamá!" The artist's voice pitches higher. "Mamá!"

I wonder which version of himself the artist is now? The little kid who cries at night?

He pulls against Tony's grip, trying to get away.

"Grab the gun, Marisol!"

I do what Tony says, lifting Graciela's gun, pointing it at the woman on the floor.

Graciela/Adora is gripping her right leg, blood spurting through her fingers. I wonder if the bullet hit an artery. She's moaning, not looking like a threat now. She's bleeding out. "Tony, did you shoot her?"

He doesn't answer—he's struggling to hold the artist still.

I inspect the statue. It's still, but I catch the gun being pulled in and away from the hole I cut.

Izzy pulled the trigger! Izzy may have saved my life. But I say nothing.

Because I trust no one.

Except Tony.

I don't want any of the personalities in this room to know the victim in the statue, my baby sister, is armed and fully prepared to kill.

Chapter Forty-Two

Day Four
4:00 A.M.
TWO AND A HALF HOURS TILL EXTRACTION

OSHUNVILLA

"Jimagua, we need to get your mother help." I make it a point to look into the artist's eyes for a couple of reasons. First, to connect. But also, to determine which personality I'm dealing with now. There's Jimagua the artist, Alejandro the groundskeeper, Luis the killer, and a kid version of himself, the boy I heard crying earlier when we arrived. And again, a few seconds ago. "Someone, watch Graciela, I mean Adora." Izzy knows I mean her. And I'm sure she knows I'm implying, shoot that woman again, if she makes a move toward any of us.

I make sure the safety is on and place Adora's gun on the artist's table, far from the old woman's reach.

"That a good idea?" Tony asks.

"Not sure." My heart vibrates like an out-of-control

washing machine. But my reporter's intuition tells me the best way to get Izzy out, and the mom help, is to appeal to the kinder, gentler side of the artist. I'm pretty sure Tony will catch on, once I start talking. We're getting good at this good cop/bad cop thing. I want to talk to the groundskeeper. "Alejandro, can you help us?"

"How do you know Alejandro?" the artist asks.

I walk to the artist and gently take both of his hands in mine.

He pulls back as if touched by a hot iron.

Tony tightens his arm around the man's chest. "Whatcha doing, Mari?" Tony asks between clenched teeth.

Tony wasn't at the Fertility Fountain with us the first time, so he doesn't know what I saw when I met the groundskeeper. Or why it's important.

I try again, moving slowly, so as not to scare the artist. I mean to handle him with care. I believe this person has suffered a lifetime of abuse, and much of what's happened to him since is a result of torture.

My fingers slide under the artist's palms.

His skin is rough and calloused, the hands of a working man, not an artist. I shiver, thinking what he's done with these hands. Not just paint. I lift both into the light, so I can see his fingers. Tony is looking, too.

"I met Alejandro when he was tending to a piece of art I accidentally broke. I recognize the tattooed fingers." The tattoos stood out. The black-inked, capital P on his left-hand pinky. E on the next finger, followed by -R-D-O-N-A-M-E-! "*Perdoname*, which means *forgive me*. It's tattooed on your flesh." My heart stretches in the achy way that makes me want to cry. "Who did this to you? Did someone brand you so you can never forget?" Or did he do this to himself as self-flagellation?

"I don't know." The artist's voice has quieted down,

become more vulnerable. "I don't remember. The ink has always been there."

"Am I speaking with Jimagua?"

"Alejandro. Jimagua wants me to speak for him. He's... he's sad."

"That his mother is hurt?" I ask.

He doesn't answer.

I'm sure it's complicated in a way I'll never understand. A wave of compassion runs through me. "If we can get my sister out of that"—I want to say sarcophagus, but instead say—"statue, we can all leave. We can drive you and your mother to the nearest hospital. We can—"

"I can help," Alejandro interrupts me. "I want to help." He starts blinking as if just waking up, and the sun is shining brightly into his eyes. He appears confused and rubs his temples. "As long as Luis doesn't come."

"How do we keep Luis from coming?"

"He's...he's... I don't know."

"I want Luis to stay away." I squeeze the artist's hands. "We'll make sure he doesn't come here." I have no freaking idea what I'm saying. But I'm hoping my words give Alejandro comfort and keep this alter ego, the groundskeeper, here and present. "Let Alejandro go, Tony."

"Mari, this man is a—"

He doesn't have to say it—this man is a killer.

But I assume the personality I'm speaking with now is not the killer. *Luis* is. I'm not sure how to keep Luis from surfacing, but I'm going to try, by keeping Alejandro busy.

I peer down at his fingers and wonder what it must be like to live with the constant reminder that your mother thinks you did something so awful you must constantly ask for forgiveness. You kill for her, but you don't get absolution. You can't bring your sister back. So, maybe you split yourself to survive? You create alter egos, or different personalities, to handle the chronic stress and trauma.

I can't help but wonder if his mother were to tell him he's forgiven, that it wasn't his fault, would it be enough for him to begin healing? Or at least stop the killings and the unnatural offerings to a goddess. Nothing I've read or heard tells me Oshun wants human sacrifices. Somewhere, somehow, the good intentions of these two tormented souls soured into something evil.

"I need a chisel and a saw," Alejandro says.

I point to the artist's table. But I wonder how this different alter ego thing works. If Jimagua is the artist and Alejandro but a groundskeeper, a protector of sorts, can he also handle this job of freeing Izzy? I search for another chisel and hammer, wanting to help him.

But then, the mother moans and moves.

"Not sure about this." Tony must have caught that movement, too. "Grab the gun on the table so he can't get it, Marisol, and keep it pointed on the mother. I'll watch the artist." Tony releases him.

The artist stumbles forward, rocking like he's about to fall. He grabs the table, slowly steadying himself. He fumbles for the chisel and picks up the saw and hammer.

Is this an act? This weakness? Is he preparing to pounce on me with the weapons he now holds? "Alejandro, we're on the same team," I say, hoping I'm winning him over.

The artist doesn't look at Tony or me as he lugs his feet over to the statue. He walks around Izzy, dragging a hand across his face, then pulls the chair to the side where I'd already hammered away at the plaster.

I hold my breath, waiting for him to question me about the hole. Waiting for Izzy to scream when he drives the chisel into her tomb-like coating. Waiting for the gun Izzy is holding to go off again.

The room grows quiet.

A single drop of sweat slides down my forehead, hovering right above my eye.

I wish I knew what was going on in Izzy's mind right now. I don't know what she's endured in this nightmare mansion, so I'll have to trust she's doing what she needs to survive.

As the artist works, Tony gets close to me and whispers, "This man has D-I-D. His mother, too, maybe."

"Multiple personality disorder, right?"

"Same thing." He shrugs. "Triggered often by prolonged trauma in childhood. I had a recent case. The kid had been kept inside his house since birth. Feral child. He developed different personalities to deal with the physical and emotional abuse of his fucked-up parents. Drug addicts."

The artist continues chiseling away at his creation, knocking out chunks that fall to the floor in clunks and thuds.

"How do we keep certain personalities from showing up?" I whisper to Tony, never taking my eyes off the mother. "I don't want to meet Luis. He's the killer."

"Good question. Stress or trauma can lead to rapid cycling between alters. Sometimes it takes only a few seconds. Fellow detective, on the psychology side, called it carousel-switching. Also heard it called rolodexing. They all mean the same thing—personality switching. I don't know how to stop it, but maybe if we stay calm, he'll stay calm."

The artist keeps up the drilling, moving in a methodical way. *Chip. Chip. Chip.* Hammer. Saw. *Chip. Chip. Chip.* Hammer. Saw.

"So, we don't know how much time we have with this alter, Alejandro."

"We don't. And we're also against the clock to get the hell out of here and get to the plane. I don't want to be left here, Mari. It won't be good."

Those words hit my stomach like poison. "What will we do with—" I search for the mother. She's leaning up against the wall, head rolled to one side, eyes closed, drool falling from one side of her partially open mouth. "Think she's dead?"

Tony walks to her, while I move the gun to cover the artist.

"Unconscious. She's got a pulse. Bleeding stopped. Good sign."

But he doesn't answer what he plans to do with the injured woman if—no, when—we get Izzy out.

"Jimagua's father never wanted him to be an artist," the artist says.

Alejandro's words stop me. First, because he's speaking about himself, while not himself. Also, interesting to watch him work the statue like a modern-day Michelangelo, but speak like the groundskeeper. It's like his voice and hands are disconnected. "What did he want the artist to be?"

"A doctor. A surgeon. 'The family needs a surgeon, not a pretty-boy painter.' He used to tell Jimagua he looked like a girl and that art was a girl's work."

"Well, I think that is wrong." And I do. "What fucked-up things parents say."

The artist gurgles, the ugly sound rising from the back of his throat. He continues to chisel and pull off pieces of plaster and tile. "I may need my drill."

"No." Tony's body tenses. "No drill."

"His mother and father fought about it every day. One day, I walked into Jimagua's bedroom, and his father had Jimagua by the heels, banging his head on the floor. Over and over and over again."

This is impossible. That Alejandro could have walked into the room. But maybe this personality disconnected so he couldn't feel the physical pain, and he witnessed it from out of body. "Didn't Adora try to stop his father?"

"He beat up Adora, too. Beat her so badly she lost a baby. Maybe that baby would have been a girl. Set Jimagua free."

"Set you free, too, Alejandro?"

"They fought all the time."

So, he's not going to answer that question.

"Adora would say Jimagua's art would make them famous and make them money. But his father made him go to Havana."

"To medical school?"

"He's a mortician."

That would explain the artist's ability to preserve bodies without the decay or smell. "Adora was right. Jimagua is world-famous. That must have pissed the father off." I'm leading the witness. But I'm running out of time.

"His father got so drunk, so mad one night, he stormed into this studio and destroyed everything Jimagua was working on. It was my job to protect the art. *My job.*"

As he'd said at the Fertility Fountain. "I'm sure you tried."

"He trashed the place, and Jimagua lost it. He took a chisel"—the artist pulls the chisel he's holding high— "and plunged it into his father's chest."

His swooping motion makes me jump back and gasp. Fortunately, it doesn't hit Izzy.

The artist takes a deep breath, blinking again, shaking his head. He looks down at the chisel, places it back on the statue, and continues his work to free my sister. "His father collapsed, cursing at us. We both stood there watching that awful man die." As he weaves the story, his motions against my sister's plaster casing grow more aggressive.

We may have to step in to keep him from hurting her. She's whimpering now. At least she's still alive.

"Jimagua cut his heart out and watched it stop beating. We watched the muscle twitch a few times, even out of the body." The artist stops again, finds my gaze.

His stare is different. More focused.

I freeze.

His body stands taller, as if he's grown an inch.

I step back. Place my finger closer to the trigger.

"That's when I met Luis for the first time."

I glance at Tony. He's got his gun pointed at the mother but, facial expressions controlled, he's watching the artist.

I don't know how Tony does it. It's like I'm the only one freaking out at how horrific this change in personality is. I have to remind myself this is Alejandro speaking about Luis like they aren't living in the same body. Or is it? Has he switched again? It's so subtle.

"Jimagua wanted to burn the heart as a sacrifice to one of the orishas. Luis had other plans. He knew Jimagua had learned a new technique of embalming in Havana."

"What's that?" I ask, even though I'm sickened by what I'm hearing, even more terrified by the mannerisms of the man before me. Chiseling away at a sarcophagus with a human inside, knowing that human is slowly dying, and telling a slasher-movie-like tale in a now calm, controlled voice. Like he's teaching one of Jimagua's mortician classes.

"Plastination is where you replace all the liquids and fats in the body with plastics," the artist says as if this is a simple explanation of a skill to learn. "It's a more difficult technique than traditional embalming, but once bodies are plastinized, they do not decay. And they are preserved in the moment they are treated, including in color and appearance."

"Like wax figures?" I ask, praying my hands will stop shaking. "So they don't smell or decompose?" Like the Bodies in Motion exhibit I once saw at Tampa's Museum of Science and Industry.

"Sometimes, the artist will showcase plastinated body parts in his works, a real eye in a fake tiled face. A heart in a mosaic body." Alejandro's voice now holds a note of reverence in it, a pride that was not there before.

Hearts in altars around town remind people what will happen if they speak the truth of Oshunvilla. I still have the business card with an evil eye and a knife through a tongue. It all makes sense now. It also makes my skin crawl.

"But mostly, he kills the girls and preserves them to live in Oshunvilla forever. Tributes to Oshun for the mother who loved him and could never have any girls of her own."

Sarcasm sours that last sentence.

"But Mandy," I say, "she was alive when we found her."

The artist slams the hammer down and the plaster breaks in two. "That's Luis's idea, too."

It takes every bit of resistance to not scream as the plastic and tile fall away from my sister. Her arms are free, but she's chained up against a metal cross and tied at the waist and shoulders, probably to keep her from falling forward or backward. Worst part, my sister is exposed, completely naked. The rage rising in me feels like a dangerous tide during a Cat Five hurricane.

I'm going to kill him for doing this to her. I don't care what kind of mental illness he has. I charge at him.

The artist raises the chisel as if to strike me.

"Mari!" Tony must read the intent on my face. I'm going to fight till one of us dies. But I stop. Far enough away the chisel can't pierce my heart. Before Tony fires to protect me. We still need the keys to unlock Izzy.

"Breathe."

I do. As my finger slides to the safety, I flick it off.

The artist is watching me, the slightest smile on his scruffy, sunken face.

We're in a standoff. But my gun trumps his chisel, and he knows it.

He is still, waiting for my next move.

Where is Tony's gun? My gaze drops to Izzy's hands. She's palming it, but her hand isn't big enough to completely hide it. If you didn't know it was there, you might not see it.

"I'm...I'm sorry?" Stand down. Buy some time for Tony

to do something. Or to come up with your own plan. "What was Luis's idea?"

Keep him talking.

The artist has shifted, so his back is to my naked sister. Like it's not a big freaking deal that an innocent young woman is naked behind him, chained and drugged. Acid rushes into my throat.

"Luis wants the women aware they are dying. He drugs them so they lose the ability to move and scream for help, but remain awake and alive."

He gives them something like roofies, the sicko.

"They die slowly, while tourists walk around them. Take pictures. That brings Luis joy."

I don't know how much more of this evil I can take.

"Sometimes the women whimper or cry for their mothers."

Another dagger to my heart. Can't even remember how many days I cried for my mamá after she was killed.

"Mari, breathe." Tony's voice makes me lift my head.

Focus. Focus on the man who has your sister chained up behind him.

"Once they stop whining, once they finally let go and accept their fate, Luis brings them into the morgue and finalizes their death. Jimagua preserves their remains. Luis made Jimagua the perfect sarcophagus design, so they are easy to open and close, moving the body in and out without disturbing his tiled artwork. He's a genius."

He's a madman who put his talent to evil deeds. "Why didn't you do that with my sister? Open her sarcophagus, unlock her, and let her free?" Instead of this show of breaking away the plaster?

"I wanted to make you suffer while I watched."

My stomach knots. That's when I know for sure I'm no longer talking to Alejandro. I'm talking to Luis.

Why waste any more time with bantering? "Luis, you need to unlock my sister. Or I will kill you."

He leers at me.

The air seems to leave the room.

"Jimagua kills out of loyalty. He hopes sacrificing lost young women to Oshun will win his absolution and make his mother happy. He's given her a family of girls always surrounding her."

Izzy's eyes are open. Tears fall from her eyes.

Tears slip down my face, too.

"But you, Luis, you kill for fun," I say.

"I love you," Izzy mouths the words.

I can't mouth them back.

"I-I do get joy out of killing innocent girls and sacrificing them to Oshun." Luis stands.

I hold my breath, waiting to see his next move. He's not reaching for keys.

The room is still, except for the whimpering of my sister. She's shivering.

A guttural, primitive wail erupts from the woman on the floor.

Luis walks slowly toward his mother.

Tony moves into the space between him and Adora, as if to protect her.

I follow the killer with my gun. To protect Tony.

Tony's gun moves toward Luis, too.

The man moves with a grace that tells me he doesn't care.

"Adora thinks I kill for her. I make sacrifices to Oshun, so maybe one day a girl will come into her life who wants to stay." The slithery smile falls from his pale face. "They never want to stay." His eyes are sparkling, alive with malevolence I didn't see before. "They all cry. Beg to leave. Pathetic. No one wants to live with you, Adora."

I glance at Izzy. She's full-out crying now, but what I

focus in on is the gun. She's no longer hiding it. She's gripping it with both hands. And the muzzle is pointing at Luis. We've got him completely covered.

"I kill for revenge, not love."

The madman talks to his mother, ignoring Tony and me, even though we're moving, with intention, toward him.

"I will surround you with dead girls, lifeless, soulless, empty shells, so you live forever in pain, realizing you will never have what you want most. The love of a female child."

I flick a glance at Tony. He's zoned in on his target, hands steady, gun in front of him.

"Jimagua cares what you think about him." The artist pivots and addresses Tony. "After Jimagua killed his father, Adora thought she was pulling the strings. And she was. Until I showed up. Now, I am in control."

The artist is so close to Tony, I'm sweating. I don't think the artist will try to kill Tony, knowing the gun is pointed right at him, but a distraction might help. "Luis, we need the keys to unlock my sister."

The artist pauses his advance and sneers at me.

His vacuum-like energy sucks the air out of the room.

A wail of rage, and in one unexpected swoop, the artist raises the chisel still gripped in his hand and slices it down, striking his mother right in her chest, in the spot where her heart beats.

Blood sprays from her chest, pumping out in spurts.

It happens before either Tony or I can pull our triggers.

The artist steps back, raises the chisel again.

Adora opens her eyes as blood bubbles from her open mouth. Her body jerks once. Twice. Her gaze finds her son, standing above her, the chisel ready.

Then, she delivers what I will always remember as the final "fuck you" to this conflicted, troubled man she damaged. "See you in hell."

Chapter Forty-Three

Day Four

OSHUNVILLA

I'm having an out-of-body experience. My brain disconnects from my hands. They tremble, but I can't think them steady.

The room wobbles, graying around the edges.

I pull in air and force it back out, but I'm suffocating.

Sweating.

Ringing in my head blocks out all other sound.

Tony and the artist glare at each other, both holding their weapons out in front of them. *Their* hands are steady.

I read Tony's lips. "What happens now, Luis?"

Surreal. Tony caught on to the artist's changing personalities.

Luis is the evil one. He's in control of the artist's mind and body now. I shake my head. Try to clear out the fog.

Focus on Izzy. She needs you. She's slumped in her restraints. The ringing subsides. I wrap my other hand around the butt of the weapon and slow the shaking.

"What happens now?" Luis asks. "I will plasticize Adora and place her in the statue I built for her."

"Why tell everyone Adora died years ago?" Tony asks.

"Adora's idea. She wanted Jimagua to tell the town she'd died, so she could rule from behind the disguise of Graciela. I wanted her to bring me girls no one would miss. I needed her to fish for me. We had an agenda that worked for both of us." The artist points back at Izzy. "Until this one arrived."

Izzy appears unconscious. She could be faking, because she's still gripping the gun.

I need to slow my heart rate and breathing. I need to steady my shaking.

Who has been controlling whom all these years?

Who has been in charge at Oshunvilla? A mother broken by grief over losing a baby girl? A son traumatized by guilt he killed his twin? Or Luis, an evil spirit, who used their broken cracks to infiltrate their minds and dictate the actions of two vulnerable human beings?

"The statue next to Oshun, the one the artist does not speak of, who is buried there?" I ask, my voice shaky, hoping since the artist is now Luis and not Jimagua, he will speak of it.

When he turns to look at me, I feel like I'm lost in the middle of a Netflix horror series. His beady eyes hold me in a death stare. "My father's ashes are part of the plaster in that statue." His eyes continue to burn with a fire that is otherworldly. "His heart sits next to baby Adora's."

I close my eyes, push back the acid reflux burning my esophagus, and an image appears in my mind. One adult heart. One child's heart. All the questions I had at the Brujeria altar in Playa Hermosa are now answered.

"My whole family will be given in tribute. The world will walk by and idolize what I have created, and no one will know, because you will not tell them who I've killed."

I'm stunned by his arrogance and lack of empathy. This is what sociopathic behavior must be like. "You really think you're going to get away with this?" I ask.

"Mari, don't." Tony knows this drill better than I do, but holy hell, are you kidding me? This guy is a psychopath, at least this version of the artist is, and I'm in his lair. And—

"The government needs me. They rely on Oshunvilla. The entire town depends on the money tourists bring in. Havana leans on Oshunvilla for money. The government feeds greedily on the blood I shed here. They turn a blind eye and will continue to do so when you leave."

My stomach heaves, rejecting itself.

"*If* I let you leave." Luis's lips curl into a smirk.

I peek at Izzy. Hair conceals her face. Her body slumps against her restraints. The lump in my throat stops a sob from escaping.

Izzy tries to move her head. It falls forward. *She's still alive. Thank you, God.*

"Are we negotiating?" Tony asks. "If so, it appears we have the upper hand."

He's referring to his gun.

But I wonder if a gun can protect from a demonic presence. My concern is for my sister, of course. She's still sagging against the belts that hold her on the metal cross. But she might be faking, because I don't see the gun. I'm thankful the artist left her hands untied.

Movement in my peripheral vision makes me jump back, reassess what the hell is—

The artist lunges at me, chisel high above his head.

My gaze is glued on his hand and what's in it. My heart thrashes against my ribs. Air stalls in my lungs. This is it. The moment my life—

Boom.

A gunshot.

I twirl my body, in case a bullet is headed my way.

Move. Move. Avoid. Live. I still have the gun in my hand. *Conyo!* Huffing, I scan the room.

The artist is on the ground grabbing his lower left leg, rocking back and forth. His eyes are wide, stunned, like he didn't know what happened. His voice different. His whimpering sounds more like the groundskeeper or Jimagua.

"Shoot me again," the artist begs. "Kill me."

I point the gun at him, approach slowly, never taking my eyes off him. I don't know where that chisel is.

"I'm a prisoner here. In my body."

That's not Luis. Or the groundskeeper, Alejandro. The artist has switched personalities again. "Jimagua?"

"Kill the evil. I can't...I can't control it," Jimagua pants.

Tony moves up next to me, and we stand close enough to see the sweat beading on the artist's forehead and the blood trickling from his leg, coating his fingers trying to stop the flow.

"I don't want to do it anymore. I'm tired." Still holding his leg, he falls back, his head against the floor now. He's bleeding, but it's obvious the bullet didn't hit an artery. He's probably not going to die here tonight. Unless we help him.

Tears hit my eyes. I believe him. I believe he wants to go. I would want to die, too, if I couldn't contain the malevolence inside.

"We can't shoot him, Marisol."

I glance at Tony. "You just did." And he has his gun still pointed at the artist.

"No, Izzy did."

"What?" I seek out my sister. She's awake, eyes wide, glaring at the artist with hatred that's unmistakable. She's also pale and trembling. "We have to get Izzy medical help." Maybe Raúl has another injectable that can reverse whatever she's been given. "What drug did you give my sister?" I walk over to the armoire I hid in, pick up a long smock, and cover Izzy with it.

She looks up at me.

I can see the effort it takes to lift her head.

Her eyes roll back, and her body slumps.

"Let's get the hell out of here." I return to Jimagua. "We need the keys. Gotta unlock her. Where are they? What did you give her? Help me, you jerk." It takes all my strength to keep from kicking him. The only thing that stops me is my compassion for the kid and the other personalities trapped inside the man's mad mind.

"End it." The artist isn't paying attention to me or my questions. He's rolling on the floor, repeating the same words. "End it. End it. End it."

"Jimagua, I need the keys." I start by holding out my hand, hoping he realizes the situation he's in and hoping it makes him cooperate. "Then I can help you."

The artist stops rolling. He's facing away from me. When he lifts the back of his smock, a few keys, attached to a ring on his belt, jangle.

I reach for them, amazed at how easy this is—

The artist flips back over, bringing his right arm over, chisel in hand, slicing through the air right toward me. I fall back on my butt, scoot away—

A gun goes off.

The artist's body jerks. He falls back, grabbing his stomach. He rips off the smock as blood spreads across the white shirt he's wearing underneath. He's been hit in the stomach.

He rolls into a fetal position, tries to sit up, but can't. Spasming now, he throws up blood, mixed with greenish stomach bile.

My stomach heaves.

He reaches for me.

I scoot fast, not fast enough. He grabs me, but his fingers slide off my sweaty skin. I use my feet and hands to push against the floor and slither out of his reach.

His mouth moves, but words don't come out, only gurgling, and bubbling of blood as it overtakes his mouth. He's trying to tell me something, fear evident in his wide gaze.

"This is what you wanted, Jimagua. May God forgive you."

The switch is happening—I see it in his gaze. Luis had come back with the intent to kill me. But now, Jimagua has returned. *To save me?*

Fear settles into acceptance. A smile, even, as he falls back against the tile. His chest rises and falls a few times with deep breaths. His chest settles, stills. His head rolls to one side. His eyes are open, staring at me. But seeing nothing.

A sound erupts from me. Half cry, half scream. Tears flow freely.

"I didn't fire," Tony says.

I turn my attention to Izzy. Clearly, she's passed out, both hands empty. Did the gun slide out of her grip and hit the floor, going off?

"What the hell?" Tony says.

I follow his gaze toward the door to the studio. "Ay Dios mio!" I can't believe *who* I'm seeing. Now I know who killed the artist.

And I understand why.

Chapter Forty-Four

Day Four
6:15 A.M.

Izzy, Tony, Orlando, Raúl, Angel, Arianna, Mandy, and I
are stuffed into Angel's 1957 Chevy. The eight of us in an
ancient car made to comfortably seat six. That's why the U.S.
Marshal and Enrique opted to stand outside.

Once again, it's a muggy, moist morning outside of
Havana.

We're all waiting for our escape plane to land on the side
of a major road in a rural town called Matanzas, about fifty
miles east of the capital on Cuba's northern coast. We've
parked the car in a wooded area off the main road, protected
by the tree line and the darkness before dawn. The trees are
thick, and the area uncharted.

We'd fled Oshunvilla as soon as we'd freed Izzy.

Raúl, Orlando, and Angel had found and unchained

Arianna from one of the artist's holding cells, and they'd done a quick look around to make sure no other missing girls would be left behind.

They'd found us in the artist's workshop and Raúl, angered at the condition he saw Izzy in, knowing what she must have been subjected to, shot the artist as soon as he'd had the chance.

Raúl had no idea what he'd stopped. Who he'd saved. He'd reacted out of pure, human emotion. He'd wanted revenge.

Can't say I blame him.

Interestingly, Orlando says he didn't record that shooting.

Security eventually confronted us in the workshop, but we outnumbered them in both bodies and weapons. We won the battle and even managed to tie them up and make sure to record on our smartphones what had taken place in the artist's workshop by recording the security footage. Then we'd sent video back home to friends via WhatsApp. Just in case we didn't make it out of Cuba tonight.

Once in the car, Raúl administered an antidote injection into Izzy, and my beautiful sister came back to life, much like Mandy.

Izzy and Raúl huddle together in the front seat. I don't know that I'll ever get over my repulsion at their intimacy—that night years ago traumatized our whole family. But I can't deny these two have a deep bond. Maybe it's even love. Maybe they've kept in touch over the years but told no one. Maybe they've waited a decade to see each other again. Maybe Raúl isn't the evil asshole I envisioned. Maybe he was a kid who would have done anything to make sure he could see his first love.

Maybe, but I'm still not ready to forgive him.

I shake my head, trying to toss away troubling thoughts to focus on the fact my sister is alive. *Izzy is alive!*

"You okay?" Tony leans in and whispers in my ear.

"Not really." He always seems to pick up on my anxiety. "You?"

"We're close, Mari." He grabs my hand and squeezes. "We're going to get out of here. All of us."

I nod. "Thank you." I roll my lips inward to keep sounds of emotion from squeaking out, embarrassing me. Don't want to break down in this crowded car, especially in front of two young women recently victimized. I force the knot of apprehension back down my throat.

"Thank me, for?" Tony asks.

"For...for...everything." *Ay Dios mio, here I go.* Tears hit my lashes. "For...for...being here. For coming with me. For risking your life." *I want to push our boundaries and see what could be with you, Tony. I want that kiss that almost was.*

"Later." His tone softens.

He wants to hold a deeper conversation for later. I agree. Inside a packed car, when I'm sitting on his lap, while also touching shoulders with Orlando, isn't the place to opine. But I'm not sure he will ever want to go deeper. He's got this wall so high, I'm not sure I'll ever scale it. I want to get closer but realize he may never let me. I take a deep breath and intentionally change my thoughts. Again. I practice this. Shifting bad thoughts to good. I stare out the window. "When is the plane supposed to land?"

"If everything goes well, in the next fifteen minutes."

"What kind of plane is it?"

"Twin Otter, I think. The kind you use to go skydiving."

Should be big enough to hold all of us—I'd been worried about that. "You heard from him?"

"From who?"

"The pilot."

"It's a her." This from the U.S. Marshal, listening through the open window. "The pilot is my wife. Former Air Force."

"Damn!" Orlando says. "Another angle to this story. Badass, man. I'm getting out. Want to film her landing."

"Can you text her?" I ask. "Make sure all's okay?"

"I could," the marshal says, "But I'm not going to take the chance someone might intercept the text."

"We're in the middle of a Tom Cruise movie," I think out loud.

"I wish. Those always end well." Orlando records with his smartphone.

"My wife knows what's she's doing."

"The video we've got already," O says.

"The story we have to tell." I turn to O. "I thought you wanted out of TV news."

"I came here with you, for you, and we will finish this story together, my Dawg."

That makes me smile. Orlando went to the University of Georgia, and I've always been his Dawg.

"We'll give our two minutes to news, but I'm shopping a longer format to Netflix. I don't care what management thinks."

I nod, taking another deep breath, wishing I didn't care. If anything happens to Orlando or Tony because they came with me to rescue Izzy, I'd...oh God, Izzy and Raúl are kissing. I lay my head back against the back seat, which is difficult considering I'm sitting on Tony's lap.

He adjusts underneath me and clears his throat.

"How's your wife going to fly into Cuban airspace without the military knowing?" I keep the conversation going, in part because I am curious, in part because Orlando is recording, and in part to keep tension down in the car.

"Do you remember the story of a Cuban refugee named Orestes Lorenzo?" the marshal asks.

"I remember the name, but not the details." The story is old. Came out of South Florida. "Wasn't there a documentary on Netflix or Prime?"

"Not sure about the documentary. He wrote a book. Back in the early 1990's, Lorenzo, a former Cuban Air Force pilot, defected from Cuba in a Soviet-built MiG. He flew to Boca Chica Naval Air Station near Key West, and he navigated the whole trip without being detected by American or Cuban radar."

"What does that say about our safety systems back then?" Orlando says.

"I know what it says about that pilot," Enrique says from the other side of the vehicle. "Says he's got giant ones."

"He left his family in Cuba, which is what many of us had to do to escape."

I struggle to turn without making it uncomfortable for Tony or me, but I want to see the marshal. "You're Cuban?"

"Born and raised."

"But I thought you were American. You work for the U.S. Marshals?"

"I came to America with nothing. The resources in your country allowed me to get an education and build a career, but my heart has always been in Cuba, along with most of my family."

"So, now you spy on the Cuban government?"

"To protect its people. *My* people."

"No judgment." I throw up both hands. "Lorenzo got out of Cuba, but at what price? He had to know he was risking his family's safety by leaving."

"We all know when we leave, we risk the safety of our family left behind. We only leave with their consent and support."

"And after Lorenzo got to America?"

"He spent months learning how to fly a Cessna. It's different flying a twin-engine. When he learned, he flew that back into Cuba."

"But how did he know how to evade detection?" Orlando asks.

"He put together a map highlighting Cuba's radar zones."

"Shit, man." O's into the story. "With technology today, imagine what he could do now."

The marshal nods. "If you know a country's weaknesses, especially when it comes to aircraft radar, you can fly in, land, fly out undetected. Drug runners do it all the time. Pick a safe road to land on, and a time when it won't be busy—"

"When he flew back, how'd he know his family would be in the right place waiting, and how'd he recognize them from the air?" I ask, wondering how his pilot wife will do the same. Even though the sun's now rising, and fingers of light stretch across the highway, it may still be hard to see us from the air.

"The family knew where to meet him, after two women visited the family home and handed his wife a note detailing Lorenzo's plan. It said, 'Look for my plane on Saturday near the beach called El Mamey. Wear an orange shirt.'"

"We aren't wearing orange shirts," I say.

"No, we aren't, but with today's technology, it's as easy as dropping a pin on your cell phone or tablet." The marshal looks down at his watch. "It's time." He opens the door to the Chevy, and we all pile out. Collectively, we look to the sky. Under the protection of the tree line, I'm unable to see the plane. But the comforting, high-pitched hum of twin turboprop engines grows louder, like a swarm of locusts coming in for a landing.

"Are you ready?" the marshal asks. "Listen up, everyone. Here's the plan. When the plane lands, we'll run out first, make sure it's safe, and afterward, Marisol, you lead your sister and the other girls to the plane. You run, okay? Don't look back."

"Okay but why, why would you say—"

The whirring of engines gets louder. The all-white, boxy,

multi-engine aircraft glides down toward the road, tires screeching as they hit the asphalt. As the aircraft comes to a stop, the props cut through the air. The engines shift into reverse; a lower-pitched whistling signals the aircraft is stopping. The cargo door slides open.

In the dawn, as the tendrils of light paint the sky and the path back to America, a chorus of insects and heavy breathing fills the air.

Until the roar of car engines erupts our anxious silence.

Two old military trucks, with URAL on the grill, fling up clay and leaves as they tear out of the wooded area to the right of us.

"Shit. How'd they know?" The marshal mumbles.

"Police or military?" I ask.

"Doesn't matter."

"What now?" Fear bubbles up in my center as the trucks speed toward the plane.

"You and the ladies run for it," the marshal yells above the noise. "We'll cover."

I glance over at Tony.

His gun is already drawn, his focus following the approaching trucks. "Go, Mari. Take the women with you. I've got a backup plan already in place. As soon as we leave the cover of these woods, it'll be activated."

Izzy wobbles up next to me. Arianna looks as weak, grasping my sister's hand. Mandy is right behind, her eyes wide and her mouth in a thin line. "Ladies, can you—"

"We're not staying here, Mari." Izzy, still dressed in a smock from the artist's workshop and barefoot, grabs Mandy with her other hand. "Let's hit it."

And with that, my courageous sister leaves the safety of cover, wobbling out into the open, pulling two other lost girls with her.

The next thing I hear is gunfire, the rippling of ear-shattering pops like I've heard before during mass shootings caught on video.

Tony and the U.S. Marshal run after Izzy, guns already in use.

I follow, my heart stuttering in time to the shots fired.

Chapter Forty-Five

MATANZAS: MEETING PLACE

Gunfire erupts from different directions.

I freeze. My legs lock as if cramping.

Something buzzes past me, so close it melts the frozen ball of fear holding me in place.

I do as the marshal said—I sprint straight toward the plane. I'm pumping my arms, taking in shallow breaths, forcing my gaze to lock into my target. Now out of the safety of the cover in the woods, there's no place to hide from a bullet. But I'm not staying in Cuba. Tony told me what happened to his grandfather imprisoned here. I've seen how the police protected a mad man and his mother.

I'm getting on that plane. Even if it means taking a bullet to get there.

Blood rockets through my veins, fueling me with much-needed oxygen. They say adrenaline is an amazing drug. I feel like I'm flying, faster than those bullets, stronger than the copper-plated steel they're made of.

The props on the twin Otter rotate with a roar. The door remains open. As I pass behind the engines humming and spitting air, Izzy helps Mandy into the plane. There are no steps, and Mandy is having trouble lifting her traumatized body into the aircraft. Arianna, already in, puts her hands under Mandy's armpits and pulls. Izzy stumbles backward as the weight is lifted off her. I make it in time to catch her. "Got you."

I steady Izzy and put my hands together to form a step. Her bare foot pushes down into my cradling hands, and she grabs onto the side of the door. Once she's ready, I boost her up. She falls forward, headfirst, into the plane.

"Move!" I yell. Using my Herculean strength, fueled by a cortisol dump, I pull myself up into the plane.

Then, I watch what's happening in front of me.

Two trucks have pulled up beside the plane. On each one, a handful of guys hold what look like AK-47 rifles—probably Russian made. Alfonso, the government watchdog, carries one of the rifles. *Of course, he's here.* He's seeing his duty right to the end.

Our gazes meet. Only for a second.

On the other side of this fight is a variety of old, rusted, vintage trucks full of kids and young men. I recognize Domingo. He's in the back of one truck, shouting instructions. His friends are also armed with cheaper looking weapons, some assault style.

Tony set this up. He must have. He must have directed Domingo and his friends to hide in the woods, armed and waiting, in case we were attacked.

Domingo stands behind a taller man, wearing a vest— maybe bulletproof—firing what looks like an assault rifle.

The boy launches something the size of a baseball at the two trucks in front of them.

Time seems to slow down.

The device lands in the truck bed and explodes on contact. A puff of smoke, a loud crack, and the back half of the truck falls to the ground, kicking up dust. The men inside go airborne, propelled up and onto the ground. One of them is Mr. White Shoes. He lands with such force his body bends unnaturally. Then falls flat.

Domingo pulls back and hurls another grenade.

The second truck kicks into reverse, spinning around to avoid the grenade. The explosive hits dirt and tosses up chunks of ground, and the driver diverts to rescue an injured man. He doesn't bother with Mr. White Shoes, confirming for me the watchdog is dead. Once the other man is in the truck, the driver hits the gas, spins his tires, then speeds off the opposite way down the road.

The threat is retreating.

But they'll be back.

I exhale.

Domingo bought us time. Time enough to get everyone on board.

"Get in!" I yell to Tony, even though I'm pretty sure they can't hear me above the sound of the spinning props.

Orlando is first to run our way. He's got a GoPro on an extended tripod in front of him, and I know he's recording.

Angel is next. He leaps into the plane like a deer leaping across a street to avoid a speeding car. As if his life depends on it. He scampers to the back of the plane.

Next, Tony.

"Enrique?" I yell at Tony.

"Not coming."

My stomach knots. I get how important it was for Tony to convince his family to come with him to America; it was his personal goal on this trip. He's leaving them all behind.

He waves me off. "Move."

I adjust so I'm behind him, but not too far away.

Tony reaches out a hand to his friend, the marshal, and pulls him in. At the same time, Raúl is trying to jump in. But something's off. He's pale, and his eyes look wild. He misses. Falls back. Tries again.

I move forward and reach out my hand. *To the enemy.* I can't leave him behind—Izzy would never forgive me. And I still need to know the whole truth. I brace my feet and hold on to the doorframe with one hand; with the other I pull Raúl in. He had momentum, taking a running start, but I'd like to think I helped.

His body hits the plane floor, and he grunts. No, it's more like a scream. My hand is stuck under his body. I drag it out. Blood.

"Hold on." The pilot's voice reminds me she's not simply a skilled person here to help us escape, she's family. The U.S. Marshal's wife. "Hold on to something. We're taking off."

"Wait!" I yell. "Raúl took a bullet." And I'm not sure he'll make it to America. If he dies on the way, he'd confirm one of the first things he said to me when we got here—that the only way he's going back to America is in a body bag. If he's going to die, and I can do nothing to stop it, I need something from him now. "Raúl, I need to know why you killed our mother."

Chapter Forty-Six

Day Four

Tony and I manage to drag Raúl into a front row seat in case we do take off. Tony pulls off his shirt, balls it up, and presses it against Raúl's wound. "Got a first aid kit?"

"I've got it," the marshal says, moving toward the back of the twin Otter.

"Why, Raúl? Why did you have to kill my mother? You have no idea how that night changed my life."

Izzy collapses next to Raúl. "*Your* life? What about ours, too?" She takes his hand and cradles it in hers. "Leave him alone, Mari. You've gotten what you want."

A chill sweeps over my heated skin. My sister, who I risked my life to rescue, is taking her lover's side. Again. "What I want? What I want is my mamá back."

"She wouldn't let me see Izzy." Raúl's voice is raspy, his skin pale. "Have you ever loved someone so much…so much, you…you would do anything for them?"

A sense of longing settles in my gut, but I fight the urge

to look at Tony.

"I brought the gun to scare her. That's it. Izzy didn't know."

"I didn't."

"Got nervous when your mom opened the door." Raúl's words are breathy. "Pulled it out. She reached for it and I… and I… It went off. I didn't mean to—we…she…I don't know how it went off."

"It was an accident, Mari," Izzy says, her gaze on me, pleading.

The edges around my vision go gray. My heart pounds like the drums in Playa Hermosa. "Why the hell didn't you both own up to that ten years ago? Why lie to me all these years?"

This could have been avoided with the simple truth. *Maybe.* Maybe I wouldn't have been mature enough to forgive *an accident.* Mamá's murder broke me.

The marshal is back with gauze and medical tape. He and Tony work to pull Raúl's shirt away from his stomach wound and stop the bleeding. But the gauze turns red, like it's a sponge pulling the life out of Raúl.

Raúl looks at Izzy. He tries to speak, but his head falls back against the chair like he's getting weaker, or maybe what Tony and the marshal are doing hurts too much for him to continue to talk.

"He ran because he was scared," Izzy picks up for him.

"He was a gangbanger. Scared, my ass." Maybe I'm still too broken to believe or forgive.

"He was scared I'd never forgive him. He was scared he'd go to jail, and I'd never speak to him again. When he got home, he told his mother the truth, and she drove him to Miami that night, hired a friend to take him by boat to Cuba the very next day. He didn't even have a chance to think. We never had a chance to say goodbye in person. He did what his mother told him to do."

"He escaped justice, Izzy. All these years he's been free here, doing whatever the hell he wanted. Probably texting with you every day."

"No, no. It wasn't until years later I found out he was still alive. Abuela Bonita ordered me to have no contact. Said it was the best for both of us. And she made me swear never to tell you. She knew if you knew what I knew, it would ruin our relationship forever."

Pretty much did, when I found out earlier this year. "Izzy, he has to face responsibility for his actions." And she hers. Izzy fled to Cuba to be with Raúl that night the cigar factory burned down in Ybor City. She chose him over me.

"He was a kid, and it was an accident. He's spent ten years living away from his mom and dad, ten years away from me. Don't you think that's punishment enough?"

My heart feels like it's lodged in my throat. "No. No, I don't." I can barely croak out the words.

"Mari."

I throw up a hand. I don't want a life lesson from anyone right now.

Orlando records us.

"Damn it, O!" I shake my head, hating that I agreed to let him document my most deep-felt, personal pain.

"What will it take for you to forgive Izzy?" Raúl croaks.

I stare at Raúl as it sinks in. He *does* love my sister because, even facing possible death, he's asking for forgiveness for Izzy, not himself.

"His parents sent him to Cuba to escape a trial and jail, but living away from everyone he loved all these years became a prison," Izzy says. "Can't we all forgive and move on? Especially after what we've survived. Think about it, Mari. Let the past go."

Izzy is gripping his hand. His fingertips are losing their

color, as are his cheeks. "If you were so happy here with Raúl, why message me to come rescue you?"

"Rescue *us*. I wanted you to rescue *us*. Girls I met here went missing. I thought if I could get you here, you could see Raúl had been trying to help them before they vanished. You would see his good side and rescue him, too. Allow him to come back to America without turning him in. We could all forgive and move forward. But I knew I'd have to use the secret sister code to make you believe I was in trouble, to get you here."

And it worked. As I watch Raúl's face, I realize he's not going to survive. Tony and the marshal must realize it, as well, because they've stopped their frantic measures to halt the bleeding. Both have stepped back to give Izzy and Raúl space.

All this time, I wanted Raúl punished for his sin, and he's been paying that penance. Holding a grudge now will only hurt my sister and me, taint our future. That's not what Abuela Bonita wanted. Izzy's the only family I have left. And yet, I still can't look Raúl in the eyes. I want to say, "*I forgive you*." I feel the words pushing themselves up from my gut into my vocal cords, but I've been fighting this fight for ten years, and I'm not sure I can—

"Hey, isn't that your relative, Tony?" Orlando's pointing to Tony's nephew, who's running toward the plane, his disabled dog in his arms. His mouth is moving, but he's too far away for us to hear what he's saying.

"We got one more coming," Tony yells at the cockpit.

"Weight might be an issue," the pilot calls back. "Calculated based on the number of people expected."

Raúl struggles to sit up. "Izzy," he says, leaning forward. Crying, she holds him up.

"Save the kid." He raises his head with immense effort. He's sweating, trembling. They lock gazes. Izzy is shaking her head. "I'm sorry," he says to her.

"I'm sorry, too."

"For everything. Let me die in Cuba." Raúl looks at me. The sincerity in his gaze rocks my center. "My sacrifice to you, Mari, is this." He pushes off Izzy and falls onto the floor of the plane. He drags and pulls himself toward the door.

None of us do anything to stop him.

Not even Izzy.

The roar of the props fills my ears. Blood pounds at my temples.

Raúl rolls out of the plane as Domingo makes it to the doorway.

Tony grabs the dog out of Domingo's arms and passes the mutt off, then reaches for Domingo.

I can't tear my gaze from Raúl. He's leaving my sister again, because he knows it's best for her. And she's letting him. Because she knows what's best, too.

Maybe they're right. I'm the only one here afraid to let go of the past and do what's right. For all of us.

"I forgive you, Raúl," I yell the words, not sure he can hear them, but he's watching me from a fetal position on the ground. I know he knows.

A car approaches that stops next to Raúl. Enrique jumps out.

Domingo squats next to me. "Enrique will take Raúl to the Santera. It's his best chance to survive."

The boy's right. And this, this feels right. To let go.

To let it all go.

Tony slams the door shut.

I fall back into my seat and adjust my seatbelt. What happens to Raúl now is out of my control. But I gave him what he asked for—I granted him forgiveness. And Tony's family should be safe, now that Mr. White Shoes is dead. Maybe these whole dramatic few days will encourage them to take those visas Tony secured and get out of Cuba. That would make Tony so happy.

My shoulders feel lighter, my burden lifted.

Izzy pulls herself into the seat next to me and puts on her seatbelt. She grabs my hand, and her cool flesh feels good against my heated skin.

I got what I came here for. I got my sister back, and we have a chance to start over. She smiles at me, even though she's still crying. I nod at her, because I understand. Leaving Raúl wasn't easy, but this time, Izzy chose me. She chose family. I won't waste this second chance with her. I won't.

I'm so proud of you. I mouth words, because the plane is accelerating down the roadway and it's getting harder to hear anything. I motion my head to the back of the plane where Mandy and Arianna sit. "You saved those girls."

We did, she mouths back.

Orlando is sitting beside them, next to a window. His GoPro is pointed outside. He's going to record us taking off, our daring escape from this communist country. What a story he'll share with the world. I have no doubt Orlando will sell a documentary that will make him famous. He'll get exactly what he's dreamed of.

Angel sits next to him, making the sign of the cross. Turns out he's a brave man after all. We'll have to help him start over in America.

Domingo and Tony embrace before they both take a seat across from us and strap in. My heart moves even higher into my throat. I'm so happy Tony gets to bring at least one family member back to America with him. He'll be a great mentor and role model for Domingo. I see great things in that kid's future, with Tony by his side.

"Everybody ready?" The plane taxis down the asphalt road. The pilot accelerates until the plane lifts off. "I'll let you know when we're out of the Cuban military zone. Forty-five minutes, and we'll be back in America."

The wheels lift and we're airborne.

Going home.

I'm grateful, because I have everything I came for. Everything I need. Nothing can touch us now.

We're flying toward a new beginning.

I gaze out the window and see Enrique driving Angel's car down the highway. *Godspeed Raúl.*

Izzy has her eyes closed, both hands resting across her heart.

The pain will ease, Izzy. But I know exactly what she and I need to do next. I lean back and think of Abuela Bonita and Mamá —they'd be so proud of Izzy and me.

You were right, Abuela. Broken girls can turn into warriors. Wait till you see what Izzy and I will create from this pain.

Chapter Forty-Seven

TAMPA, FLORIDA

Izzy kneels at the Wishing Wall. But it's not the infamous one at Oshunvilla, thank God. That wall survived, despite the death of the artist, Jimagua. Tourists still come from all over the world to leave wishes. In fact, after Jimagua's death, Oshunvilla became even more famous and revered. *Condé Nast* listed the beach town as the number one tourist destination in the world this year.

That might change after Netflix releases Orlando's and my documentary, called *Oshunvilla, The True Story*.

We are debuting it today, right after we cut the ribbon at our new home for troubled young women. We've named the facility "Izzy's House." We were able to build it on the land where the cigar factory used to stand in Ybor City. Andreas Santiago, an old enemy, and new friend financed it.

"The media's ready," Mandy Peacher says. She's Izzy's

new assistant, Vice President of Izzy's House.

The media is ready for me. Interesting. I've spent a decade working as a TV reporter, covering news conferences like this one, and now *I'm* the person who called the media here with an unusual and newsworthy story to tell.

Not sure I'll have a job in TV news after this.

My boss and I have been butting heads over whether I can be both an objective reporter and a news maker at the same time. And, covering my own sister's new home for troubled girls crosses the line, he says. I disagree. But today, my reporter's hat is off. I'm Izzy's assistant. Orlando's partner.

"I'm coming, thanks."

Orlando already quit TV news, intent on making our documentary the best creative project he's ever put together. I'm sure he's done it. But we're about to find out.

"You okay?" Mandy places a hand on my shoulder.

"I am. How about you?"

"Never been prouder. We have four people scheduled to speak. Orlando will start. Followed by Arianna, then Teddy's mother."

As soon as we got back to America, I'd called Teddy's mother, the one I'd met at Oshunvilla, and detailed what we'd learned about her daughter's death. Just as I promised her I would. Her mother came today, to speak in honor of her daughter. A clinical psychologist will end the presentation. And we have a waiting list of young women referred to us by the Department of Children and Families. We are ready to help.

Gratitude rushes through me, a river with powerful lift.

"Let's do this." I walk over to Izzy and place a gentle hand on her shoulder. She'd recently learned Raúl passed away. He'd suffered numerous setbacks after he got shot while we tried to escape Cuba. His death certificate reads death by sepsis. But I'll always believe he died of a broken heart that wouldn't heal.

I observe my kneeling sister, grateful she's been able to turn her grief into passion and her pain into purpose. She's been the leader in every aspect, bringing this home, this mental health retreat, into existence. Young women will stay here for free, supported by grants Izzy and Mandy learned how to apply for. The Wishing Wall will have new meaning at Izzy's House. When a young woman dedicates herself to self-transformation, when she commits to the program, she will begin by writing her most heartfelt wish on the Wishing Wall.

I'm curious to see what Izzy wrote, so I read her note.

Here, Broken Girls will Blossom into Warriors.

My hand flies to cover my heart. That's what Abuela Bonita said in the letter she wrote to me to be opened after her death. I'd never shared that with Izzy. Did I? Cool air sweeps past me, and I glance at a picture of Abuela Bonita that Izzy hung on the wall near the entrance.

Mandy squeezes me. "She's here with both of you today."

I roll my lips in, embarrassed at the hot tears building in my eyes. Abuela Bonita and Mamá must be here. I feel the energy of both.

"Mari, what do you think?"

"What?" I'm so in my own head, I'm not sure what Izzy's referring to.

"The first message on the Wishing Wall." Her fingers trace the words written in marker on the whiteboard. "It's important I get this right."

I smile at her. "It's perfect. Exactly what I would have wished for." Because this is the message every broken girl wants to hear.

You *can* blossom into a warrior. And we will help you.

Maybe we could have helped Adora, had we known about her tortured childhood at the hands of a sadistic mother and then an abusive husband. All details we learned from a journal Orlando confiscated from Oshunvilla while searching for the missing girls. Adora carried on a vicious cycle of abuse, because it's what she learned at a very young age.

The cycle must stop. It takes a strong woman to break it. I reach out my hand to Izzy. "Time for the news conference."

She takes my hand, and I pull her to her feet. We walk through the fifteen-bedroom facility. Through the kitchen, past the meditation den, through the lab room, where counseling will take place, through the lobby. Once outside, Izzy and Arianna, Andreas Santiago, Tony, and Teddy's mom move to stand behind the red ribbon, ready to cut it and open the doors to Izzy's House.

Orlando is in front of them, recording.

I scan the room, assessing about thirty media representatives present. Pretty good. My heart swells with pride and gratitude. We're going to make a difference.

Izzy steps up to the mic. "Welcome to Izzy's House. Before we begin, I'd like to thank a few people. First, my sister Marisol Alvarez, who gave me the idea for a house where broken girls could learn to not only survive but thrive. You are not only my sister, but my best friend."

I blow her a kiss, my body buzzing with adrenaline. *Okay, I'm not going to cry.*

"To Andreas Santiago, thank you for giving us this land and financing our dream. I promise you we will make you proud. And to Orlando Jones, who has been documenting the most amazing story of lost girls gone missing and a twisted, talented serial killer. He will introduce you to a Norman Bates for the new generation, a mentally disturbed man, who made innocent victims into living pieces of sacrificial art. Encapsulating them into mosaic statues at his world famous Oshunvilla, where they die, hidden in plain sight, as tributes to his monstrous mother."

The crowd buzzes. This is not what they expected at a ribbon cutting. I smile. It's going exactly as I planned.

"We invite you to stay after the ribbon cutting. Join us in the theater room to watch a preview of a documentary called *Oshunvilla, The True Story.* And learn the real reason behind the murders that took place there, and what we can do to help others with mental health issues before they follow that same sad, sadistic path. And how we can also help their victims heal."

Chapter Forty-Eight

Orlando stands on the stage in our multipurpose room at Izzy's House. He's at the podium introducing our documentary. Tony, who took the day off work to be here, sits in the audience next to me. I want to reach over and touch him, slip my fingers between his, make that physical connection again.

We haven't really seen that much of each other since our return. Tony dove into work, maybe to hide from the trauma of what we'd all been through. He spent most of his free time with Domingo, helping him learn the ways of our country, guiding him through months of school.

I had my hands full with Izzy, and Mandy, who moved in with us. Arianna went home to a grateful family. We committed ourselves to creating Izzy's House. I also had to go back to work.

We all focused on surviving.

But I'm not sure we've been thriving.

That's why I invited Tony here today. To be a part of this. He needs to see how far we've come and see how much a part of this he was. I want him to feel good about what we accomplished, despite the horror we experienced to get to this point.

And honestly, I miss him. I long for that unusual connection we get whenever we're working together. It's magic. Me, the good cop. Him, the bad cop. Our synergy on fire. I wonder if my prayer to Oshun while in Cuba will ever come true. Is there a time limit on these prayers or wishes?

"The purpose of this documentary is not to make evil villains out of either the artist or his mother," Orlando continues his address to the audience.

I know how important it is for him to get that message across. We don't mock or disparage those with mental health issues—no matter the terror they may have created. We aim to heal, before any harm can be done to someone else.

"We are trying to show the world what can happen when we ignore mental health. We have grown numb to visuals of mass shootings and terrorist attacks. Humans hurting other humans because their own brains are broken. Or, they are abused in childhood and become perpetrators, because of the intergenerational trauma. We have an expert here to delve into domestic violence, to explain this type of cruelty doesn't happen in a vacuum. We want to show the world how generations of traumatic events—some no fault of anyone's—leads to decades of mental illness hidden under the mask of masterpieces the world adores."

Still adores.

"You will meet Adora, the controlling mother, who could never accept the loss of her baby girl," Orlando continues. "A victim of abuse by her own cruel mother and later her husband, Adora followed a pattern and abused her son, attacking him with guilt until he broke. It doesn't take a leather belt to scar someone."

I'm so proud of O! He spent years behind the TV camera,

never wanting to stand in front of the audience. Look at him now. He's done his homework, and it's magnificent to see the results.

"You will also meet Graciela, the manager of Oshunvilla and the enabler of the killer. Graciela's purpose was to protect the secrets of Oshunvilla. At all costs. Because if people ever found out the truth of the world she'd created to protect her son and herself, the real world would have been mortified, the two of them vilified. She protected Jimagua, because he became the moneymaker—a world famous, reclusive artist the Cuban government protected as well. You will learn Adora and Graciela are one and the same, but I will argue this was *not* a case of dissociative identity disorder, commonly referred to as multiple personality disorder. Adora *chose* for the world to believe she died, so she could continue to control her world under the disguise of another personality. But to her son, Jimagua, at night, she became Adora again, the abusive mother, who kept her son under her thumb by blaming him for his sister's death, repeatedly for years. Around others, she love-bombed Jimaugua. Behind closed doors, she tortured her son.

"That caused Jimagua's personality to split. He is, we believe, a true victim of personality disorder called DID.

"Jimagua the artist made art to assuage his guilt for killing his baby sister in the womb. He spent his life trying to pay tribute to the Santeria saint Oshun. He built a town of masterful pieces of art in her honor, all to gain forgiveness from his mother and God or Oshun. Killing to please his mother and earn her validation. Why kill the girls? He'd been accused of being a killer of girls since before he was even born.

"Can you imagine that kind of pressure? Every day? That is why we, and the experts we've interviewed, believe Jimagua developed multiple personalities. To survive. You will meet Jimagua's alter egos, Alejandro, the groundskeeper, another personality—the child version of himself who cried at night. You will meet Luis, the killer, the personality that did what had to be done. Unlike Jimagua, who is tortured about what his mother is forcing him to do, Luis takes joy in killing. It's his way of torturing his mother and payback for her torturing him. This is the sadistic side of the artist, the abused child continuing the cycle in adulthood, copying what he knows.

"It's complicated, a twisted tale of love and hate and murder. And the lesson of Oshunvilla is that we can't turn a blind eye to the problem that is now destroying our world. We must take care of mental health issues before they destroy us. Izzy's House is but one step forward. Please watch *Oshunvilla, The True Story* with an open mind and an empathetic heart."

When Orlando stops speaking, you can hear an ant crawl across the floor, that's how quiet the room is.

The lights flick off.

The opening credits roll.

I'm pretty sure our lives will never be the same.

Chapter Forty-Nine

The three of us, Tony, Orlando, and I walk out of Izzy's House into the parking lot transformed into a festival worthy of any grand opening. We're silent, but the festivities are loud and alive. The local band Orchestra Fuente plays salsa, two food trucks serve up Latin dishes, and Spanish escalates from the flock of West Tampa and Ybor City locals we invited to the grand opening after-party.

My clothes stick to me in the Tampa humidity. That asphalt is so hot, my expensive, red-bottomed heels sink a bit as I walk across it.

No one is paying attention to our entrance. Just like we'd hoped. Many of the people crowding into the roped-off area are dancing, driving their limbs outward and around, a flurry of colors moving against the heat: yellow, white, some in red. The droning of conga drums from the salsa band lulls me into a hypnotic state of happiness.

We have come full circle, Tony, Orlando, and I.

"What in the voodoo drums is going on here?" Orlando asks.

I laugh, remembering how he said the very same thing the day we first arrived in Playa Hermosa, Cuba. We chose September eighth to open and debut our documentary on Oshunvilla before Netflix airs it, because it's the day we entered Cuba a year ago. We decided we needed to change the emotions and the feel of that day, so we wouldn't dread it forever. We're detoxing the past all together—letting it go— with one grand party.

My gaze is drawn to Izzy, Mandy, and Arianna, the three beauties spinning around each other, oblivious to anything else. They're dressed in colorful dresses, swirling their skirts, and twirling in an increasing frenzy. Their movements and their facial features express joy.

I grab Tony's arm to steady myself. My stomach is turning, maybe from the dizzying dancing, maybe from the stress of helping Izzy put together this event, maybe from the lack of sleep over the past two days. Or maybe because I dreamed of seeing my sister back in Tampa, happy and carefree. I squeeze his arm, nails digging in.

He side-eyes me but says nothing. The drums make speaking nearly impossible. He smiles, and I feel it all through my body. I'm so glad he's here. I want to tell him that, but don't. Our relationship has been *interesting* over the last year.

"I've got something for you," he says.

"You do?"

Tony isn't usually one for surprises.

He hands me a box. A jewelry box.

Ay Dios mio. My heart skips. Maybe my prayer to Oshun is about to come true. I take the tiny, unwrapped container. My hands tremble as I open it. Usually, I'd avoid showing any vulnerability, like the fact I'm nervous to see what's inside. But after that trip to Cuba, I realized being vulnerable isn't a weakness, it's a strength, especially when you learn to share your fears and trust others to help you work through them. Otherwise, you'll spend your life alone. If not literally, figuratively.

Inside the box is an azabache charm and bracelet. I exhale. He's replacing the one I lost in Cuba. Exactly what I want right now. Tony showing me he accepts me for who I am, superstitions and all. "Thank you." I tear up. This time I don't fight it. If I cry, I cry.

"I've had it for a while."

I'm about to ask why he waited until now to give it to me, but decide better. For once, the reporter is going to keep her mouth shut.

"I bought it right after we returned. But—"

I wait to let him unbox his feelings.

"But I needed to put some space between what happened in Cuba and—"

"Hey, Marisol. I've got some breaking news." Orlando puts one hand on my shoulder and one on Tony's.

"You recording?" I ask.

"Always," he says. "The Netflix contact told me they want a follow-up. They're contracting me for another documentary."

"What?"

"Not sure what it's going to be about yet, but—"

"Oh O, that's amazing." I throw my arms around him and hug him tight. "I'm so proud of you." As I say this, I pick up tension in Tony. Instinctively, I reach for his hand, clutch it, afraid to let him go.

"Looks like I'm interrupting something," O says, stepping back, giving me the knowing eye.

"You are." I'm tired of trying to hide my feelings. "Give us a minute, please."

"K." Orlando pats Tony on the back and smiles. He looks at me and points. "I'll be right over—"

I laugh. "I'll find you." I give him a playful shove and

wait for him to get out of hearing distance. "Sorry, you were saying?" My heart is dancing all over my ribs, lightly tap dancing, hoping Tony is about to—

"Would you like to have dinner with me tomorrow night?"

I try to fight back a smile. I don't want to…ah, screw it. I smile and clap my hands together. "Are you asking me out on a date, Tony?"

His eyes sparkle at me. He nods.

"What's changed?" I have to ask. I mean, I'm a reporter after all, and it's been a damn year.

"I have."

I can't wait to hear more. "Me, too." I also have so much to share.

"Sorry to interrupt." Mandy is rushing to my side, a phone in her hand. It's the cell phone we bought for Izzy's House. "Someone's asking to speak with you. Says it's urgent."

"Me?" I ask.

Mandy nods.

I turn to Tony and let my shoulders drop, so he sees my frustration.

He shrugs but is still smiling.

"First of all, yes. I want to have dinner with you tomorrow night."

Mandy cocks her head and whistles. "Oh baby!"

I shake my head, grab the phone, and wave her away. "I'll take the call inside."

He nods.

I skip inside, close the door, thinking about what I should wear tomorrow night. "Hi, it's Mari." I have a new sundress that is sexy but still professional. Nah, forget professional.

"Hello, Mari. I've been watching you on TV."

I freeze.

"This time you're not reporting the story. *You* are the

story."

My whole body goes ice cold.

"It's you." The last time I saw this serial killer was in this very location, as the cigar factory that used to be here burned to the ground. His body was never recovered. His whereabouts remain unknown.

"Your mother's murderer is dead," he says.

How the hell would he know about Raúl? "Where are you?" I scan the celebration through the glass front doors. How does he know I'm here? How does he have the facility's new number?

"Has justice been served like you think it was deserved?" he asks.

"What do you mean?" I know exactly what he means. *Keep him on the phone.* I open the door, wait to catch Tony's gaze, and gesture wildly to him.

"Don't bother with a trace. I won't be on long enough."

"What do you want?" I need to know his intentions before he hangs up.

"Do you know where Detective Garcia's Cuban cousin is?"

Air stops in my lungs. I scan the parking lot. I don't see Domingo or his dog. The teen they'd rescued had been here, hadn't he? *Come to think of it, I haven't seen him today.* My stomach drops a thousand feet.

"I blame both you and Tony for my fate. Isabella and Orlando, too. Almost burned alive. Now living in the shadows. I can't even attend Gasparilla. You know, the parade is always my favorite day of the year."

Tony strides through the door.

I cover the phone and mouth the name of the killer we took down together over a year ago.

Tony reaches for the phone.

I flip around, turning my back to him. If Tony knew the

killer had his cousin…he'd lose it. I need to remain in control. Get more information.

"You may have forgiven and moved on with your life," the killer on the phone says, "but I haven't."

"What are you planning?" It has something to do with Gasparilla. Maybe the parade? The masquerade ball?

"I plan to teach a new Cuban friend about old-school American justice."

My breath catches, as does my gaze when it meets Tony's. He and his cousin have grown tight since they'd come back. Like father and son. This will kill Tony. He'll blame himself.

"I'm going to seek my revenge against all of you. This is just the beginning. You have twenty-four hours to save the kid and his dog. Come find me, Mari *rhymes with sorry*. And bring your detective lover. If you dare."

Click.

My heart explodes, the cortisol dump underway. The room spins. I can't swallow. I scan the room for a clock. None. I remember Tony always wears an Apple watch. I grab his wrist and turn it.

Three o'clock p.m., Friday September eighth.

The clock starts ticking.

Again.

Acknowledgments

I have an amazing network of friends and supporters, and I want to thank you.

In the beginning, authors Kelly Coon, Katherine Caldwell, Veronica Forand, Deborah Evans, Jaime Lynn Hendricks, and editors Gretchen Stelter and Jacquelyn Lancaster took time from their own careers to read and offer input on my rough draft.

My fabulous editor Robin Haseltine helps me make magic every time!

Morgan Barse, Wing Woman extraordinaire, thank you for your assistance and your social media and brand excellence.

Barbara Rosenberg, you are a joy to work with. Thank you for your guidance as my agent.

Jessica and Lizzie, you are part of the genius behind Entangled Publishing, and I am thrilled to work with you on this series.

Thank you to my readers. I cannot do this without your support. I love and appreciate you.

Don't be mad at me for this cliffhanger! Here's the first chapter in Book Three: *The Phantom Pirate of Gasparilla.*

Chapter One

Cannons fire, one after the other, from the pirate parade floats moving at a snail's pace down Bayshore Boulevard. High school drummers pound out loud, staccato beats while various songs blare from float speakers. Chaotic sounds wash ashore, a musical monsoon, erupting during Tampa, Florida's annual Children's Gasparilla parade.

None of the reporters and anchors standing near me on our TV station's parade float acknowledge the unusual noise slicing through the familiar sea of sounds. But, in a warm rush of air, a bullet whizzes past me during our live TV coverage. I don't recognize it as a gunshot at first. Why would I? But, when the bullet lodges itself in my photographer's shoulder, and the impact pushes him back against a walled-in parade float Porta Potty I know.

I know.

My photographer's eyes go wide. A trickle of blood escapes, weaving a crooked, red trail down his white Channel 15 shirt.

The air stalls in my lungs. I'm halfway through a sentence.

My words vaporize. I'm the deer caught in the headlights on live TV. For once in my decade-long career I do not know what to say.

His camera drops. The heavy equipment lands on his right foot.

I cringe, phantom pain shooting through me.

His mouth opens, but no words form. Like agony holds his scream hostage.

I freeze. Still speechless. Time slows, and I'm suspended in it. *It's happening, isn't it. Just like that murderer promised.* Just like I'd warned the police chief and our boss before today's parade. They'd upped security but refused to call off the parade based on my phone call with the serial killer.

A phone call only I heard. A phone call no one could confirm. Not even Tony Garcia, homicide detective, who stood right next to me at the time.

A round of staccato shots, at assault-rifle speed, incites screams and chaotic movement. People dart away from our float as if a bomb exploded. They fan out, shrapnel dispersing in every direction.

"What is that?"

"Gunshots. Get down!"

"Shooter!"

A shrill voice rises above the shattering screams.

"Active shooter. Run!"

Bill, a hired security guard, rushes toward my photographer.

The photog falls to his knees and pitches facedown onto the floor of the float, landing on his own equipment. He's passed out, but his back still rises and falls.

"Medic," I scream, my body tingling from my ears all the way down to my toes. "We need a paramedic." I push past my colleagues.

Most shove me out of their way, trying to get into the

bathroom stall. Others throw their bodies flat on the floor.

I step over them, get to the side, grab the rail, search the street for first responders.

The thick crowd streaks away from Bayshore, pulled like an outgoing tide. Costumed people rush over immaculately groomed landscapes in front of the magnificent mansions lining one of Tampa's richest streets. I scan the crowd for help. Or for the killer I fingered.

I know that devil is here.

I also know I won't find him. Too many pirates, dressed in eye patches and puffy pants, faces made up with fake blood and man-made scars.

Unrecognizable.

A perfect day for a killer to hide in plain sight.

A high-end baby stroller falls over in front of our float. A mother slaps hands over her cheeks, while an older man swipes the baby up off the concrete. High school band members, in black and red uniforms that say WARRIORS, stumble past our float, zombie-like, leaving their instruments abandoned, cluttering the street, like an alien-led shockwave just vaporized everyone.

Kids scream in various octaves, a choir of terror.

Hot tears blur my vision, but I catch the yellow vest of a— "Hey!" My heart leaps. "Over here." I gesture with both hands knowing he can't hear—

Tack. Tack. Tack. Boom. Boom. Boom.

I drop to my knees. Pull my arms over my head. *The shooter is firing this way!* My heart slams my ribs with such force I'm afraid my bones will break. *Can't catch my breath.*

One of my coworkers falls next to me. She rolls over, eyes wide.

I'm screaming now, too. It hits me.

Not a bullet, but the truth.

He's targeting me. The serial killer I helped bust is

coming for me. He told me he would. But I had no idea he'd take out innocent people in the process during a *children's parade*. Stars spin in my peripheral vision. I pray my racing heart doesn't explode. The float whirls around me.

Ding.

My cellphone. I jerk it out of my pocket, read the incoming text.

It's me.

My throat is dry, and yet I'm sweating.

I type back. *What do you want?*

You know what I want.

Sirens get louder. Tires screech to a stop. I peek out between the railing. An army of cop cars and first responders fill the side streets. Some vested cops jump out of their patrol car and file in a single line toward us. Others stay put, crouching behind their patrol car doors. All hold up weapons.

"We're trying to find where the shots are coming from." A voice over a loudspeaker—probably Tampa Police. "Can anyone identify a location?"

The microphone. Maybe there's still a chance. He hasn't fired again. He's waiting. I have seconds. I crawl back to the center of the float, moving over bodies, all warm and still alive, but with nowhere to hide. Nowhere to go.

Before my live hit, I'd been using the mic to talk with the crowd, get them to cheer— raise their hands for the colorful beads we throw out each year. I see a black cord protruding from under the photographer's body. I exhale. Close my eyes for a second. The mic is under the body of—? *Ay Dios mio.* The photog is so new I don't even know his name. I just know that his body, blood pooling under it, is covering what I need. Where did the damn security guard go? I need him to lift the body.

The body.

My stomach heaves.

No time. No time. He's waiting for my reply.

I reach under the photog. His body is heavy, and my fingers feel for the mic. It's wet and sticky. I jerk it out. Pray it still works. "Channel 15. Channel 15 float. Two down. We've got two down. Maybe more. Need medics." My voice cracks. The mic touches my mouth. I jerk away, cringing at the taste of warm, fresh blood.

The photog moans.

He's alive!

Snap. Snap. Snap. Another barrage of shots, like out-of-control fireworks.

"See those flashes? They're coming from that house." More words blasting through the police loudspeaker.

I crawl to the rail. Look through it. Flashes pop from an upstairs window across the street from me, almost in time with another barrage of snapping sounds. "Second story—new mansion at Bayshore and Lumpkin." I yell into the mic. If he's going to kill me, I'm going to make sure he doesn't get away with it.

"Control three—we need all streets leading away from Bayshore shut down. And we need backup at Bayshore and Lumpkin. Active shooter. Active shooter."

Another slurry of snaps.

What the hell is he doing? I thought he wanted to hurt me and Tony, the homicide detective who helped finger him. Also, Orlando, my former TV news photographer, and my sister, Izzy. People I love. I thought he wanted to—

My community. He's hitting my community—the kids. The kids parade because he knows that will hurt me. My brain burns, ignited by fire. *The bastard.*

"I got shot. I'm shot."

It's the coworker who fell next to me earlier. She's moving now. "Where?"

"My arm."

"Okay. Okay. Where?"

I grab the cord from the mic still in my hand. "Might hurt." I tie the cord around her upper arm, above the bleeding, using it as a tourniquet. I pull tight and tie a knot best that I can.

"Get down!"

"Get back. Behind somewhere!"

"Anjoli. Anjoli, baby, where are you?"

I'm attacked by a barrage of frightened voices coming from faces I can't see.

"Why'd I come?" The coworker is crying now, loud and hard and fast. "Why?"

She's going to pass out again. I scoot down from her, my own emotions bubbling over, too. I need to keep my shit together. I need to-

This is all my fault.

"You okay?"

My gaze directs itself toward that voice, as if dehydrated—the voice—water. *Tony is here!* He crouches down next to me on the float. When did my detective arrive? My heart flutters, and I really want him to hold me, so I can dissolve into the good cry I've been holding back. After the call from the killer, Tony asked me not to attend the parade.

I did anyway.

"He's behind this," I yell. "He warned me he was coming for us. Maybe if I hadn't come. If I'd listened to you."

"Stop," Tony says. He turns my face toward his and wipes away tears that escaped my tight control.

"What do we do?" No telling how many are dead. "I'm still alive because this is a game, and the serial killer we outed wants me to play." *Why do I put everyone I love I in danger?* "I've got to engage."

Tony shakes off my idea.

I reach down to my azabache charm bracelet, the one

Tony gave me, and rip it off. Throw it over the float rail. The black gemstone has not provided me or anyone here with protection. Or maybe it has. I am still alive. I glance at Tony. I see disappointment in his eyes. Because I threw his gift away? Or because I put myself and maybe everyone else in danger by showing up today?

I look through the cracks. No telling where the charm fell. Too many different sized feet kicking around the street. Scrambling, oblivious to anything but getting to safety.

"Where's the injured?"

A paramedic—young—probably just out of high school—walks over those sprawled on the float's floor. "Here." I point to my coworker on the other side of Tony.

The paramedic pulls out his radio to—

Clack. Clack. Clack.

The paramedic drops, his lanky limbs slapping me as he falls.

"Stop," I scream. "Stop." *I have to end this.* I want this murderer to be captured, brought to justice. Kept out of society. Nothing can change a truly evil person. Except incarceration or death. *This I know.*

Ding.

I want you to stand. If you do, I'll stop firing. At least at other people.

His words punch me like a boxing glove. I can save some of my friends. I can save other people I don't know. All I need to do is stand. And maybe take a bullet. *Do I have the guts to commit suicide?*

I don't have a choice. I'm going to give this madman what he wants.

I don't tell Tony. He'll stop me. I know he will. He's always been my hero.

I stand and twist to face the mansion on Bayshore where I think the killer is firing from.

I don't need to say a word.
I know that predator will zero in on me.
He probably already has.
I raise both hands in surrender.

• • •

Want to know what happens next?

Join my newsletter: https://bit.ly/Bondnewsletter

About the Author

By day, Linda Hurtado Bond is an Emmy and Edward R. Murrow award-winning journalist. By night, she's an author of James Bond like adventures and heart-stopping thrillers. Linda met her husband Jorge on assignment in Cuba, twenty-some years later they've raised a doctor, a nurse, a pilot, a paramedic firefighter, and an aspiring psychologist. A breast cancer survivor, she's active in the Tampa community raising money and awareness. When not working she finds time for her passions, her husband Jorge, world travel, classic movies, and solving a good mystery. Visit Linda at lindabond.com.

Also by Linda Bond…

ALL THE BROKEN GIRLS

THE INVESTIGATORS

ALIVE AT 5

CUBA UNDERCOVER

FLATLINE

Discover more romance from Entangled...

The Poet
a novel by Lisa Renee Jones

Some call him friend or boss. Some call him husband or dad. Some call him son. But the only title that matters to him is a name he earned from the written words he leaves behind after he kills, words that are as dark and mysterious as the reason he chooses his victims. A secret that only Detective Samantha Jazz can solve. He's writing this story for her. She just doesn't know it yet.

Tough Justice
a K-9 Special Ops novel by Tee O'Fallon

A deadly batch of opioids just hit the streets of Denver, filling Dr. Tori Sampson's ER with victims. With no sign of the epidemic stopping, Tori has a choice: work with annoyingly hot DEA agent Adam Decker and his K-9, Thor, or watch more innocent people die. She has her reasons for not trusting the DEA, but there's more to these overdoses. There's a killer on the loose... and they're closer to Tori than she knows.

AMARA
an imprint of Entangled Publishing LLC